THE
DALEMARK
QUARTET
CART AND CWIDDER

HarperCollins *Children's Books*

For Rachel

First published in Great Britain by Macmillan London Ltd in 1975
This edition published by HarperCollins *Children's Books* in 2016
HarperCollins *Children's Books* is a division of HarperCollins*Publishers* Ltd,
1 London Bridge Street
London SE1 9GF

The HarperCollins *Children's Books* website address is
www.harpercollins.co.uk

1

ISBN 978-0-00-817062-2

Printed and bound in England by
Clays Ltd, St Ives plc

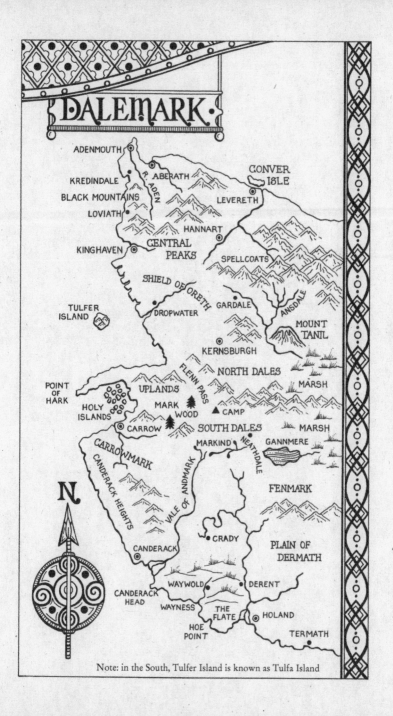

Note: in the South, Tulfer Island is known as Tulfa Island

CHAPTER ONE

"DO COME OUT of that dream, Moril," Lenina said. "Glad rags, Moril," said Brid. "We're nearly in Derent."

Moril sighed reproachfully. He had not been in a dream, and he felt it was unfair of his mother to call it that. He had merely been gazing at the white road as it wandered northwards, thinking how glad he was to be going that way again, and how glad he would be to get out of the South. It was spring, and it was already far too hot. But that was not the worst of the South. The worst, to Moril's mind, was the need to be careful. You dared not put a foot, or a word, out of place for fear of being clapped in jail. People were watching all the time to report what you said. It gave Moril the creeps. And it irked him that there were songs his father dared not sing in the South for fear of sounding seditious. They were the best songs, too, to Moril's mind. They all came from the North. Moril himself had been born in the North, in the earldom of Hannart. And his favourite hero, the Adon, had once upon a time been Earl of Hannart.

"You're dreaming again!" Lenina said sharply.

"No, I'm not," said Moril. He left his perch behind the driving seat and climbed hastily into the covered back of the cart. His mother and his sister were already changed into their cheap tinsel-trimmed show dresses. Lenina, who was pale and blonde and still very beautiful, was in silver and pale gold. Brid, who was darker and browner, had a glimmering peacock dress. Lenina hung Moril's suit above the rack of musical instruments, and Moril squeezed up to that end to change, very careful not to bang a cwidder or scrape the hand organ. Each instrument was shiny with use and gleaming with care. Each had its special place. Everything in the cart did. Clennen insisted on it. He said that life in a small cart would otherwise become impossible.

Once Moril was changed, he emerged from the cart as a very flamboyant figure, for his suit was the same peacock as Brid's dress and his hair was red – a bright, wild red. He had inherited Lenina's paleness. His face was white, with a few red freckles.

"You know, Mother," Brid said, as she had said before every show since they left Holand, "I don't think I like that colour on Moril."

"It makes people notice him," said Lenina, and went to take the reins while Clennen and Dagner changed in their turn.

Moril went to walk in the damp springing grass on the roadside, which was rough-soft under his toes, where he could have a good view of the cart that was his home. It was painted in a number of noticeable colours, principally pink and gold. Picked out in gold and sky blue along the sides were the words *Clennen the Singer*. Moril knew it was garish, but he loved this cart all the same. It moved softly, because it was well sprung and well oiled, and ran easily behind Olob, the glistening brown horse. Clennen always said he would not part with Olob for an earldom. Olob – his real name was Barangarolob, because Clennen loved long names – was harnessed in pink and scarlet, with a great deal of polished brass, and looked as magnificent as the rest of the turnout. Moril was just thinking that his mother and Brid on the driving seat looked like two queens – or perhaps a queen and a princess – when Clennen stuck his head out of the canvas at the back.

"Admiring us, are you?" he called cheerfully. Moril smiled and nodded. "It's like life," Clennen said. "You may wonder what goes on inside, but what matters is the look of it and the kind of performance we give. Remember that." His head popped back inside again.

Moril went on smiling. His father was always giving them odd thoughts to remember. He would probably want this one repeated to him in a day or so. Moril thought about it – in the dreamy way in which he usually gave his attention to anything – and he could not see that their turnout was like life. Life was not pink and gold. At least, some of theirs was, he supposed, but that was only saying the cart *was* life.

He was still pondering when they came under some big trees covered with pale buds, and the canvas cover went down with a bit of a clatter, revealing Clennen and Dagner dressed in scarlet and ready for the show. Moril scampered back and climbed up with them. Clennen smiled jovially. Dagner, whose face was tight and pinched, as it always was before a show, pushed Moril's cwidder into his hands and Moril into the right place without a word. He handed the big old cwidder to Clennen and the panhorn to Brid, and took up a pipe and a long, thin drum himself. By the time they were all settled, Olob was clopping smoothly into the main square of Derent.

"Ready," said Clennen. "Two, three." And they struck up.

Derent was not a big place. The number of people who came into the square in response to their opening song was not encouraging. There was a trickle of children and ten adults at the most. True, the people sitting outside the tavern turned their chairs round to get a better view, but Moril had a vague feeling, all the same, that they were wasting their talents on Derent. He said so to Brid, while Lenina was reaching past him to receive the hand organ from Dagner.

"All your feelings are vague!" Lenina said, overhearing. "Be quiet."

Undaunted by the sparse crowd, Clennen began his usual patter. "Ladies and gentlemen, come and listen! I am Clennen the Singer, on my way from Holand to the North. I bring you news, views, songs and tales, things old and things new. Roll up, draw up chairs, come near and listen!" Clennen had a fine rolling voice, speaking or singing. It rumbled round the square. Eyes were drawn to him, for his presence matched his voice. He was a big man, and not a thin one, though the scarlet suit made his paunch look bigger than it really was. He had a good sharp curl of ginger beard, which made up for the bald patch at the back of his head – now hidden by his scarlet hat. But the main thing about him was his enormous, jovial, total good humour. It seemed to fetch people by magic or multiply those there out of thin air. Before his speech was over, there were forty or fifty people listening to it.

"So there!" Brid said to Moril.

Before the performance could start, however, someone pushed up to the cart, calling, "Have you got any news from Holand, Clennen?" So they had to wait. They were used to this. Moril thought of it as part of the performance – and it certainly seemed to be one of their duties – to bring news from one part of Dalemark to the others. In the South particularly, there were few other ways in which people could get to know what was happening in the next lordship, let alone the next earldom.

"Now, let's see," said Clennen. "There's been a new earl invested for the South Dales – the old one's grandson.

And they tell me Hadd has fallen out with Henda again."
This surprised nobody. They were two very quarrelsome
earls. "And I *hear*," said Clennen, stressing the *hear,* to
show that he was not trying to stir up trouble, "I *hear*
the cause of it had something to do with a shipload of
Northmen that came into harbour at Holand last month."
This caused confused and careful muttering. Nobody
knew what to make of a ship from the North coming into
Holand, or whether they were breaking the law to think
of it at all. Clennen passed on to other news. "The Earl of
Waywold is making new money – copper and goodness
knows what else in it – worth nothing. You get more than
two thousand to one gold. Now the price on the Porter –
you've all heard of the Porter, I suppose?" Everyone had.
The Porter was a notorious spy, much wanted by the earls
of the South for passing illegal information and stirring up
discontent. Not one of the earls had been able to catch him.
"The price on the Porter's head now being two thousand
gold," said Clennen, "it's to be hoped that he's not
taken in Waywold, or you'll have to collect your reward
in a wagon." This caused some cautious laughter. "And
the storm last month carried off the lord's roof in
Bradbrook, not to speak of my tent," said Clennen.

Lenina, by this time, had sorted out the strips of

paper on which she had written messages from people in other places to friends and relatives in Derent. She began calling them out. "Is there someone called Coran here? I've a message from his uncle at Pennet." A red-faced young man pushed forwards. He confessed, as if he were ashamed of it, that he could read, and was handed the paper. "Is there a Granny Ben here?"

"She's sick, but I'll tell her," someone called.

So it went on. Lenina handed out messages to those who could read, and read them out to those who could not. More people hurried into the square, hearing there was news. Shortly there was a fair throng of people, all in great good humour, all telling one another the latest news from Holand.

Then Clennen called out: "Now I'm putting my hat on the ground here. If you want a song of us too, do us the favour of filling it with silver." The scarlet hat spun neatly on to the cobblestones and waited, looking empty and expectant. Clennen waited too, with rather the same look. And after a second the red-faced Coran, grateful for his message, tossed a silver coin into it. Another followed, and another. Lenina, watching expertly, muttered to Brid that it looked like good takings.

After that the performance began in earnest. Moril did

not have much time even for vague thinking. Though he did not do much of the singing, his job was to play treble to the low sweet notes of his father's big cwidder, and he was kept fairly busy. His fingers grew hot and tingly, and he leant over and blew on them to cool them as he played. Clennen, as he had promised the crowd, gave them old favourites and new favourites – ballads, love songs, and comic songs – and some songs that were entirely new. Several of these were his own. Clennen was a great maker of songs. Brid and Dagner joined him for some of them, or played panhorn, drum and third cwidder, and Lenina played stolidly on the hand organ. She played well – since Clennen had taught her – but always rather mechanically, as if her mind were elsewhere. And Moril fingered away busily, his left hand sliding up and down the long, inlaid arm of his cwidder, his right thrumming on the strings until his fingertips glowed.

Every so often Clennen would pause and send a cheerfully reproachful look towards his hat. This usually caused a hand to come out from the crowd and drop a small, shamed coin in with the others. Then Clennen would beam round at everyone and go on again. When the hat was more than half full, he said: "Now I think the time has come for some of the songs out of our past.

As you may know, the history of Dalemark is full of fine singers, but, to my mind, there have never been two to compare with the Adon and Osfameron. Neither has ever been equalled. But Osfameron was an ancestor of mine. I happen to be descended from him in a direct line, father to son. And it was said of Osfameron that he could charm the rocks from the mountains, the dead from their sleep and the gold from men's purses." Here a slight raising of Clennen's sandy eyebrows in the direction of the hat called forth an apologetic penny and a ripple of laughter from everyone. "So, ladies and gentlemen," said Clennen, "I shall now sing four songs by Osfameron."

Moril sighed and leant his cwidder carefully against the side of the cart. The old songs only needed the big cwidder, so he could have a rest. In spite of this, he wished his father would not sing them. Moril much preferred the new, full-bodied music. The old required a fingering which made even the big mellow cwidder sound cracked and thin, and Clennen seemed to find it necessary to change his deep singing voice until it became thin, high and peculiar. As for the words – Moril listened to the first song and wondered what Osfameron had been on about.

"The Adon's hall was open. Through it
Swallows darted. The soul flies through life.
Osfameron in his mind's eye knew it.
The bird's life is not the man's life."

But the crowd appreciated it. Moril heard someone say: "I do like to hear the old songs done in the right way." And when they were over, there was a round of applause and a few more coins.

Then Dagner, with his face more tight and pinched than ever, took up his cwidder. Clennen said, "I now introduce my eldest son, Dastgandlen Handagner." This was Dagner's full name. Clennen loved long names. "He will sing you some of his own songs," said Clennen, and waved Dagner forwards into the centre of the cart. Dagner, with a grimace of pure nervousness, bowed to the crowd and began to sing. Moril could never understand why this part was such a torment to Dagner. He knew his brother would have died rather than miss his part in the performance, yet he was never happy until it was over. Perhaps it was because Dagner had made the songs himself.

They were strange, moody little songs, with odd rhythms. Dagner made them even odder, by singing now loud, now soft, for no real reason, unless it was nerves. And they had a haunting something. The tunes stuck in your head and you hummed them when you thought you had long forgotten them. Moril listened and watched, and envied Dagner this gift of making songs. He would have given – well – his toes, anyway, to be able to compose anything.

"*The colour in your head*
The colour in your mind
Is dead
If you follow it blind,"

Dagner sang, and the crowd grew to like it. Dagner was not remarkable to look at – he was thin and sandy-haired, with a large Adam's apple – and people expected his songs to be unremarkable too. But when he finished, there was applause and some more coins. Dagner flushed pale purple with pleasure and was almost at ease for the rest of the show.

There was not much more. The whole family sang a few more songs together and wound up with *Jolly Holanders*. They always finished with that in the South, and the audience always joined in. Then it was a matter of putting away the instruments and replying to the things people came up to say.

This was always rather a confused time. There were the usual number of people who seemed to know Clennen well; the usual giggly girls who wanted Dagner to tell them how he composed songs, a thing Dagner could never explain and always tried to do; the usual kind people who told Moril he was quite a musician for a youngster; and the usual gentlemen who drifted up to Lenina and Brid and tried to murmur sweet nothings to them. Clennen was always very quick to notice these gentlemen, particularly those who approached Brid. Poor Brid looked older than she was in her show clothes – she was really only just thirteen – and she did not know how to deal with murmuring gentlemen at all.

"Well, you see, my father taught me," Moril explained.

"They come into my head like – er – ideas," Dagner explained.

"It is Lenina, isn't it?" murmured a gentleman at the head of the cart.

"It is," said Lenina.

"I didn't quite hear what you said," Brid said rather desperately to another gentleman.

"I don't go to Hannart. I had a little disagreement with

19

the Earl," said Clennen. He swung round and, with one comprehensive look, disposed of the man Brid could not hear and also the one who thought Lenina was herself. "But I'm going through Dropwater and beyond," he continued, turning back to his friends.

Lenina had collected the money and was counting it. "Good," she said. "We can stay at the inn here. I fancy a roof over my head."

Moril and Brid fancied it too. It was the height of luxury. There would be feather beds, a proper bath and real food cooked indoors. Brid licked her lips and gave Moril a delighted grin. Moril smiled back in his milky, sleepy way.

"No. No time," said Clennen, when at last he was free to be asked. "We have to press on. We're picking up a passenger on the road."

Lenina said nothing. It was not her way. While Brid, Moril and even Dagner protested, she simply picked up the reins and encouraged Olob to move.

CHAPTER TWO

"WHERE ARE WE picking up the passenger?" Brid enquired when they were three miles or so beyond Derent and her discontent had worn off somewhat. She was back in her everyday blue check and looked rather younger than she was.

"Couple of miles on. I'll tell you where," Clennen said to Dagner, who was driving.

"Going North, is he?" Dagner said.

"That's right," said Clennen.

Moril, in the ordinary rust-coloured clothes he preferred, and in which, to Brid's mind, he looked a great deal nicer, trotted along beside the cart and hoped vaguely that the passenger would be agreeable. They had taken a woman last year who had driven him nearly crazy with boredom. She had known a hundred little boys, and they were all better than Moril in some way, and she had at least two long stories about each boy to prove it. They took someone most years, going North. Since North and South had begun their long disagreement, very little traffic went between. Those who had no horse – and to walk meant the risk of being taken up as a vagrant and clapped into jail – had to rely on such people as the licensed singers to take them as paying passengers.

The disagreement had begun so far in the past that not many people knew its cause: the North had one version, the South another. But it was certain that three kings of Dalemark had died, one after another, without leaving a proper heir to the throne. And almost every earl in the land had some kind of claim to be king. Even before the last king ruled from Hannart in the North, there had been quarrels and wars, and the country showed signs of breaking up into two. And when the Adon, who was the last king, died, his heirs were not to be found. Civil war began in earnest.

Since then the only rulers of Dalemark had been the

earls, each in his own earldom, with the lords under them. No one now wanted a king. Keril, the present Earl of Hannart, said publicly that he had no claim to the throne. But the disagreement ran deeper than ever. The men of the North claimed that half the land was enslaved, and the earls of the South said the North was plotting against them. The year Brid was born, Keril, Earl of Hannart, had been proclaimed a public enemy by every earl and lord in the South. After that the only people who dared travel between were accredited traders and licensed singers, and they had to prove that their business was harmless or they might be arrested anywhere in the South.

Moril had met some of the traders and quite a few of the singers. Clennen did not speak highly of any of them, except perhaps the singer Hestefan, whom Moril had not met. But Moril had never heard any of them complain of having to take passengers. He thought they must all be very patient people.

"What about payment?" asked Lenina.

"You wait and see," said Clennen, with a laugh.

"That's all very well," said Brid, returning to her discontent. "But why do we always have to take someone? Why can't the stupid North make friends with the silly South?"

"You tell me," said Clennen. And after Brid had stammered for a minute, he laughed and said, "Would *you* make friends with someone you knew would stab you in the back if he got the chance? Remember that. Mind you, there was a time when the South was as free a place as the North. Remember that too."

This was a bold thing to say in the South. The last rebellion had been stamped out very harshly indeed, and the strict laws were still in force. You did not say anything that suggested you were discontented with the ways of the South. The countryside was known to be full of spies and informers, watching and listening to give warning of rebellious thoughts.

That was why, when Clennen spoke of North, South and freedom in the same breath, Moril saw Lenina look round the hedges to make sure no one was listening. He found himself doing the same.

But the hedges, though the leaves were already dusty, were still thin enough to see through. Nothing moved in them but birds. The only people they saw, for the next mile or so, were in the distance, planting vines on a hillside, until they came to where a road branched off to another vineyard. There, on the triangle made by the turning, a man was waiting. At his feet he had a huge round bottle half encased in a straw basket. He waved, and Dagner drew up. Olob turned his head and looked at the huge bottle with evident misgiving.

"Evening, Flind," said Clennen. "Is that our payment there, by your feet?" The man nodded. He seemed disinclined to smile, though Clennen smiled broadly at him. "I hoped it was," said Clennen. "Where's the passenger?"

Flind jerked a thumb. The passenger, probably in an attempt to keep out of the sun, was sitting behind the bottle in its shadow. He looked very hot, very untidy, rather discontented and rather younger than Dagner.

"Help him into the cart," Clennen said to Moril.

Moril did his best, but the passenger shook off his helping hand. "I can get in by myself," he said, "I'm not a cripple." He climbed in very nimbly and sat on the floor. The canvas cover was half up, and he seemed glad of its shade. Moril looked vaguely after him and hoped it was the heat that made him feel so disagreeable. He knew from bitter experience that someone around Dagner's age could make life very unpleasant if he was steadily disagreeable for some hundreds of miles. This could be worse than the woman last year. He looked at Brid, who made her squeezed-lemon face back.

Clennen and Flind, meanwhile, were heaving the huge jar through the tailgate of the cart. It took a good deal of effort, and a lot of space once it was in. Olob almost laid his head backwards over his shoulders in an attempt to show his strong disapproval of it.

"Are you really taking our payment in wine?" said Lenina.

"Can you think of a better one?" said Clennen. "My dear girl, there's only beer to drink in the North! Count your blessings. We'll broach it this evening, shall we? Or would you rather wait until we're going through Markind?"

"Oh – this evening," said Lenina, smiling a little.

Clennen latched the tailgate, waved to Flind, and they went on. Olob made a very expressive business of getting the cart under way again. Brid was quite sorry for him, straining in front of all that extra weight, but everyone else knew that the cart was so well sprung and greased that Olob could hardly feel the difference. Dagner made no bones about flicking him with the whip.

"What a lazy horse!" exclaimed the passenger.

"They're often the wisest ones," said Clennen.

The passenger, realising he had been snubbed, put his chin on his knees and sighed gustily. Brid and Moril took turns at eyeing him through the gap in the tailgate. He was burlier than Dagner, though he was younger, and much the same height. But he was more remarkable-looking, because he was a queer combination of dark and fair. His hair was tawny-fair, and there was a lot of it, like a lion's mane, only rather more untidy, and his eyes were a pale blue-green. But his eyebrows were thick and black and his skin very brown. His nose put them in mind of an eagle. He still had that fed-up look, which they decided must be due to more than the heat.

"Perhaps his grandfather's dying, and they sent for him, and he doesn't want to go," Brid speculated. Moril was content to leave it vague. He simply hoped the passenger would not vent his annoyance on them.

A mile or so further on Clennen said: "We haven't got your name, lad. There's a lot in a name, I always think. What is it?"

"It's Kialan," said the passenger. "With a K."

"Even with a K, it's not half long enough for me," said Clennen.

"Well, what do you expect me to say? It's really my name!" the passenger protested.

"I like longer names," Clennen explained. "Clennen's too short for me too. Lenina – my wife's name – is too short. But my children all have good spreading names, because I could choose them myself. The lad driving is Dastgandlen Handagner, my daughter is Cennoreth Manaliabrid, and the one with the red hair is Osfameron Tanamoril."

Moril ground his teeth and waited for the passenger to laugh. But, in fact, he looked rather awed. "Oh," he said. "Er, do you call them all that when you want to speak to them?"

"And the lazy-wise horse is Barangarolob," Clennen added, perfectly seriously, as if he were simply anxious for Kialan to know. Dagner gave a little whinny of laughter, which might have come from Olob. Kialan looked piteous.

"Take no notice," said Lenina. "They're Dagner, Brid and Moril for short. And the horse is Olob."

Kialan looked relieved. He gave another gusty sigh or so and took off his coat. He must have been hot in it, because it was a thick coat, of good cloth. Brid whispered that it must be his best one, but Moril had lost interest in Kialan by then and did not care. Kialan folded the coat – not as carefully as such a good garment deserved – and used it as a pillow while he pretended to go to sleep. Brid knew he was only pretending, because he started up every time any travellers passed them and looked through the opening of the cover to see who they were.

There was not much traffic on the road. Mostly it was slow wagons, which Olob trotted past without any difficulty, sending spurts of white grit from beneath the cartwheels, until Moril, trotting in the rear, seemed to have hair the same colour as Clennen's. But there were a few horsemen, and these overtook Olob as easily as Olob overtook the wagons. Once, quite a group of riders came past, raising a whirl of white dust, and were scanned by Kialan with great interest. One of the group seemed equally interested in them. He craned round in his saddle as he passed to get a good look at the cart.

"Who was that fellow?" Clennen said to Lenina.

"I couldn't say," she answered.

"Funny," said Clennen, "I seem to have seen him before." But since the man was a perfectly neutral-looking person, neither dark nor fair and neither young nor old, Clennen could not place him and gave up the attempt.

Shortly after that, as the sun was getting low, Olob left the road of his own accord and jolted the cart among gorse bushes into a heathy meadow. He stopped near a stream.

"Olob thinks this'll do," Dagner said to Clennen. "Will it?"

"You don't really let your horse choose where to stop!" Kialan exclaimed.

"He doesn't often let us down," said Clennen, surveying the meadow. "Yes, very nice. Horses have a gift for stopping, Kialan. Remember that."

The fed-up look settled on Kialan's face, and he watched, a little scornfully, while Dagner unharnessed Olob and led him off to drink. He watched Moril wiping the dust off the cart and Brid collecting firewood.

"Don't offer to help, will you?" Brid muttered in his direction.

While Lenina was cooking supper, Clennen fetched the big cwidder down, polished it, tuned it carefully and beckoned Moril. Moril came reluctantly. He was rather in awe of the big cwidder. Its shining round belly was even more imposing than Clennen's. The inlaid patterns on the front and arm, made of pearl and ivory and various coloured woods, puzzled him by their strangeness. And its voice when you played it was so surprisingly sweet and quite unlike that of the other cwidders. Clennen took such care of it that Moril still sometimes thought – as he had when he was little – that this cwidder was an extra, special part of Clennen, more important than his father's arm or leg – something on the lines of a wooden soul.

"Let's have that song of Osfameron's," said Clennen.

Moril liked the old songs so little that he was making very heavy weather of learning them. Clennen corrected him, made him go back to the beginning, and twice stopped him in the middle of the second verse. To make matters worse, Kialan came over and stood himself in front of Moril, listening. Moril, in self-defence, went into a dream between two notes, and stopped. He was with the Adon, on a green road in the North.

"Do you really need to teach him?" said Kialan.

"How else," asked Clennen, "do you think he'd learn?"

Kialan seemed a bit confused. "Well – I sort of supposed they picked it up–from giving shows," he said.

"Or it grew naturally, along with hair and fingernails?" Clennen suggested.

"No – I – Oh, that's silly!" said Kialan, and to Moril's relief, he drifted away. But he drifted back when Moril had finished and Brid took his place. Kialan caught Moril's sleeve. "I say, you all know all this music, but I suppose you can't even read and write, can you?"

Moril removed his sleeve. "Of course I can," he

said. "My mother taught us." Before Kialan could ask any more impertinent questions, he scurried off among the gorse bushes to the stream. He stayed there, lost in vagueness, watching the bright water hurry over the different brightness of the stones beneath, until he heard Brid shouting.

"Supper! *Wash*, Moril!"

Supper was not very good, and what little bread they had was stale. "I say, this tastes peculiar!" Kialan said, pushing his share about on his plate.

Lenina's face, which never had much expression, went quite blank. "I meant to buy bread and onions in Derent," she said. "But there was no time."

There was a heavy pause. Then Clennen said, "Look, lad, we've got to travel more than a hundred and fifty miles together, you and us. It needs a little give and take, don't you think? I'd hate to have to break a good cwidder over your head."

The sun was setting then, and the light was red. But Moril thought that this did not entirely account for the colour of Kialan's face. Kialan, however, said nothing. He silently accepted some of the wine and drank it, but he did not speak again until much later. By then Clennen had become very jolly with the wine. Beaming in the firelight, he leant back against the wheel of the cart and said to Dagner, "Give us that new song of yours."

"It's not quite ready yet," said Dagner. But, since this was not a performance, he willingly fetched his cwidder and picked out a sketch of what Moril thought was a very promising tune. And without a trace of nervousness, he half sang, half spoke the words.

"Come with me, come with me.
The blackbird asks you, 'Follow me.'
No one will know, no one will know,
Wherever you go, I shall go.
Come with me. Morning spreads,
Clouds are high in milky threads,
The moon looks like a white thumbnail,
Larks are singing up the dale.
The sun is up, so follow me.
I'd like us to go secretly
Along the road, across the hill
Where water runs and woods are still."

"And then I think the first four lines again," Dagner said, looking up at Clennen.

"No," said Clennen. "Won't do."

"Well, I needn't have them again," Dagner said humbly.

"I mean the whole thing won't do," said Clennen.

Dagner looked very dashed. Kialan seemed unable to stop himself saying indignantly: "Why? I thought it was going to be a jolly good song."

"The tune's all right, as far as it's gone," said Clennen. "But why spoil a tune like that with those words?"

"They're jolly good words," Kialan insisted. "I liked them."

"It's the words I seem to want," Dagner said diffidently.

"I see," said Clennen. "Then in that case don't utter them again until we're in the North – unless you want us taken up for rebels."

Dagner tried to explain. "But I – it wasn't. I was just trying to say how much I liked travelling in the cart and – and so on."

"Were you?" said Clennen. "And haven't you heard the songs the freedom fighters used to sing here the year of the rebellion – oh, it'll be sixteen years ago now, the year you were born? They never dared say a thing straight out, so it was all put sideways – *Follow the lark* was one, *Free as air and secret* another went, and the best known was *Come up the dale with me*. The lords here still hang a man on the spot for singing words like that."

"And I do think that's ridiculous!" Kialan burst out. "Why can't people sing what they want here? What's the matter with everyone?"

Brid and Moril looked at his firelit face with interest. It began to seem as if Kialan might be a freedom fighter. They felt they could forgive him much if he was. Clennen, however, simply seemed amused.

"I hope there's not someone behind the gorse listening to you," he said. Kialan's head jerked round towards the nearest looming bush. "See?" said Clennen. "That's why, in one easy lesson, lad. No one can trust anyone any more. It comes of uneasy rulers paying uneasy men to make the rest uneasy too. It's not always been like that, you know. Dagner, what did I say outside Derent?"

Dagner's mind was woefully on his unsuitable song. "Oh – er – something about life being only a performance, I think."

"I knew I could trust you to get the wrong saying – and the wrong saying wrong," Clennen said tolerantly. "Anyone?"

"You said the South was once as free as the North," said Brid. "You said it to me, really."

"Then remember it," said Clennen.

CHAPTER THREE

AFTER ONE NIGHT attempting to share the smaller tent with Kialan and Dagner, Moril took to creeping into the cart along with Brid and the wine jar. As he told Brid, even the wine jar took up less space than Kialan, and it did not have knees and elbows. Moril had woken up three times to find himself out among the guy ropes in the dew. He resented it. He resented Kialan, and he wished Dagner joy of him. It was hard to tell if Dagner got on with Kialan or not, because he was such an untalkative person. Dagner was like Lenina in that way. It was quite impossible to tell what Lenina thought about Kialan –

or, indeed, about anything else.

Kialan, in spite of Clennen's rebuke, seemed unable to stop making outspoken remarks. "You know, that cart is really horribly garish," he said, on the second morning. Perhaps he had some excuse. It was standing against the dawn sky, as he saw it, and Moril's red head was just emerging from it. The effect was undeniably colourful, but Brid was keenly offended.

"It isn't!" she said.

"I expect you're too young to have much taste," Kialan replied. Brid swore to Moril that she was Kialan's enemy for life after that one.

What Moril resented most – apart from Kialan's elbows and the fact that Kialan never made the slightest attempt to help with any of the chores – was the superior way Kialan stood by and listened in whenever Moril had a music lesson. Unfortunately he had them fairly frequently in the next few days. They were taking – perhaps for Kialan's benefit – a more direct route to Flennpass and the North than usual. It meant that they did not pass through any large towns and only two villages. Lenina bought supplies in the first, but they did not perform in either. Clennen took the opportunity to grind away at the old songs with Moril, to keep Brid hard at the panhorn and to rehearse a number of songs with all of them.

Kialan stood by and put Moril off continually. Moril came so to resent it that he took refuge in more than usual vagueness. He would sit on his perch behind the driving seat, staring up the white road unreeling ahead between the grey-green slopes of the South, basking in the hot sun – which never tanned him however long he sat in it – and dream of his birthplace in the North. It always saddened Moril that his father would never go to Hannart because of his disagreement with Earl Keril. He longed to see it, and he had built up in his mind a complete image of what it was like. There was an old grey castle in it, rowan trees and blue hills of a certain spiky shape. Moril saw it clearly. He saw the whole North with it, spread over the grey-green Southern landscape as if it were painted on a window: dark woods and emerald dales, the queer green roads from olden days which led to places that were not important any longer, hard grey rocks, and the great waterfall at Dropwater. In it lived all the stories of magic and adventure that seemed to go with the North. The South had nothing to compare with them.

Hearing Kialan talking behind him, Moril thought that the North had one new advantage. Kialan would leave them there.

"I've said that six times now," Kialan said. "Do you spend *all* your time a thousand miles away?"

Moril was annoyed. His family could accuse him of dreaminess if they wanted, but Kialan was a stranger. "You've no right to say that," he said.

It was possible Kialan did not realise how annoyed Moril was. "You see," Brid explained to him later, a good long way behind the cart, "even when you're angry, you always look so sleepy and – and *milky,* that he probably didn't even notice you were attending. Not," she added tartly, "that he'd have noticed anybody's feelings but his own, mind you."

What Kialan had replied was: "Oh, good grief! I know you're the fool of the family by now, but you don't have to be rude as well as stupid!"

"And the same to you!" Moril retorted, and took Kialan completely by surprise by butting him in the stomach. Kialan fell backwards heavily – and painfully, Moril hoped – on to the wine jar. Whereupon Moril found the prudent thing to do was to hop out of the cart double quick and scud off down the road behind it. And for the rest of the day he was forced to walk well in the rear for fear of Kialan's vengeance.

But it was Clennen who took the vengeance. When

they camped for the night, he beckoned both Kialan and Moril up to him. "Are you two going to make up and apologise?" he enquired. Moril looked warily at Kialan, and Kialan looked most unlovingly back. Neither answered. "Very well then," said Clennen, and banged their heads together. Nothing seems harder than another person's head. Moril could only hope that Kialan had seen as many stars as he had. He was rather surprised that Kialan did not say anything to Clennen. "Next time, I'll do it harder," Clennen promised. Then, as if nothing had happened, he went on to give Moril a lesson. And to Moril's annoyance, Kialan stood by and listened just as usual.

The following day they reached a market town called Crady, and it came on to rain – big warm drops that seemed like part of the air and very little to do with the moist white sky. The raindrops made dark brown circles in the dust of the road and raised a delicious smell of wet earth. But it meant everyone crowding into the cart to change in great discomfort. Moril was not surprised that Kialan got out.

"I'm not really interested in your show," he said to Clennen. "I'll meet you on the other side of Crady, shall I?"

"If you like, lad," Clennen said cheerfully. Brid and Moril exchanged seething glances in the hot dim space under the cover and wondered why Clennen did not box Kialan's ears for him. But the only thing which seemed to perturb Clennen was the rain. "We shall have no audience in the open," he said. "I'll see what I can do. We'll go in with the cover up."

It was lucky that they did. By the time they came to the marketplace, the rain was coming in white rods and bouncing up off the flagstones. Olob was wearing his most long-suffering expression, and there was not a soul in sight. But Clennen had friends in Crady, just as he had everywhere else. Half an hour later they were installed under the great beams of a warehouse on the corner of the marketplace, and a crowd, damp but interested, was gathering into it.

They gave an indoor kind of show. After Clennen had told everyone about Hadd and Henda, the Waywold money, the price on the Porter's head and the cost of corn in Derent, and the usual messages had been handed out, they sang songs with a chorus that the audience could join in. Dagner did his part early. Then, when good humour and attention were at their peak, Clennen told one of the old tales. This pleased Moril highly. He always felt rather too hot indoors, and playing the cwidder made him hotter still. But during a tale he was only needed once or twice. All the stories had places where there was a song. For the rest of the time Moril could sit on the dusty chaff of the floor with his arms wrapped round his knees and drink the story in.

Clennen chose to tell a branch of the story of the Adon. It had to be only a branch because, as Clennen was fond of saying, stories clustered round the Adon and Osfameron like bees swarming. The songs which came in where the story needed them were the Adon's own, or Osfameron's. Moril always thought the old songs sounded rather better set in their proper stories, though he still wished the silly fellows had tried to sing more naturally. But their doings made splendid tales. Moril listened avidly to how Lagan wounded the Adon and the wound would not heal until Manaliabrid came out of the East to him. Then came the story of the love of both Lagan and the Adon for Manaliabrid, and how the Adon fled with her to the South. Lagan followed, but Osfameron helped them by singing a certain song in the passes of the mountains, so that the mountains walked and blocked the way through. And Lagan was forced to turn back.

Here Clennen lowered his rich voice to say: "I shall not sing you the song Osfameron sang then, for fear of moving the mountains again. But it is true that since that day the only pass to the North is Flennpass."

The Adon for a time roamed the South with Manaliabrid, singing for a living, until Lagan found where they were. Then he stole away Kastri, the Adon's son by his first wife, and the Adon followed. But Lagan was something of a magician. He made Kastri invisible and took on the shape of Kastri himself. And when the Adon came up to him, unsuspecting, Lagan stabbed him through the heart.

Here came Manaliabrid's lament, which Moril was supposed to sing. He took up his cwidder for it, glancing as he did so into the warm blue-grey depths of the barn at the attentive audience. To his surprise, Kialan was there. He was standing at the back, very wet and draggled, listening with as much interest as anyone there. Moril supposed he had decided he preferred a performance to a soaking after all. And he was annoyed with Kialan for coming. His head was full of grand things, journeys, flights, fighting and the magic North of once-upon-a-time. Kialan was the everyday world with a vengeance. Moril felt as if he had a foot on two different worlds, which were spinning apart from one another. It was not a pleasant feeling. He took his eyes off Kialan and concentrated on his cwidder.

Then Clennen went on to how Manaliabrid asked Osfameron for help. Osfameron sang, and made Kastri visible. Then he took up his cwidder and journeyed by a way that only he knew, to the borders of the Dark Land. There he played such music that all the dead crowded in multitudes to hear him. Once they were gathered, Osfameron sang and called the soul of the Adon to him. And – this part always gave Moril a delicious shiver – Clennen once more lowered his voice to say: "I shall not sing you the song Osfameron sang then, for fear of calling the dead again."

Osfameron led the Adon's soul back and restored it to his body. The Adon arose, defeated Lagan, and reigned as the last King of Dalemark. He was the last king because Manaliabrid's son, who was to have been king after him, chose instead to go back to his mother's country. "And since that time," said Clennen, "there have been no kings in Dalemark. Nor will there be, until the sons of Manaliabrid return."

Moril gave an entranced sigh. He had hardly the heart, after such a story, to join in *Jolly Holanders*, and he only managed to sing with an effort. After it he crept away to the other end of the barn to avoid the usual crowd, and sat under the cart, brooding, while Clennen greeted his friends and Dagner failed to explain how he made up songs. *If only such things happened nowadays!* Moril thought. It seemed such a waste to be descended from the singer Osfameron, who knew the Adon and could call up the dead, and to live such a dull life. The world had gone so ordinary. Compare the Adon, who lived such a splendid life, with the present-day Earl of Hannart, who could think of nothing better to do than to stir up a rebellion, so that he dared not show his face in the South. Or you only had to think of the difference between that Osfameron, Moril brooded, and this one, Osfameron Tanamoril, to see how very plain and ordinary people had become lately. If only –

Here the plain and ordinary life interrupted in the person of Lenina, carrying the chinking hat to the cart. She was followed by the usual kind of murmuring gentleman. "And it must be sixteen years now…" this gentleman was murmuring.

"Seventeen," Lenina said briskly. "Moril, come out of that dream and count this money."

Moril unwillingly scrambled out from under the cart. As he did so, Clennen turned his head, and his voice boomed across the barn. "No, I didn't care for him at all, last time I was in Neathdale." With his voice came a look that caused the murmuring gentleman to wither away into the crowd. Moril watched him wither, a little puzzled. He seemed to be the twin of the murmuring gentleman in Derent.

The takings were not bad, which pleased Lenina. And Clennen was in good humour because an old friend of his had made him a present of a beefsteak. It was beautifully red and tender and wrapped in leaves to keep it fresh. Clennen stowed it carefully in a locker. He talked jovially of supper as they drove through Crady in the slackening drizzle. Kialan, to Brid's contempt, was waiting for them under a tree just beyond the town.

"Huh!" said Brid. "Not interested in our shows, isn't Mr High-and-Mighty! Did you see him, Moril? Drinking in every word!"

"Yes," said Moril.

While the red steak fizzled over the fire, Brid said mock-innocently to Kialan: "Father told one of the Adon stories at the show. Do you know them at all?"

"Yes. And a dead bore they are too," said Kialan. "All that magic!"

"You *would* say that!" said Moril. "I saw—"

"Silence!" said Clennen. "You're interrupting the steak. Not another word until it's ready to eat."

The steak was certainly worthy of respect. Even Kialan had nothing to say against it. They went on again after supper. In his carefree way, Clennen seemed to be quite as anxious as Moril to see the North again. He refused to let Olob choose them a meadow until the sun was nearly down and the sky ahead and to the left was a mass of lilac clouds barred with red.

"Imagine *that* over the peaks of the North Dales," he said. "But even in the South, Mark Wood is fine at this time of year. There's nothing to beat a tall beech in spring. And do you know the Marsh at all, Kialan?"

"A little," said Kialan.

"If we'd time, I'd take you through it just for the flowers," said Clennen. "But it's too far east, more's the pity. The ducks there make your mouth water."

"There are rabbits in the South Dales," Dagner suggested.

"So there are," said Clennen. "Look the snares out tomorrow."

By the end of the following day the landscape had begun to change. The rolling grey-green slopes gave way to higher, greener hills, and there were more trees.

It was like a foretaste of the North. Moril began to feel pleasantly excited, although he knew that they were only entering the South Dales. Tholian, Earl of the South Dales, was reputed to be a tyrant fiercer even than Henda. It was still a long way to the North. Beyond these green hills lay the Uplands and Mark Wood, before they came to Flennpass and the North at last.

Nevertheless, budding apple trees made a pleasant change from rows of vines. The nights were slightly cooler, and rabbits were plentiful. Every night Dagner went off to set snares round about the camp, and to Moril's surprise, Kialan made his first helpful gesture and went with Dagner.

"It's only because he likes killing things," Brid said. "He's that type."

Whatever the reason, Kialan was surprisingly good at catching and skinning rabbits, and Lenina was good at rabbit stew. Since they had wine as well, they fed very well for the next few days. Moril was almost grateful to Kialan. But Brid was not in the least grateful because every time they stopped in a town or village to give a show, Kialan would put on his act of not being interested and announce that he would meet them outside the town. And every time, unfailingly, they would see him among the audience, as interested as anyone there.

"Two-faced hypocrite!" Brid said indignantly. "He's just trying to make us feel small."

"That wouldn't do you any harm," Lenina said, in her dry way. Brid was more indignant than ever. It was becoming clear that Lenina rather approved of Kialan. Not that she said anything. It was more that she did not say any of the things she might have done. And when Kialan tore his good coat in the wood, Lenina mended it for him with careful neat stitches.

Kialan seemed far more surprised than grateful when Lenina handed him the mended coat. "Oh – thanks," he said. "You shouldn't have bothered." His face was red, and he seemed actually a little scornful of Lenina for doing it.

"Nothing to what I am!" said Brid. "He can go in rags for all I care."

The day after this they entered the part of the South Dales which was the lordship of Markind. They never gave shows in Markind. Brid's dislike of Kialan came to a head while Olob was patiently dragging the cart up and down the steep little hills of this lordship. The reason was that Clennen, who never disdained an audience, began to explain to Kialan exactly why he always hurried through

Markind without giving a performance.

"I took Lenina from here, you see," he said. "From the very middle of Markind, out of the Lord's own hall. Didn't I, Lenina?"

"You did," said Lenina. She always looked very noncommittal whenever Clennen told this story.

"She was betrothed to the Lord's son. What was his name? Pennan – that was it. And a wet young idiot he was too," Clennen said reminiscently. "I was asked in to sing at the betrothal – I had quite a name, even in those days, and I was a good deal in demand for occasions like that, let me tell you. Well, no sooner did I come into the hall and set eyes on Lenina than I knew she was the woman for me. Wasted on that idiot Fenner. That was his name, wasn't it, Lenina?"

"He was called Ganner," said Lenina.

"Oh, yes," said Clennen. "I remember he reminded me of a goose somehow. It must have been the name. I'd thought it was his scraggy neck or those button eyes of his. Anyway, I thought I'd rely on my looks being better than his and deal with Master Gosler later. For the first thing, I concentrated on Lenina. I sang – I've never sung better, before or since – and Lenina here couldn't take her eyes off me. Well, I don't blame her, because I don't mind admitting that I was a fine-looking man in those days, and gifted, too – which Flapper wasn't. So I asked Lenina in a song whether she'd marry me instead of this Honker fellow, and when I came up to get my reward for my singing, she said Yes. So then I dealt with him. I turned to him. 'Lording,' I said, most respectful, 'Lording, what gift will you give me?' And he said 'Anything you want. You're a great singer' – which was the only sensible thing he said that evening. So I said, 'I'll take what you have in your right hand.' He was holding Lenina's hand, you see. I still laugh when I think of the look on his face."

While the story went on – and it made a long one, for Clennen went over it several times, embroidering the details – Brid and Moril walked by the roadside out of earshot, watching the fed-up look settle on Kialan's face. They had both heard the story more times than they could remember.

"I suppose the thing about being a singer is that you like telling the same story a hundred times," Brid said rather acidly. "But you'd think Father would remember Ganner's name by this time."

"That's all part of it," said Moril. "I always wonder," he added dreamily, "what would happen if we met Ganner while we were going through Markind. Would he arrest Father?"

"Of course he wouldn't," said Brid. "I don't suppose it's true, anyway. And even if it did happen, Ganner must have grown into a big fat lord by now and forgotten Mother ever existed."

Since this was Brid's true opinion of the matter, it was a little unreasonable of her to be so angry when she found Kialan shared it. But one is seldom reasonable when one dislikes someone. They stopped for lunch, and Clennen, thoroughly in his stride, went on embroidering the story.

"Lenina's a real lady," he said, leaning comfortably against the pink and scarlet wheel of the cart. "She's Tholian's niece, you know. But he cast her off for running away with me. And it was all my fault for playing that trick on Gander. 'Lording,' I said to him, 'give me what you have in your right hand.' Oh, I shall never forget his face! Never!" And he burst out laughing.

Kialan had heard this at least three times by then. Moril had rarely seen him look so fed up. While Clennen was laughing, Kialan got up quickly to avoid hearing any more, and stumped off without looking where he was going. He nearly fell over Moril and Brid and became more fed up than ever.

"Blinking bore your father is!" he said. "I'd be quite sorry for Ganner if I thought there was a word of truth in it!"

"How dare you!" said Brid. "How *dare* you say that! I've a good mind to punch your nose in!"

"I don't fight with girls," Kialan said loftily. "All I meant was I'm sick of hearing about Ganner. If your father remembers it that well, why on earth can't he get the poor fellow's name right?"

"It's part of the *story*!" screamed Brid, and threw herself at Kialan.

Kialan, for a second or so, tried to keep up his claim not to fight girls, with the result that Brid punched his nose twice and then boxed his ears in perfect freedom. "You spiteful cat!" said Kialan, and grabbed both her wrists. It was in self-defence. On the other hand, he squeezed her wrists so painfully that he hurt Brid rather more than if he had hit her. She lashed out at his legs with her bare feet, but finding that made no impression on Kialan, she sank her teeth into the hand round her wrists. At this, Kialan lost his temper completely and punched Brid with his free hand.

Dagner never let people hit Brid. He surged up from his seat in the hedgerow and fell on Kialan. Moril, since

Dagner seemed to be doing his best to strangle Kialan, thought he had better get Brid out from between them and entered the fray too. They made a grunting furious bundle. Brid would not unfasten her teeth and Kialan would not let go of Brid. Clennen heaved himself up, strolled over, and wrenched Dagner away from Kialan and Kialan away from Brid. Everyone, including Moril, fell with heavy thumps, this way and that. Clennen might have been fat, but he was also strong.

"Now stop!" said Clennen. "And if you've anything more to say about my story, Kialan, say it to me." He looked cheerfully down at Kialan, angrily sprawled on the roadside sucking his bleeding knuckles. "Well?"

"All right!" said Kialan. "All *right*!" Moril could see he was nearly crying. Brid was crying. "You can keep on saying you'll never forget Ganner – or whatever he's called – all you like," said Kialan. "I don't believe you've even met him! You wouldn't know him if he came walking down the road this minute! So there!"

The cheerfulness died out of Clennen's face. It was replaced by a very odd look. Kialan noticeably tensed at it. "Do you know Ganner then?" Clennen said.

"No, of course I don't!" said Kialan. "How could I? I don't suppose he exists."

"Oh, he exists all right," said Clennen. "And I'm sure you don't know him. Yet you're right. I've seen Ganner three times this month and not known him till this minute." He laughed again, and Kialan relaxed considerably. "Not a face that stands out in a crowd," he said. "Eh, Lenina?"

"I suppose not," agreed Lenina, and continued calmly slicing cold sausage.

"*You* knew him though, didn't you?" Clennen said. "In Derent, and on the road, and again in Crady?"

"Not till he said who he was," Lenina said, quite unperturbed.

There seemed suddenly to be a situation ten times worse. All through lunch Clennen looked at Lenina in a tense, troubled way. He seemed to be expecting her to say something and, at the same time, carefully not saying all sorts of things himself. And Lenina said nothing. She said nothing so positively and obviously that the air seemed sticky with her silence. It was hateful. The rest of them picked awkwardly at their food, and no one spoke much. Kialan did not say anything. It was obvious, even to Brid, that he was kicking himself for causing the situation – as well he might, Moril thought.

When the food was finished and the cart packed again,

they went on, still in the same heavy silence. At last Clennen could bear it no longer.

"Lenina," he said, "you're not regretting all that, are you? If you want that kind of life – if you'd rather have Ganner – just say the word and I'll turn Olob towards Markind this moment."

Moril gasped. Brid's mouth came open in her tear-stained face. They looked at Clennen and found he seemed quite serious. Then they looked at Lenina, expecting her to laugh. It was so silly. Lenina was as much part of their life as Olob or the cart. But Lenina did not laugh, nor did she say anything. Not only Brid and Moril, but Dagner, Kialan and Clennen too, stared at her in increasing anxiety.

They came to a fork in the road. One branch led west, and the milestone said MARKIND 10. "Do I turn here?" asked Clennen.

Lenina gave herself an impatient shake. "Oh no," she said. "Clennen Mendakersson, you must be a very big fool indeed to think such a thing of me."

Clennen burst into a roll of relieved laughter. He shook the reins, and Olob trotted past the turning. "I must say," he said, laughing still, "I can't see how you could prefer Ganner to me. He couldn't have made the songs I've made to you, not if his life depended on it."

"Then why did you think I did?" Lenina asked coldly. The trouble was not over yet.

"Well," Clennen said awkwardly. "Money and all that. And it's what you were bred to, after all."

"I see," said Lenina. There was silence again for quite half an hour, except for the plopping of Olob's hooves and the light rumble of the cart. Kialan was unable to bear it. He got out and walked ahead, whistling the *Second March* rather defiantly. The others sat with their heads hanging, wishing Lenina would make peace. At last she said, "Oh, Clennen, do stop sitting there watching me like a dog! I'm not going to take wings and fly, am I? It's lucky Olob has more sense than you, or we'd be in the ditch by now!"

Then the trouble seemed to be over. Clennen was shortly laughing and talking again. And Lenina, if she was silent, was silent in her usual way, which everyone was used to. Brid and Moril got out of the cart too, though they did not go near Kialan. Brid was still too angry with him.

CHAPTER FOUR

THAT NIGHT THEY camped in one of the many little valleys Markind abounded in. There were woods up its steep sides and a meadow in the bottom, containing a small peaceful lake full of newly hatched tadpoles. Dagner and Kialan went off to set their snares. Lenina put herbs on the fire against the midges, and the fragrant smoke streamed sideways and settled across the lake in bands. Brid and Moril, quite unworried by insects, waded into the shallows of the lake and tried enthusiastically to collect tadpoles in an old pickle jar. Moril had just lost most of them by accident when he looked up to find his father watching them.

"You want a bigger jar," Clennen said. "And both of you want to remember what I said to Kialan about give-and-take."

"*He* doesn't remember it," Brid said sulkily.

"He's never had to learn it before," said Clennen. "That's his trouble. But it's not yours, Brid. A fight takes two."

"Did you hear what he said?" Moril demanded.

"I'm not deaf," said Clennen. "He's entitled to his opinion, like everyone else. And it wouldn't hurt you to find some opinions of your own instead of borrowing Brid's, Moril. Now get that slime off your fingers before you touch my cwidder."

While Moril was having his lesson, Kialan came out of the woods and into the lake, where he tried to teach Dagner to swim. The sight of them splashing about was a great distraction to Moril. It grew worse when Kialan tried to persuade Brid to learn to swim too. Brid claimed to be afraid of leeches. Nothing would induce her to go above her knees in water, but she agreed to learn the arm movements. Moril could hear her laughing. It looked as if Kialan were trying to make friends.

Moril became more distracted than ever. Perhaps, after

all, Kialan was not bad at heart – only tactless. Moril tried to decide what he thought. It really rankled with him that Clennen believed he borrowed Brid's opinions. Moril considered that he thought long and deeply – if rather vaguely – about most things. But he knew he had agreed with Brid, quite unquestioningly, both about Kialan and about the Ganner story. And it looked as if Brid had been wrong about both. Moril did not know what he thought.

"I suppose I ought to be used to you being up in the clouds by now," said Clennen. "Do you want to swim too?"

"No," said Moril. "Yes. I mean, is that story about Ganner true, then?"

"Word of honour," said Clennen. "Except it's the fellow's face I seem to have forgotten, not his name. I may embroider a detail here and there, but I never tell a story that isn't true, Moril. Remember that. Now go and swim if you want to."

Clennen was clearly very relieved that Lenina was not leaving for Markind. He drank a great deal of the wine that night to celebrate. The level in the huge bottle was almost down to the straw basket when he finally rolled into the larger tent and fell asleep. He was still asleep next morning when Dagner and Kialan went off to look at their snares. When Brid and Moril got up, they could hear him snoring, though Lenina was up and combing out her soft fair hair by the lake. Brid attended to the fire, and Moril tried to attend to Olob. Olob, for some reason, was tetchy. He kept flinging up his head and shying at shadows.

"What's the matter with him?" Moril asked his mother.

Lenina's comb had hit a tangle. She was lugging at it fiercely and not really attending. "No idea," she said. "Leave him be."

So Moril left off trying to groom Olob and turned to put the currycomb back in the cart. He found himself looking at a number of men, who were pushing their way through the last of the wood into the clear space by the lake. They were out almost as soon as Moril saw them, six of them. They stood in a group, looking at Moril, Brid kneeling by the fire, Lenina by the lake, the cart and the tents.

"Clennen the Singer," one of them said. "Where is he?"

Olob tossed his head and trotted away round the lake.

"He's not here," said Brid.

Moril thought he would have said the same. The men alarmed him. It was odd to see six well-dressed men outside a wood in the middle of nowhere. They were very well dressed. They wore cloth as good as Kialan's coat, and all of them had that sleek look that comes from always living in style. Each of them wore a sword in a well-kept leather scabbard, belted over the good cloth of their coats, and Moril did not like the way the hilts of those swords looked smooth with frequent use. But the truly alarming thing about them was that they had an air of purpose, all of them, which hit Moril like a gust of cold wind and frightened him.

"My father won't be back for ages," he said, hoping they would go away.

"Then we'll wait for him," said the man who had asked. Moril liked him least of all. He was fair and light-eyed, and there was an odd look in those eyes which Moril did not trust.

Lenina evidently felt the same. "Suppose you give me your message for Clennen," she said, coming forwards with her hair still loose.

"You wouldn't like it, lady," said the man. "We'll wait."

"Moril," said Lenina. "Go round the lake and fetch your father."

Moril thought that was clever of her. It would deceive

the men, and Dagner and Kialan might be some help. He tossed the currycomb into the cart and set off at a trot. But Clennen chose that moment to crawl out of the tent like a badger. He stood up, with his eyes red and blinking inside a tousled frill of hair and beard.

"Somebody call me?" he said sleepily.

Moril stopped, helpless. Everything went so quickly that he could hardly believe it was happening. The six men pushed forwards in a body, overwhelming Lenina for a moment, and then leaving her in the open, clutching Brid. Their swords caught the pink early sun. The group round Clennen trampled a bit. Clennen, sleepy as he was, must have put up something of a fight. A man stumbled sideways into the lake. Another fell in with a splash. Then the six men, swords sheathed again, went running away from the lake in a group. One glanced into Clennen's tent and then the smaller one. Another took a quick look into the cart as they passed.

"Nothing here," he called.

"Look in the woods, then," said the fair one. And they were gone.

Clennen lay where he had fallen, half in the lake, with blood running out of him into the water.

Before Moril could move, there was a thumping of

racing feet. Dagner shot past him round the lake and surged on to his knees in the water beside Clennen. "Have they killed him?"

"Not quite," said Lenina. "Help me move him."

Moril stood where he was, some distance away, and watched them heave his father out of the calm sunny water. Brid's face was greyish white, and her teeth were chattering. Dagner's mouth kept twisting about. Moril could see his hands shaking. But Lenina was quite calm and no paler than usual. As they turned Clennen over, Moril saw a cut in his chest. Bright red blood was gushing from it as fast as the river ran in Dropwater, steaming a little in the cold air over the surface of the lake.

At the sight, the bright trees, the lake and the sunny sky dipped and swung in front of Moril. Everything turned sour and grey and distant. He could not move from the spot. Up in the woods behind him, he could dimly hear the six men crashing about and calling to one another, but they could have been on the moon for all the fear and interest Moril felt. His eyes stared, so widely that they hurt, at the group by the water.

Lenina, without abating her calm, tore a big strip from her petticoat, and another, to stop the bleeding. "Give me yours," she said to Brid, and while Brid, shaking and shivering, was getting out of her petticoat, Lenina said in the same calm way to Dagner, "Get the small flask from the cart."

Moril stared at his mother working and telling Brid what to do. The only sign of emotion Lenina showed was when her hair trailed in the way of the bandages. "Bother the stuff!" she said. "Brid, tie it back for me."

Brid was still trying to get a ribbon round Lenina's hair when Dagner scudded back with the flask. "Do you think you can save him?" he asked, as if he were pleading with Lenina.

She looked up at him calmly. "No, Dagner. The most I can do is keep him with you for a while. He'll want to have his say. He always did." She took the flask from Dagner and uncorked it.

Moril desolately watched her trying to get some of the liquid from the flask into Clennen's mouth. It was not fair. He felt it was not fair on his father at all, to die like this, first thing in the morning, miles from anywhere. He ought to have had warning. Dying was a thing someone like Clennen ought to do properly, in front of a crowd, with music playing if possible.

Music was possible, of course. Moril found himself beside the cart, without quite knowing how he had got there. He scrambled up and seized the nearest cwidder. It happened to be the big one. In the ordinary way, Moril would not have chosen it. But being inside the cart made him feel sick and queer, so he simply took what came first to hand and backed hastily down with it.

While he was getting its strap over his back, he realised that Clennen's eyes were open. And it was clear that Clennen shared Moril's opinion. Moril heard him say, rather thickly, but quite strongly, "This came out of the blue, didn't it? I'd have preferred to have notice."

Moril put his hands to the strings and began to play, very softly, the weird broken little tune of *Manaliabrid's Lament*. The cwidder responded sweetly. The old song seemed more melodious than usual, and because of the water, it carried out across the lake until the valley seemed full of it. Moril heard its echo from the woods opposite.

His ears were so full of the sound that he did not hear much else of what Clennen said. Clennen's voice became weaker, anyway, after that first remark, and he spoke to Lenina in what was only a murmur. Then he spoke to Brid for a while, reaching out to hold her hand, which made Brid cry. After that, it was Dagner's turn. Clennen was very weak by then. Dagner had to put his head right down near his father's face in order to hear him.

Moril played on, as softly as he could, watching Dagner listening and nodding, and wondered vaguely at the amount Clennen seemed to have to say. Then Dagner looked up and beckoned to Moril.

"He wants to talk to you. Quickly."

Moril did not dare take off the cwidder for fear of wasting time. He hurried over to Clennen with it bumping at his thighs and knees, and hoisted it away sideways as he knelt down. Clennen's face was paler than Moril had ever seen a face before. His eyes did not seem to reflect the sky, or Moril bending over him, though it was clear he could see Moril.

"Got the big cwidder, have you?" Clennen said. Moril nodded. He could not manage to speak. "Keep it carefully," said Clennen. "It's yours now. Always meant to give it to you, Moril, because I think you've got the ability. Or will have. But you have to come to terms with it, and with yourself. Understand?" Moril nodded again, though he did not understand in the least. "You're in two halves at present," Clennen went on. "Often thought so. Come together, Moril, and there's no knowing what you might do. There's power in that cwidder, if you can use it. Used to be Osfameron's. He could use it. Handed down to me. I couldn't use it. Only found the power once, when I—" Clennen paused for breath. Moril waited for him to go on, but nothing happened. Clennen stayed as he was, with his eyes open looking at Moril, and his lips parted. After a while, Moril realised that this was all there would be. He got up and carefully, very carefully, put the cwidder back in its place inside the cart.

Brid was crying loudly. Lenina was standing very upright beside the lake, as calm as ever. Dagner seemed to have frozen into the same sort of calmness, facing her. And Kialan was coming slowly towards them round the lake with a bundle of dead rabbits.

When he reached them, Kialan stopped. He looked at Clennen and, for once, seemed not to know what to say. "I'm – terribly sorry," he said at length.

"It was going to happen sometime," said Lenina. "Will you help us dig a grave, please?"

"Of course," said Kialan. "Here?"

"Why not?" said Lenina. "Clennen never had a home after he left Hannart, and we can't take him there."

"Very well," said Kialan, and he laid the rabbits down and unhooked the spade from its clips beneath the cart. Dagner went and fetched the pickaxe, and the two set to work. Lenina watched and seemed ready to take Kialan's advice, as if, in some odd way, Kialan were in charge just then. "I think we should mark the spot," Kialan said as he dug.

"How?" said Lenina.

"Is there a spare board in the cart?" Kialan asked.

"Find him one, Moril," said Lenina.

Moril managed to work free one of the spare boards Clennen always carried under the floor of the cart, and on Kialan's instructions, he sawed off a piece about three feet long. Then he relieved Kialan at the digging for a while. Kialan took out his sheath knife and carved away at the board, quickly and competently, as if this were another thing he was good at. When he had finished, the board had letters deeply and neatly cut into it. CLENNEN THE SINGER.

"That do?" said Kialan.

"Very well," said Lenina.

When the grave was ready, Kialan, Dagner and Brid put Clennen into it. Moril did not like to see his father topple into the hole. Nor did he like to see the earth going in on top of Clennen's face and clothes. Rather than watch, he fetched his own cwidder and stood back a little, playing another lament, a newer one that had been made for an earl of Dropwater killed in battle. He went on playing while Brid put the turf back in place and Kialan trenched his board in until it was standing upright at the head of the grave, as it should. And now that there was nothing but a grave to be seen, Moril began to feel that something was missing. They should all be feeling and doing something else. They should be angry. Clennen had been murdered. They should be trying to bring the murderers to justice. But none of them thought of it. It was out of the question, here in the South. The six men had been far too well dressed.

"There," said Kialan, wiping his hands on his coat.

"Thank you," said Lenina. "Now I must change. This dress has blood on it. And you too, Brid. Kialan, I think it would be a good idea if you changed your coat for Dagner's old one."

Kialan agreed to this, although Moril did not think Kialan's good coat was more than a little earthy. When everyone was changed and cleaned, Lenina told Dagner to catch Olob and harness him to the cart. Kialan picked up his bundle of rabbits.

"Leave those," said Lenina. "We don't need them."

"Well, I don't fancy them at the moment, either," said Kialan. "But—"

"Leave them," said Lenina. Kialan did as he was bid. Now Lenina seemed to be definitely in charge. It was she who took the reins when Olob was ready and drove out of the valley.

Brid and Moril looked back. It was a very beautiful valley. Probably, Moril thought, it was a good place to be buried, if one had to be. Brid cried. Dagner did not look back. He had sunk into a silence as profound as any of Lenina's. He did not look at anything, and no one liked to speak to him.

Lenina drove northwards for a mile or so, until she came to a road that turned off to the left. Then, to Moril's surprise, she swung the cart into it.

"Hey! Where are we going?" said Moril.

"Markind," said Lenina.

"What? Not to Ganner!" demanded Brid, halting in the middle of a sob.

"Yes. To Ganner," said Lenina. "He said he would have me and mine if ever I was free, and I know he meant it."

"Oh, but no! You can't!" said Moril. "Not just like that!"

"Why not?" Lenina asked. "How do you think we shall live, without a singer to earn us money?"

"We can manage," said Moril. "I can sing. Dagner can – Dagner…" His voice tailed away as he thought of Dagner and himself trying to perform as Clennen did. He just could not see Dagner doing it. He did not know what to say, so he stopped, fearing he might be hurting Dagner's feelings. But it looked as if Dagner was not listening. "Father wouldn't like us to go to Markind," Moril asserted. He was sure of that, at least.

"I can't see that your father has much say in the matter now," Lenina answered drily. "Get this clear, Moril. I know well enough that your father was a good man, and the best singer in Dalemark, and I've done my duty by him for seventeen years. That's half my lifetime, Moril. I've gone barefoot and learnt to cook and make music. I've lived in a cart in all weathers, and never complained. I've mended and cleaned and looked after you all. There were things your father did that I didn't agree with at all, but I never argued with him or crossed him. I did my duty exactly in every way, and I've nothing to reproach myself with. But Clennen's dead now, so I'm free to do as I choose. What I'm choosing is my birthright and yours too. Do you understand?"

"I suppose so," Moril mumbled. He had never heard Lenina say anything like this before. He was frightened and rather shocked to see that she must have been *not* saying it for longer than he had lived. He thought it was wrong of her, but he could not have said why. He thought she was altogether wrong, but he could not find any words to set against her. All he could do was to exchange a scared, helpless look with Brid. Brid said nothing either.

It was Kialan who spoke. He sounded rather embarrassed. "It's not my place to object," he said. "But I do have to get to Hannart, Lenina."

"I know," said Lenina. "I've thought of that. You can pose as my son for the moment, and I'll find someone to take you North as soon as I can, I promise. Hestefan's in the South, I know, and Fredlan may be too."

Kialan looked exasperated as well as embarrassed. "But Ganner must know how many children you've got!"

"I shouldn't think so," Lenina said calmly. "People who haven't got children themselves never bother to count other people's. If he wonders, I'll say you've been ill and we'd left you at Fledden."

Kialan sighed. "Oh well. Thanks, anyway."

"Remember that," Lenina said to Moril, Brid and Dagner, and Moril felt very queer, because "Remember that" was such a favourite saying of Clennen's. "Kialan's your brother. If anyone asks, he's been ill in Fledden."

Olob plodded towards Markind. He did not look happy either, Moril thought, looking at the droop of

Olob's head. Moril was so miserable himself that he could almost hear it, like a droning in his ears, and he could not hide away in vagueness, much as he tried. He felt vividly and horribly attentive to everything, from the leaves in the hedge to the shape of Kialan's nose. Kialan's eagle nose was so different from Dagner's, Brid's, or Moril's that surely anyone could tell at a glance he was no relation? Why did he have to be a relation, anyway? And had Clennen known he wanted to go to Hannart? Clennen would not have gone there because he never went to Hannart. And why had the six men killed Clennen? Who were they, and what were they looking for in the wood? And why, why, why above all, had Clennen given Moril a cwidder he did not want in the least?

I shall never play it, Moril thought. *I'll polish it and string it, and maybe tune it from time to time, but I don't want to play it. I know I should be grateful, because it must be very valuable – though it* can't *be old enough to have belonged to Osfameron; he's long ago in a story – but I don't like it and I don't want it.*

Markind came into view at the other end of a valley. Without meaning to, Moril looked at it as he always looked at a new town. *Sleepy and respectable*, he thought. *Bad takings*. Then he remembered he was supposed to be going here to live, not to sing, and tried very hard to look at the pile of yellowish-grey houses with interest. He found he was more interested in the villainously freckled cows which were grazing in the small green meadows outside the town.

Lenina looked at these cows with pleasure. "I remember I always liked those speckles," she said. She encouraged Olob to trot, and the grey and yellow houses approached swiftly. Moril's heart sank rather – and he had thought it was low enough before.

Soon they were winding up a gravelly street between quiet old houses. The houses were tall and cold and shuttered. There were very few people about. Even when they came to the main square and found a market going on under the high plane trees, there were still very few people, and these all sober citizens who looked at the gay cart with strong disapproval. Lenina drove past the stalls looking neither to right nor to left, and drew Olob up in front of a round-topped gateway in a massive yellow wall. Two men who seemed to be on guard at the gate peered round it at the cart in evident astonishment.

"Had you business here?" one of them asked Lenina.

"Certainly," Lenina answered haughtily. "Go and tell Ganner Sagersson that Lenina Thornsdaughter is here."

They looked at her in even more astonishment at that. But one of them went off into the spaces behind the thick yellow wall. The other stayed, frowning wonderingly at Lenina, the cart and her family, until Moril scarcely knew where to look.

"What's the betting we get a message back to say, Not Today, Thank You?" whispered Brid.

"Be quiet, Brid!" said Lenina. "Behave properly, can't you!"

Brid would have lost her bet. The man who had gone with the message came back at a run, and they could hear a number of people behind the gate, running too. The two halves of the gate were flung wide open.

"Please drive in," said the man.

Lenina smiled graciously and shook the reins. Olob plodded forwards, disapproval in every line of his ears and back, into a small deep courtyard lined with interested faces. Ganner was standing in the middle of it, smiling delightedly.

"Welcome back, Lenina!" he said. "I never thought I'd see you so soon. What happened?"

"Some men killed Clennen this morning," said Lenina. "They looked like the pick of somebody's hearthmen to me."

"Not really!" exclaimed Ganner. Then he looked a little worried and asked, "Does that mean it happened in my lordship then?"

"Yes," said Lenina. "At Medmere."

"I'd better send some hearthmen over to investigate," said Ganner. "Anyway, come down and come in. Are these your children?"

"My three sons and my daughter," said Lenina.

"What a lot of them!" said Ganner, looking a little daunted. But he smiled gallantly at all four. "I'll do my best to look after you all," he said. Moril could not find it in his heart to dislike Ganner, much as he had intended to. It was so plain he meant well. If, to someone who had been used to Clennen, he seemed a very ordinary person, then that was hardly Ganner's fault, Moril supposed.

"He doesn't look much like a goose," Brid whispered, in some disappointment. Kialan had to bite his lip. Moril looked at Ganner gallantly helping Lenina down from the cart and smiling at her in a way that showed he adored her. Apart from that smile, he really seemed perfectly normal and ungooselike.

"Oh dear, oh dear!" Ganner exclaimed, as they all got down. "Shoes! Boots! Can you only afford one pair of boots?"

Lenina glanced along their line of bare feet, interrupted by Kialan's scuffed boots. "We don't usually bother with them," she explained. "But Collen has tender feet."

"I must make sure you all have shoes this instant!" Ganner exclaimed distractedly.

"You know, I think he may be a goose after all," Brid said, with considerable satisfaction.

CHAPTER FIVE

B Y THAT AFTERNOON Moril was wondering if it was
only that morning they had left Clennen buried
by the lake. It felt like last century. There had been so
many changes. After a good breakfast, followed by the
attentions of a tailor, a bootmaker and Ganner's old
nurse, followed in turn by an astonishingly good lunch,
Moril scarcely knew himself. He looked in a mirror – it
was a thing he seldom had the chance of doing, so he
looked long and often – and he saw a smoothly combed
red-haired boy in a suit of good blue cloth and a pair
of soft rust-coloured boots. The boots, to tell the truth,

pleased him enormously. But he did not look in the least like his idea of himself. Dagner and Kialan had become spruce, gentlemanly figures in the same kind of blue clothes, and Brid a young lady in bright cherry colour. They were all four behaving very soberly and politely, not because Ganner insisted on it – because he did not – but simply because Markind was the sort of place where you could behave in no other way.

The biggest change was to Lenina. She was splendidly dressed too, and she had done her hair the way ladies did. Her cheeks were pinker than usual, and she laughed and chattered and hurried about with Ganner on a hundred errands. Moril had not often seen her laugh, and he had certainly never seen her so talkative. She was like a different person. That troubled him. It troubled him far more than learning she was going to marry Ganner that same evening.

Moril quite liked Ganner. Ganner told Moril he could do just what he liked and go anywhere he wanted, and obviously meant it. He was a very good-natured man. Moril quite liked the other people in the house too. He liked Ganner's old nurse specially. She fussed rather, and she said rather too often that she had always known Lenina Thornsdaughter would come back to them, but she called Moril "My duck" and said he was a "blessing". And while she was dressing him, she told Moril a story about a lord of Markind who had been outlawed. Moril had not heard the story before, and he drank it up. But he felt strange. Everything felt strange.

Moril took Ganner at his word and explored the house. He found two gardens and the kitchens. He looked at the cellars and the small rooms under the roof, but in between each exploration he found himself drifting into the stableyard. The cart had been put away in a coach house there, just as it was, wine jar, cwidders and all, down to the string of onions under the driving seat. It was just the same, yet somehow it already looked smaller and dustier and a little faded. Moril spent a lot of time talking to Olob, who was standing dejectedly in a stall nearby and seemed glad of his company. Moril stole sugar for him from the kitchen, which was easy to do because everyone there was in a great bustle, preparing for the wedding feast. Olob ate it politely, but he looked sad, and he was sweating rather.

"Poor fellow," Moril said sadly. "I'm hot too. It's being in a house."

As the afternoon drew on, Moril became hotter still. Being between walls so oppressed him that he wondered whether to go out and walk in the town. But Markind had not inspired him with any wish to see more of it. He wandered to the stableyard and then into one of the gardens. Brid was there. She was feeling much the same, for she had taken off her cherry-coloured boots and was sitting with her feet in one of the goldfish ponds.

They exchanged sad, polite smiles, and Moril went on into the second garden. Behind him he heard Ganner's voice.

"My dear little girl! You'll catch your death like that! Do please dry your feet and put your boots on. You'll worry your mother."

Moril felt sorry for Brid. Then he suddenly felt even more – desperately – sorry for himself. He needed to be somewhere else, out in the open. He looked round wildly, upwards, everywhere. And a sturdy creeper growing up the thick yellow wall of the house gave him an idea. He slung himself on to it and started to climb.

It was extremely easy, except for the last bit, which needed a long stride and a heave across some crumbly stonework. Then he was on the wide, leaded roofs. It was splendid. Moril looked round, into the town, out across the valley, and over to valleys beyond. He turned north and looked at the misty blue peaks there, where he had so longed to go, and Kialan – lucky Kialan! – was going soon. But that made him sad. So, presently, Moril began to patter about across the leads and among the chimneys. He skirted courtyards and looked down into the gardens. Then he ran along a narrow part to another wing and looked down into another court.

And there was Ganner, horrified and gesturing below. "Come down! Come down at once!"

Moril looked. There was a lead pipe and an easy flight of windows. Obediently he swung his legs over the edge of the roof.

Ganner stopped him with a hoarse shriek. "No! Stop! Do you want to break your neck? Wait!" He ran away and presently ran back with a crowd of men carrying a ladder. With them ran a group of horrified maids and the old nurse, wringing her hands.

"My duck! Oh, my duck!"

Moril sat sadly on the edge of the roof, swinging his legs and watching them all pothering with the ladder. He knew what was wrong with Ganner now. He was a fusspot.

The ladder finally thumped against the wall beside him. "You can come down now," Ganner called. "Go very carefully."

Moril sighed and got on to the ladder. He came down rather slowly out of sheer perverseness. He decided when he got near enough he would say to Ganner, "But you told me I could go anywhere I wanted." When he judged he was low enough for it to be most effective, he turned round to say it.

A man was just coming in through the door to the courtyard – a fair man with light, untrustworthy eyes, who checked for a moment when he saw Moril twenty feet up a long ladder, staring at him. Shrugging slightly, the man strolled over to Ganner and said something to him. Ganner replied. The man shrugged again, said another word or so to Ganner, and strolled out of the courtyard.

Moril forgot what he intended to say. Instead, as soon as he was down on the ground, he said, "Who was that man here just now? The fair one, who spoke to you."

Ganner looked uneasy, so uneasy that Moril's chest went tight and he felt sick. "Oh – er – just someone who's my guest here," said Ganner. "Now you are absolutely *not* to get on the roof again! It's extremely high, and the leads are quite unsafe. You might have been killed!"

"Killed, my duck!" said his nurse.

Moril bore with a long scold from both Ganner and

the nurse, without listening to a word. Both of them would have scolded anyway, but Moril was fairly sure that Ganner was scolding mostly as an excuse not to discuss the fair man. Moril did not want to discuss him. His one desire was to get away and find Lenina.

Lenina was in the great hall of the house. Presumably it was the same place where Clennen had sung and then played the trick on Ganner seventeen years before. Lenina was gaily organising the tables for the wedding feast, and doing it as if she had done nothing else all her life. Moril had to pull her sleeve to get her to attend to him.

"Mother! One of the men who killed Father! He's staying here."

"Oh, Moril, don't interrupt me with stupid stories!" Lenina said impatiently.

"But I saw him," said Moril.

"You must have made a mistake," said Lenina. She pulled her sleeve away and went back to the tables.

Moril stood, shocked and troubled, in the middle of the hall. He saw quite clearly that his mother did not want to believe him. She had put Clennen and all that part of her life behind her and she did not want to be reminded of it. Yet if Ganner had had a hand in killing Clennen, this was the last place she ought to be – the last place any of them ought to be. Moril looked at gay, busy Lenina, shook his head desolately, and hurried away to find Brid.

Brid was hurrying through the garden in the opposite direction. "Moril—!"

"One of the men who killed Father," said Moril. "He's staying here."

"I know. I saw him," said Brid. "Did you try to tell Mother?"

"Yes. She wouldn't listen."

"She wouldn't listen to me either," said Brid. "She doesn't want to know, I think. Moril, what are we going to do? We can't stay here, can we? Do you think Ganner had Father killed?"

Moril thought about it. He remembered that though Ganner had obviously been very pleased to see Lenina, he had not perhaps been entirely surprised. And he did not like it at all. "I don't know. He *could* have done. Only he's a bit too feeble to think of it, isn't he?"

"And why not do it years ago if he felt that bad about Father stealing Mother off him?" said Brid. "But I don't care whether he did or not. I'm not staying here, and that's final!"

"Mother *is* staying," said Moril. "I'm afraid that's final too."

"Then we'll have to do without her," said Brid. "I can cook, and we've got good clothes now. The only thing is, I'm not very good on the hand organ."

Moril did not feel as if they had come to a decision. It was as if he had known all along that they would leave. "But can we manage?" he said. "Give shows and all without even Dagner?"

"Dagner will have to come too," stated Brid. "He'll have to. He's Father's heir, and he ought to. Besides, he shouldn't stay here even more than us. If it was old days, he'd have to avenge Father."

Moril was dubious. Wherever Brid thought Dagner's duty lay, Moril knew Dagner would want to stay with Lenina. He knew, without knowing how he knew, that Dagner had always been closer to his mother than to Clennen. And how could Dagner take up the singer's trade when he was terrified and nervous at every show? "But would Dagner do it – on his own? I mean—"

"I know just what you mean," said Brid. "But I can manage Dagner. I can always manage him when there aren't any parents around to interfere."

"Let's go and find him, then," said Moril.

Neither of them had seen Dagner for a considerable while. Since they had not the least idea where to start looking, they drifted quite naturally to the stableyard first, to have a look at Olob and the cart.

Dagner was in the stableyard, polishing Olob's harness, and Kialan was helping him. Both of them looked a little blank when Moril and Brid came in.

"Do you two haunt this yard, or something?" Kialan said irritably.

Moril decided to take the bull by the horns. "We're taking the cart and leaving," he said. "Are you two coming?" Kialan was clearly astonished and stared at Moril with all the annoyance of someone who cannot believe his ears.

"I've got to go anyway," said Dagner. "Father asked me to take Kialan to Hannart. But there's no need for you two to come."

"Oh, yes, there is!" said Brid. "One of the men who killed Father is in this house, and if that isn't a reason for going, give me a better one!"

Dagner and Kialan exchanged glances, and Kialan screwed his mouth up. "True?" Dagner said to Moril.

"I saw him," said Moril. "The fair one with queer eyes. But you didn't see them, did—"

"Yes, I did," said Dagner. "We were only in the woods. That one was the leader. Kialan, I think that settles it, don't you? We'd better leave at once, as soon as I've said goodbye to Mother."

"Don't be an idiot!" said Moril. "If you tell Mother we're going, she'll tell Ganner. And he's such a big fusspot that he's bound to say it's dangerous and stop us going."

Kialan and Dagner looked at one another again. "He's got a point there, Dagner," Kialan said. "Ganner is an awful old woman. He's bound to come after us, anyway. What do you say to waiting until the wedding feast has started and he's too busy to notice we're missing?"

Dagner pondered anxiously. He looked purple and bent with worry. "No," he said at length. "No, we daren't. Not if this other fellow's here." He jerked his head to the end of the yard. There was a big old gate in the wall there, bolted and peeling. "We've found out that leads to a back street. You two get those bolts back while I harness Olob, but don't open it till I'm ready."

Kialan helped Dagner pull out the cart and back Olob between its shafts, so they were ready almost as soon as Brid and Moril had done their part. The bolts were very stiff and rusty. Brid wanted to fetch the oil from the cart, but Moril would not let her. "No," he said. "I've an idea to fool Ganner." It took them quite a while, and cost Brid a pinched finger, to waggle the bolts back without.

"Ready," said Dagner. Olob came towards the gate, almost dancing with pleasure at being at the work he was used to. Brid and Moril swung the gate creaking open. Brid went up into the cart, with the easy spring of long practice, and sat down to get her boots off. The cart rumbled through and crunched on the gravel of the lane outside, which was so narrow that Olob for a moment seemed likely to run into the shuttered house opposite. Moril stayed inside the stableyard and carefully bolted the gate again. It looked, to his satisfaction, as if it had never been opened at all. He took a running jump at it and managed to hook his fingers in the top, where the gate did not quite meet the wall above. From there, he swarmed up on to the thick top of the wall itself. Kialan stood up in the cart to help him jump down.

"Good idea," he said. "Let's hope Ganner wastes a lot of time trying to find out which way we went."

CHAPTER SIX

IN THE LATE afternoon Markind seemed to be deserted. As they clattered northwards through its shuttered, respectable streets, Moril was ready to swear that there was no one around to notice even such a noticeable cart as theirs. Nevertheless, Dagner was as tense as if he were giving a performance. He did not relax even when they were out of Markind. Instead of looking for a main road, he struck into the first small lane that went north and kept turning round uneasily as he drove to see if Ganner was following them.

Olob clattered along with a will, with his ears gaily

pricked. The lane, and then the other lanes they took after it, led through apple orchards where the trees were bursting into bloom. The sun was mild and warm. Moril sat smiling sleepily and happily, listening to the familiar beat of Olob's hooves, the wine sloshing about in the great jar behind him, and the blackbirds singing in the apple trees. This was the life! He was sure they could manage, whatever Lenina thought. A cuckoo sang out, cutting across the songs of the blackbirds.

"O—oh!" said Brid. Tears began rolling down her cheeks. "Father said to me – by the lake – he hadn't heard a cuckoo yet this year. And he was sorry he was going to miss it." Her face screwed up, and her tears ran faster than ever. "He told me to listen for him, on the way North. And Mother goes and drives straight off to Markind! How could she!"

"Shut up, Brid," said Dagner uncomfortably.

"I shan't! I can't!" cried Brid. "How could she! How could she! Ganner's so stupid. How *could* she!"

"Will you be quiet!" said Dagner. "You don't understand."

"Yes, I *do*!" Brid cried. "Ganner and Mother arranged to have Father murdered – that's what happened!"

"Don't talk such blinking nonsense!" Kialan said

sharply. "That had nothing to do with either of them."

"How do *you* know?" Brid wept. "Why did she go straight off to Ganner like that?"

"Because she's always wanted to, of course!" said Dagner. "Only she couldn't, because she thought it wasn't honourable. I *told* you you didn't understand," he went on, in an odd, agitated way. "You're too young to notice. But I've seen – oh, enough to know Mother hated living in a cart. She wasn't brought up to it like we are. It was all right while we were in the Earl of Hannart's household – we had a roof over our heads and that wasn't too bad for her – but – I suppose you don't remember."

"Not very well," Brid admitted, sniffing. "I was only three when we left."

"Well, I do," said Dagner. "And Father *would* leave, though he knew Mother didn't want to go. And in the cart she had to bring us up and keep us clean and cook – and she'd never done anything like that in her life till then. And sometimes there was no money at all, and we were always on the move and always – well, there were other things she didn't like Father doing. But Father always got his own way over them. Mother never had a say in anything. She just did the work. Then she saw Ganner again in Derent, after all those years, and she told me it had brought her old life back to her and made her feel terrible. I just don't blame her for going back to what she was used to. You can see Ganner's not going to order her around like Father did."

"Father didn't order her around!" Brid protested. "He even offered to take her back to Ganner."

"Yes, and I thought Mother was really going to call his bluff for a moment then," said Dagner. "He knew darned well Mother wouldn't go, because it wasn't her duty, but he had an anxious moment all the same, didn't he? And then he took good care to point out how much cleverer he was than Ganner."

"That was just his way," said Brid.

"It was all just his way," said Dagner. "Look, Brid, I don't want to pull Father to pieces any more than you do, but in some ways he was – oh, maddening. And if you think about it, you'll see he and Mother weren't at all well matched."

Moril was blinking a little at all this. It was so unlike Dagner to talk so much or so clearly. He marvelled at the way Dagner managed to put into words things Moril had known all his life but not truly noticed till this moment. "Don't you think Mother was fond of Father at all?" he asked dolefully.

"Not in the way we were," said Dagner.

"In that case, why did she run off with him like that?" Brid asked triumphantly, as if that clinched the matter.

Dagner looked pensively at a new vista of apple trees coming into view beyond Olob's ears. "I'm not sure," he said, "but I *think* that cwidder had something to do with it."

Moril swivelled round and cast an apprehensive look at the gleaming belly of the old cwidder, resting in its place in the rack. "Why do you think that?" he asked nervously.

"Something Mother said once," said Dagner. "And Father told you there was power in it, didn't he?"

"There probably is, if it belonged to Osfameron," Kialan observed in a matter-of-fact way.

"Don't be silly! It can't be that old!" Moril protested.

"Osfameron lived not quite two hundred years ago," said Kialan, and he really seemed to know. "He was born the same year as King Labbard died, so it can't be more than that. A cwidder'd surely last as long as that if you took care of it. Why, we've – I've seen one that's four hundred years old – though, mind you, it looks ready to drop apart if you breathed on it."

Moril cast another look, even more apprehensive, at

the quiet, prosperous shape of the old cwidder. "It can't be!" he said.

"Well," Dagner said diffidently, "you get used to thinking things like that were only around long ago, but – I'll tell you, Moril – didn't you get the impression you kept Father alive with it this morning?" Moril stared at Dagner with his mouth open. "I thought so," Dagner said, a trifle apologetically. "I've never heard it sound like it did then. And – and Father was dead awfully quickly after you left off, wasn't he?"

Moril was appalled. "Whatever am I going to do with a thing like that!" he almost wailed.

"I don't know. Learn to use it, perhaps," said Dagner. "I must say I was glad Father didn't give it to me."

Everyone subsided into thoughtfulness. Brid sniffed wretchedly. Olob clopped steadily on for a mile or so. Then he took a look at the sinking sun and decided to choose them a camping ground. Dagner dissuaded him. He refused to let Olob turn off the road three times, until Olob got the point and did not try again. They went on and on and on, downhill, uphill, through small valleys, pastures and orchards. The sky died from blue to pink and from pink to purple, and Brid could bear no more.

"Oh, do let's *stop*, Dagner! Today seems to have gone

on for about a hundred years!"

"I know," said Dagner. "But I want to get a really good start."

"Do you think Ganner will really follow us?" said Moril. "He ought to be glad we've gone. Then he needn't fuss about roofs and things."

"He's bound to," said Kialan. "A man with a conscience – that's Ganner. He'll probably send some of his hearthmen out tonight and set out himself first thing tomorrow. That's what – I mean, if it had been just Dagner and me, he—"

"Go on. Say it. You think Moril and I shouldn't have come," Brid said bitterly.

"I didn't *say* that!" snapped Kialan.

"Just meant it," said Brid.

"No, he didn't," said Dagner. "Stop being stupid, Brid. The thing is, I left without explaining to Mother, and even if I had explained, she wouldn't have wanted you two to go. So I know she'll ask Ganner to come after us. If he does catch us up, you and Moril will have to go back, I'm afraid."

"Oh *no*!" said Brid, and Moril felt equally mutinous.

"That's why I hope he doesn't catch us," Dagner said. "Because I don't think I could give a show on my own, and I was wondering how on earth I'd manage."

This admission mollified Brid greatly. She refrained from grumbling, although they went on until the light was all but gone. Then Dagner at last permitted Olob to select them a spot on top of a hill. This meant their camp was windy, a fact which Brid bitterly pointed out while they were fumbling around trying to put up the tent in the breezy semi-dark.

"Yes, but we can see people coming," said Dagner.

"And there are thistles. I've just trodden on one," Brid complained.

"Then why on earth don't you put your boots on?" demanded Kialan.

"Oh, I couldn't! I'd spoil them," Brid said, quite shocked.

Kialan roared with laughter, which seemed to restore Brid's frayed temper. She took it quite cheerfully when Moril discovered the only food they had was bread and onions.

"I *knew* we'd need those rabbits," Kialan said dejectedly.

"We all had a good lunch," said Brid.

Moril had the notion of frying the bread and onions together. Unfortunately it was then so dark that he could not see to fry. The mixture he turned out of the frying pan was extremely singed, and it was only eaten because everyone was very hungry. Then they settled down to sleep. It seemed to Moril, waking and resettling himself round the wine jar during the night, that Kialan and Dagner kept watch, turn and turn about, until dawn broke. Certainly they both looked very jaded in the morning.

Nevertheless, as soon as the sun was up and Olob fed, Dagner had the cart on the move again. They ate the last of the bread as they went. Brid moaned a little, and Dagner promised they would buy more food in the next village they came to.

"What with?" said Brid.

That was a nasty moment. There was no money in the locker where Lenina usually kept it. She must have taken it out in Markind. And none of them had any money in the pockets of their fine new clothes. For a while, it looked as if they would have to give a show before they could eat. Then Brid thought of going through the clothes locker, turning out pockets. There were a few coins in the pockets of Clennen's scarlet suit, and a further few fell out of Kialan's old good coat when Brid picked it up.

"May we use these? We'll pay you back," she said.

"Of course," said Kialan. "I'd forgotten I'd got any."

When they came to a village, Dagner drew up on the outskirts and sent Brid and Moril shopping, shouting after them at the last minute that there were no more oats for Olob. The rule was that you bought oats first – for where would you be with Olob undernourished? – and they were dear in those parts at that season. Brid and Moril came glumly back with oats, a loaf, half a can of milk, a cold black sausage and a cabbage. Knowing that Dagner would certainly put off giving a performance if he could, Brid prepared to do battle.

"That's all we could afford. If we don't give a show tomorrow, we'll starve," she announced, dumping the meagre purchases in the cart.

"We're going to," Dagner said, to her surprise. "Father said we were to be sure to perform in Neathdale, and I think we'll be there by tomorrow. Have you found it?" he asked Kialan, who was frowning over the map. It was not a good map. Clennen knew Dalemark like the back of his hand and only kept a map for emergencies.

"If this place *is* Cindow, Neathdale's quite a way to the north-west," said Kialan. "Is it worth it? It would be almost as easy to go by the Marshes from here."

"Yes, I've got to go. And he said we'd be bound to

get news there," said Dagner. "Let's get going. And," he added, "I suppose we'd better have a bit of a practice this evening."

As Olob went on, Moril, sighing rather, went and fetched the old cwidder. When he had vowed not to play it, he had been thinking of an idle life in Markind – if he had thought of the future at all – but now, whether Dagner played pipes or treble cwidder, and Brid pipes or panhorn, someone was going to have to play tenor to them. That meant Moril on the big cwidder. And he had always been in awe of it, and never more than now. By way of coming to terms with it, he laid it on his knees and polished it as Clennen had taught him. Brid gave him the note on the panhorn, and he tuned it. And tuned it again. And re-tuned it. As fast as he got a string to the right pitch, it went off again. All he could produce was the moaning twang of slack strings.

"I think the pegs are slipping," he said helplessly.

"Let me have a go," Brid said competently. But she could not get it tuned either.

"Let me look at the pegs," said Kialan. He looked, and seemed fairly knowledgeable, but he could not see anything wrong. He handed it on to Dagner. Dagner, who knew most of all, hitched the reins round his knees and spent half an hour trying to get the cwidder tuned. In the end he was forced to hand it back to Moril in the same state as before.

"Isn't that all we needed!" said Brid. "Perhaps it's in mourning. After all, we all should be, and look at us!"

"Try playing a lament," Kialan said thoughtfully.

"Why?" said Moril. "Anyway, I hate the old songs."

"Any lament," said Dagner. "You played your own treble over the grave, didn't you?"

Moril tried it. He began singing the *Lament for the Earl of Dropwater*, and brought the cwidder in as softly as he could after the first line. The discord was horrible. Brid shuddered. But Dagner took up the song too, and the cwidder seemed almost to follow his lead. The notes came right as Dagner sang them. To Moril's astonishment and secret terror, the cwidder was in tune by the end of the first verse. He sang the chorus, and first Brid, then Kialan, joined in.

> *"This was a man above all other,*
> *Kanart the Earl, Kanart the Earl!*
> *You'll never find his equal, brother.*
> *He was a man above all other."*

The cwidder sang on, as sweetly as it had for Clennen. Tears poured down Brid's face. Moril felt tearful too. They sang lustily through the whole song, and sad though it made them, they felt heartened too. The oddest effect was on Olob. His pace dropped to a slow, rhythmic walk, and he went for all the world as if the cart was a hearse.

"Put it away," said Dagner, "or we'll never get to Neathdale."

Moril put the alarming cwidder carefully back, and they made better progress. As before, Dagner would not let Olob stop at the usual time or in the usual kind of place. A little before sunset he took Olob right off the road into a high, lonely field full of big stones, where they could see a good way in most directions.

"There hasn't been a sign of Ganner!" Moril protested.

"Well, there won't be, until we see him arriving, will there?" said Kialan.

They demolished the sausage and held their practice. To Moril's relief, the big cwidder now behaved perfectly. But there were other difficulties. Without Clennen or Lenina, they found they could not do half the songs in the way they were used to. They had to work everything out afresh. And Dagner did not in any way take Clennen's place. He refused to do more than a third of the singing, and that was the only thing he was firm about. Otherwise, he simply made suggestions, and he was quite ready to be overruled by Brid or Moril. The younger two felt lost. They were used to Clennen's kind but entirely firm way of telling them exactly what to do. Sometimes they were annoyed, and several times they were tempted to get very silly. It was only the grim thought that their next meal depended on this practice that kept them from breaking into loud arguments or louder laughter. Moril felt he had never truly missed Clennen till then.

Yet, in the middle of thinking that, he remembered what Dagner had said about Clennen's always having his own way. It occurred to him to wonder if Clennen had not, in fact, kept them all a little too dependent on him. Maybe this was why it seemed so hard to manage without him.

While they practised, Kialan lay full length on a rock above them, listening and also, Moril suspected, acting as lookout. This elaborate caution began to irritate Moril. After all, it was Moril and Brid who stood to lose if Ganner found them, not Dagner and Kialan. In the morning he was exasperated to see that they had been on watch again. Both of them looked tired out.

Brid was furious. "How on earth do you think you're

going to give a performance, Dagner, if you can hardly keep your eyes open? I've never known you so silly! We *depend* on you!"

"All right," Dagner said wearily. "You drive and I'll have a sleep in the cart. But wake me if – if – "

"If *what*?" snapped Brid.

"If anything happens," said Dagner, and lay down beside the wine jar with a groan. Kialan flopped down on the other side of the jar, and both of them fell asleep before Olob had the cart in motion.

It was left to Brid and Moril to find the way to Neathdale. They did it too, half cross and half proud of themselves. The map did not help much. They were forced to follow their noses across country, turning into any road that seemed to go north-west and hoping for the best. Once they arrived in a farmyard and had to back out of it, pursued by the barking of dogs and the squalling of hens and roosters. Kialan and Dagner did not even stir. "Stupid fools," said Brid. They were still asleep when the cart came out on a rise above Neathdale.

"We did it!" said Moril.

"Unless Olob knew the way," Brid said, trying to be fair. "But I don't think even he can have come to it this way before."

Neathdale was a big cheerful-looking town lying across the main road north to Flennpass, in the last level ground before the Uplands. They could look across even its tallest buildings from where they were to where the South Dales mounted like stairs to the Mark Wood plateau.

"Say four days, and we'll be in the North," Moril said yearningly.

"Four days," said Brid promptly.

The scuffle that followed on the driving seat woke Dagner and Kialan at last. "What's the matter? What's going on?"

"Nothing. Only Neathdale," said Brid. Dagner's sleepy face at once became pinched and tense and mauvish. Brid set herself to soothe him. "We always used to get good takings here," she said. "There must be hundreds of people who remember us and know Father. I'm going to do the talking, mind, and I shall talk about Father and say who we are – though they can read that on the cart anyway."

"The cart ought to be repainted with Dagner's name," Moril observed. He did not think Brid was soothing Dagner in the slightest, but he did not mind helping.

"You'd hardly get the name on," Brid said brightly.

"Dastgandlen down one side and Handagner up the other, I suppose."

"Isn't Neathdale the seat of Earl Tholian?" Kialan asked, tactlessly cutting through the soothing.

"Not really. His place is outside a bit, over to the east," Dagner said. He pointed with a hand that shook noticeably. A great white house was just visible, among trees, on the other side of Neathdale.

"Blast you, Kialan!" said Brid. Kialan looked at her in surprise. "Oh, it doesn't matter," said Brid. "Just if this show goes wrong, I'll blame you. Dagner, I think we'd better put on our glad rags now."

"No," said Dagner.

"What do you mean?" said Brid.

"Just no," said Dagner. "We'll give the show as we are. We're quite respectable."

"Yes, but we always change," Brid protested. "It gives you a feel."

"That was Father's idea," said Dagner. "And he was right in a way. It went with his style to come rolling in, singing and glittering. He could live up to it. But if I go in dressed in tinsel and singing my head off, people are just going to laugh."

"You think that because you're nervous," Brid said

persuasively. "You'll feel better once you're changed."

"No, I won't," said Dagner. "I'll feel ten times worse. Brid, I just haven't got Father's personality, and I can't do the same things. I'll have to do them my way, or not at all. See?"

Brid, by this time, was near tears. "Do you mean you're not going to give a show at all then?"

"Not Father's kind," said Dagner, "because I can't. We'll give a show all right, because we'll starve if we don't, and you can introduce us and explain what's happened, and maybe it'll be all right. But if I find you boasting and ranting about us – that goes for you too, Moril – I'll stop. We'll just have to be plain, because we're not Father."

Brid sighed heavily. "All right. But I'm going to put my boots on, anyway. I need a feel." She brightened a little. "I've always hated the colour of your suit, Moril. You look nicer like that."

"Thank you," Moril said politely. Dagner had suddenly brought it home to him that, for the first time in their lives, they were about to give a show entirely on their own. He had never, as far as he knew, been nervous before. Now he was. As Brid drove downhill towards Neathdale, Moril sat clutching the big cwidder with hands that were icy cold and sweating at once, and it would have been hard to say whether he or Dagner was the more nervous. The houses came nearer. Quite desperate, Moril laid his cheek against the smooth wood of the cwidder. "Oh, please help me!" he whispered to it. "I'll never manage. I can't!"

"Can you stop a moment?" said Kialan.

Brid drew up. Kialan immediately swung down from the cart to the road. Brid looked at him sombrely. "Now you're going to give us that about not being interested in our shows, aren't you? Well, don't. I won't believe you. I've seen you listening to every show we've given."

Kialan looked up at Brid's stormy face and seemed nonplussed. Then he laughed. "All right. I won't give you that. But I'm going to meet you on the other side of Neathdale all the same. See you." He set off at a good swinging pace towards the town, with his hands in his pockets, whistling *Jolly Holanders.*

"I give up!" said Brid. But both her brothers were too nervous to reply.

CHAPTER SEVEN

THE MAIN SQUARE at Neathdale was always busy. It was not very large, but it had a handsome fountain in the middle and four inns on three of its sides. There was also a corn exchange and two guildhalls, which added to the coming and going. The fourth side was occupied by the grey frowning block of the jail. When Brid drove the cart into the square, it seemed busier even than they had remembered. It was packed with people. The reason, they saw, as Olob patiently shouldered his way towards the fountain, was that there had been a public hanging that morning. The gallows was still there, outside the jail, and so was the hanged man. A number of people outside the inns were raising tankards jeeringly in his direction.

The dangling figure made them all feel sick, although it meant a good crowd. Dagner turned green. Moril clutched his cwidder hard and swallowed. Brid could not resist leaning down and asking the nearest person who it was who had been hanged.

"Friend of the Porter's," was the cheerful reply. It was a cheerful whiskery man Brid had chosen to ask, and he looked as if he had enjoyed every second of the hanging. "Some say he *was* the Porter," he added, "but you can't tell. He wouldn't admit to anything. Taken up last week, he was, on the new Earl's orders."

"Oh, is there a new Earl?" Brid said blankly, trying to keep her eyes from the swinging criminal.

"Sure," said the man. "Old Tholian died more than a month back. The new Earl's the grandson. Got a real nose for the Porter and his like, he has. Good luck to him too!"

"Oh, yes. Very good luck," Brid said hurriedly, terrified of being arrested for disloyalty to the new Earl.

"Leave off, Brid, and let's get started," Dagner said irritably.

Brid smiled rather falsely at the whiskery man and

hitched up the reins so that Olob knew to stand still. Then she blew a blast on the panhorn for attention. When sufficient people had turned their way, she stood up and spoke. Moril marvelled at how cool she was. But Brid was like Clennen that way. An audience was meat and drink to her.

"Ladies and gentlemen," she called, "please come and listen. You see the cart I'm standing in? Many of you will know it quite well. If you do, you'll know it belongs to Clennen the Singer. You'll have seen it coming through Neathdale, year after year, on its way North. Most of you will know Clennen the Singer—"

She had aroused people's interest by then. Moril heard someone say, "It's Clennen the Singer."

"No, it isn't," said someone else. "Who's the pretty little lass?"

"Where's Clennen, then? It isn't Clennen," said other people. Finally, someone was puzzled enough to call out, "Where is Clennen, lass? Isn't he with you?"

"I'll tell you," said Brid. "I'll tell you all." Then she stopped and simply stood there, upright and conspicuous in her cherry dress. Moril could see she was trying not to cry. But he could also see she was making it plain to the crowd that she was trying not to cry. He marvelled at the way she could use real feelings for what was in fact a show. He knew he could not have done it.

Brid stood there silent long enough for murmurs of interest to gather and grow but not long enough for them to die away. Then she said: "I'll tell you. Clennen – my father – was killed two days ago." And she stood silent again, struggling with tears, listening attentively to murmurs of sympathy. "He was killed before our eyes," she said. At the height of a loud murmur, she came in again loudly, but in such a calm way that Moril and most of the people present thought she was speaking quietly. They hushed to hear her. "We are the children of Clennen the Singer – Brid, Moril and Dastgandlen Handagner – and we're doing our best to carry on without him. I hope you'll spare time to listen to us. We know our show will not be the same without Clennen, but – but we'll try to please you. We hope you'll forgive any faults in – in memory of my father."

She got a round of applause for that. "Put your hat out, then, and let's hear you!" someone shouted. Brid, with tears running down her cheeks, picked up the hat she had ready and tossed it on the ground. Several people put money into it at once, out of pure sympathy for them.

Brid could not help feeling pleased with herself. She had made a considerable effect without boasting once – in fact, she had done the opposite, which, she thought, ought to please Dagner.

Though Dagner was far too nervous to show any pleasure at all, Brid knew he was not displeased because he left her to do all the announcing. That meant that Brid could more or less choose what they sang. She did her best to put together the things they had practised in the order she thought would be most impressive. She began them with general favourites. Moril felt terrible. Without the deep rolling voice of Clennen, they sounded to him thin and strange, and they lacked the body Lenina usually gave them on the hand organ. Moril began to feel they had nothing to offer the crowd, except perhaps some well-trained playing on cwidder and panhorn.

Brid felt much the same. To encourage them, she announced that they would now play, in trio, the *Seven Marches*. That was one thing she was sure they could do well. And they did. The most successful part was when Dagner, on the spur of the moment, signalled to Brid to play soft during the *Fourth March*, and played his treble cwidder in double time against Moril's slow and mellow tenor. They looked at one another while they were doing it. Moril knew they were neither of them exactly enjoying it, but they were both by then desperate for some applause from the silent crowd, and they had the dour kind of satisfaction of knowing they were giving an exhibition of real skill. They were rewarded by a burst of clapping and a little shower of coins falling into the hat.

Then they did Clennen's *Cuckoo Song*, which always made people laugh. After that Brid, feeling that the sooner Dagner got his part over, the better he would be for the rest of the show, announced that Dagner would now sing some of his own songs.

Brid was glad she had said "some". Dagner was so nervous that he only managed three. If she had not said "some", it was probable that he would only have sung one. Moril was disappointed and Brid exasperated, and it was altogether a pity, because the crowd liked Dagner's songs. *The Colour in Your Head* went down particularly well. Brid could tell he had the crowd's sympathy. They thought of him as bravely following in Clennen's footsteps and wanted to encourage him. But Dagner was mauve and shaking, and he stopped.

Crossly Brid took the centre of the cart and sang herself. Moril, without being told, came to her aid on the cwidder, while Dagner gasped to himself in the background. Brid did well. An audience always helped her. She sang a number of ballads, though she was forced to avoid *The Hanging of Filli Ray*, which she did best, because of the corpse dangling on the gallows behind the crowd. Her success was undoubtedly the patter song, *Cow-Calling*, which she did instead of *Filli Ray*. Brid always enjoyed it. You started with a sort of yodelling cry, to the whole herd, then you called the cows one by one, and each verse you added a new one.

> "*Red cow, red cow, my lord's thoroughbred cow,*
> *Brown cow, brown cow, the woman in the*
> *town's cow,*"

Brid sang, and no one looking at her could have realised that she was frantically wondering what else she could put into their unusually short show before her voice gave out. At *Old cow, old cow*, inspiration came. Brid bowed at the end of the song. Coins clattered into the hat.

"Now, ladies and gentlemen, my brother Moril will sing four songs of Osfameron."

Moril gulped and glared at Brid. He had never performed any of the old songs in public before. But

Brid had gone and announced him, so he was forced to take the centre of the cart, with his wet hands shaking on the cwidder. To make matters worse, he suddenly met Kialan's eye. Kialan was standing near the fountain, looking cool, attentive and slightly critical. From where Moril stood, the hanged man on the gallows appeared to be dangling over Kialan's head. Moril took his eyes off both of them and began to play. He knew he was going to make wretched work of it.

For a short while he could attend to nothing but the queer fingering and the odd, old-fashioned rhythms. Then his tension abated a little, and he was surprised to discover that his performance was pleasing him. As Moril's voice was naturally high, he did not need to sound cracked and strained, the way Clennen did. And not being yet expert and not anyway liking the noise the old fingering made, he found he had been unconsciously modifying it, into a style which was not old, nor new, but different. Osfameron's jerky rhythms became smoother, and Moril felt that if he could have spared time to attend to them, he might almost have understood the words:

*"The Adon's hall was open. Through it
Swallows darted. The soul flies through life.*

Osfameron in his mind's eye knew it.
The bird's life is not the man's life.

"Osfameron walked in the eye
Of his mind. The blackbird flew there.
He would not let the blackbird's song go by.
His mind's life can keep the bird there."

It sounded good to Moril. And it was his own doing, he was positive, and not the cwidder's. When he had finished, however, there was silence in the square. The crowd had never heard the old songs done that way and did not know what to think. Kialan made up their minds for them by clapping loudly. Other people clapped. Then came a burst of applause which made Moril feel ashamed of himself – he was only a learner, after all – and more coins went into the hat.

The applause seemed to worry Olob. From then on he became restive. He tossed his head, he stamped, he tried to go forwards, and he threatened to back. Brid pulled him up, and he backed in earnest, throwing Moril into Dagner. Brid had to take the reins up again, which put her half out of action. Seeing this, Dagner pulled himself together and led into some songs with rousing choruses, hoping the crowd would join in. He had little luck. People were in the mood for listening. But they had come to the end of all they had practised, so Dagner was forced to go on to *Jolly Holanders* and finish.

Olob was still behaving like a colt, so Moril got down and went to his head. The crowd shifted away from the cart. Moril heard Brid say to Dagner, "Shall I go shopping? I know what to get," and the hat chinking.

"No, I'll go," said Dagner. He still seemed nervous, although the show was over. He took the hat and climbed down from the cart. Almost at once, several men that Moril recognised as friends of Clennen's came up and crowded round Dagner.

"What's this, Dagner? What's this about Clennen?"

The upshot was that Dagner went off to have a drink with them, taking the hat. Moril did not see which inn they went to because he found himself being talked to by a kindly man just then. This man first gave Moril a pie, then told him – in a fatherly way – that he had sung the old songs all wrong, and things were going to the dogs if people could take those kind of liberties.

Moril took a leaf out of Dagner's book. "Yes, but I can't do it like my father did," he said with his mouth full. He was extremely grateful for the pie, or he would have told the man his real opinion of the old songs.

When the man had gone, muttering that he didn't know what the young were coming to, Moril remembered that Brid would be a prey to murmuring gentlemen. He looked up at the cart, wondering what he would do if she was. There was – or had been – a murmuring gentleman. Brid was glaring at him like a tiger, and the gentleman was retreating, very red in the face. "I do hope Dagner remembers the shopping," Brid said to Moril, pretending the gentleman had never existed.

So did Moril. They waited, and waited, Moril at Olob's restive head and Brid in the cart, for well over an hour. Moril saw Kialan at intervals, hanging about in the square, evidently waiting too. But Kialan made no attempt to come near them. Moril rather irritably wondered why not.

Olob tossed his head furiously. Brid said, "There's Dagner!" Moril saw Dagner hurrying back across the square with the empty hat rolled up in one hand. "Where's the shopping?" Brid wondered. Dagner waved cheerfully and came hurrying on. He had almost reached the cart when two large men advanced, quietly and purposefully, on either side of Dagner. One took Dagner's shoulder in a large hand.

"What—?" said Dagner, trying to shake free.

"You're under arrest, in the Earl's name," said the man. "Come on quietly and don't make any trouble now."

For a moment Moril had another glimpse of Kialan, looking absolutely horrified, in the crowd beyond the fountain. The people near, seeing someone being arrested, drifted quickly away from around the cart. Kialan seemed to get lost in a moving group and was gone the next second. Moril stood by Olob's head in an empty space, quite irrationally angry with Kialan. Not that anyone could do anything if the Earl took it into his head to have Dagner arrested, but even Kialan would have been better than no one. He looked despairingly at Dagner. Dagner had only time for one hopeless look back before the two men led him away across the square towards the jail. The crowd hurried away from all three – as if Dagner had a disease, Moril thought angrily. He wished Dagner would walk upright, instead of going bent and guilty-looking.

"I've never been so furious in my life!" said Brid. "Never! Of all the unjust—" She stopped, and looked uneasily round the empty space by the fountain, realising she was on the way to getting herself arrested too.

The two men vanished with Dagner inside the frowning jail. Moril had never felt more lonely. "I've just realised," he said. "We didn't have a licence to sing, did we?"

"We're entitled to operate on Father's for six months," said Brid. "Father told me, and I *know* that's the law. I hope Dagner remembers. They can't *do* this! They're just trying—"

A man approached across the empty space, rather grudgingly, carrying what looked like a sack of oats. He stopped some way off the cart. "Your brother ordered this," he said. "Do I take it away again?"

"You'll do no such thing!" Brid said haughtily. "It's paid for – that I do know. Put it in the cart."

"Please yourself," said the man unpleasantly. He dumped the sack on the flagstones and went away.

That was nasty, somehow. Moril saw that everyone was going to avoid them now. Angrily he supposed that Kialan had deserted them in the same way. He left Olob, who seemed to be quietening down, and dragged the sack over to the cart. "What shall we *do*, Brid?"

"Do?" said Brid, more furious than ever. "I'll tell you what to do. I'll have to stay here, in case Dagner ordered anything else, but you're to go over to the jail at *once* and ask to see Dagner. Go on. Tell them he's related to the Earl. Say Mother's Tholian's niece. Make a fuss. Ask them to send for Ganner. Make it quite clear that we're well connected. And when you see Dagner, tell him to do the same. Go on. They're just trying to frighten us into paying for another licence, I know they are!"

Obediently Moril scurried off across the square. He was so shaken that he could think of nothing else to do, even though he knew in his heart that it was no good. In the South, when they arrested people, even for small offences, it took more than a boy talking about noble relatives to get them out of prison. At the least it took a lot of money. And as they had not got a lot of money, the doors of the jail could well have closed on Dagner for good. Moril wished Ganner had found them, after all. By the time he reached the cold archway into the jail, he was heartily wishing they had never left Markind.

"Please," he said to the man on duty there, "I want to see my brother."

The man looked down at him, not unkindly. "Clennen the Singer's son?" Moril nodded. "And how old are you, lad?" asked the man.

"Eleven," said Moril.

"Eleven, are you?" said the man. "They don't hang your kind till they're fifteen, you know, so you're lucky." Moril thought this was meant to be a joke and smiled politely. "Look, lad," said the man. "Take some good advice. Get in that cart of yours and drive off. You won't do any good here."

Moril looked up at him in helpless irritation. "But—"

"Be off!" said the man, urgently. Footsteps were coming through the dark passage behind him. Moril could see the man meant kindly, but he did not move. He waited to see if the person coming would let him see Dagner.

The man who came was one of the two who had arrested Dagner. He glanced at Moril, without seeming very interested. Then he looked again – sharply. "That's another of them, isn't it?"

"Yes, sir," said the man at the gate, and he gave Moril a reproachful look, as much as to say, "Now see what you've done."

"Come with me, lad," said the other man. Moril, with his stomach hopping as it had never done before, even before this last show, followed him into the dark passageway, through a dismal courtyard and up some stone stairs. They went into a blank room with yellow walls and a bench by one of the walls, where the man told him to sit and wait. Then he went out and locked the door.

Moril sat on the bench for some time, feeling terrible.

He wondered if he was arrested too. It looked like it. He tried to see out of the window, but it was high up and barred. He dragged the bench over to it, but he still could not see much except grey walls. There was no hope of wriggling out between the bars. He dragged the bench back to its original position and sat on it again.

Then the most dreadful part began. He could not bear being shut between walls. He was hot. He was trapped. The room seemed to get smaller every second and the ceiling seemed to be moving down on him. He thought he would have to scream. He nearly did scream, when a fortunate stain on the wall opposite caught his attention. It was almost the shape of the mountains between Dropwater and Hannart.

Moril thankfully escaped into a dream. He imagined snow-capped mountains and forgot he was too hot. He imagined wide valleys and the sky overhead, and the small room became easier to bear. He thought of the old green roads of the North and of Osfameron and the Adon walking along them. He became Osfameron himself. He and his friend the Adon made their way to imaginary Hannart. On the mountain, they were ambushed by enemies and fought their way clear. Then they went down into Hannart and strolled under the rowan trees outside the old grey castle, composing a song of victory together.

The door opened, and another man told Moril to come along now, quickly.

Moril came back to the present with a jump. He was scared and vibrating and small. He was aware of every stone and stain in that oppressive room, of the grain in the wood of the door, and the dirt in the fingernails of the man's hand holding it open. He even knew there were six hairs in the mole on the man's nose. As he got up, he suddenly remembered Clennen by the lake, saying, "You're in two halves at present." And he wondered if this was what Clennen had meant.

The man ushered him into a large, imposing room, with a heavy old table at one end. An elderly man sat behind the table, with a younger one who was taking notes. Moril could see by the gold chain round the elderly one's neck that he was a Justice.

"Stand in front of the table and answer clearly," said the younger man, pausing in his writing and pointing his pen at Moril.

Moril did as he was told, still vibrating. He knew every bulge in the rather pointless carving on the wall above the Justice. He could tell how many wrinkles there were in the forehead of the Justice – fifteen yellowish folds.

The Justice wrinkled these folds up and looked at Moril. "Full name?"

"Osfameron Tanamoril Clennensson," said Moril. "I'd like to see my brother, please."

"Quite a mouthful," remarked the Justice, while the other man wrote it down. "Osfameron?"

"He's my ancestor," said Moril. Seeing that the yellow folds of the Justice were lifted towards him with slight interest, he explained, "I was called after him. And could I see Dagner, please?" The yellow folds drew closer together. "My brother," Moril said patiently.

"Your brother?" said the Justice. The other man passed him a sheaf of papers, and he drew the folds of his forehead together over them until it looked like smocking. "Some other mouthful down here," he said.

Moril, with a little wobble to his stomach, realised the papers must be Dagner's answers to the questions they had asked him. He wondered what Dagner had said and wished he knew. For if he gave different answers from Dagner's, the Justice might well convict Dagner of all sorts of things he had never done. "We call him Dagner for short," he explained carefully. "And I'd like to see him, please."

"You can see him presently, if you answer my questions

truthfully," said the Justice. "You come of a family of singers, is that true?"

"Yes," said Moril.

"And you travelled with your father, giving shows?"

"Yes," said Moril.

"How long have you been doing that?"

"All my life," said Moril.

"Which is how long?"

"Eleven years," said Moril.

The younger man leant over. "The elder boy said ten years."

The Justice smocked his forehead at Moril, calculating how old he was. He looked weary and shrewd, and Moril was just a doubtful fact to him. Moril saw that to follow Brid's advice and talk of being related to the Earl and to Ganner would do no good, simply no good at all. He knew Brid would have done it. But he was not going to try.

"I was a baby when we started," he explained.

"From Hannart?" said the Justice sharply.

"Yes, but I don't remember," Moril said, knowing well enough that if he admitted to his true feelings about Hannart here, he could convict both himself and Dagner. "My father said he had a quarrel with Earl Keril."

They checked that off against Dagner's answers, and it seemed to be right, to Moril's relief. But they seemed dissatisfied, and they became more dissatisfied as the questions went on.

"Where did you last perform before Neathdale?"

Moril thought. It seemed very long ago. Fledden? Yes, because that was the last place before they were in the Markind lordship and stopped performing. That was where Lenina had mended Kialan's coat. "Fledden," he said.

"Who did your brother talk to in Fledden?"

"Nobody," said Moril. He remembered particularly, because no girls had come up to Dagner for once, and he had talked to Dagner himself.

"But you weren't with him every moment you were in Fledden, were you?" said the younger man.

"Yes, I was," said Moril. "We were all in the cart, you see. Father always made us stay in the cart together in towns."

"Always?" said the Justice, smocking his folds severely. "You don't mean to tell me your brother never went off on his own."

Moril realised he could convict Dagner of poaching rabbits unless he was careful. "No, never," he said.

"Dagner's not interested in anything much except making up songs." And to divert attention from the idea of poaching, he added, "Dagner hasn't done anything you could arrest him for – and our licence is in order, honestly."

The Justice sighed irritably. "I'm not concerned with your licence, boy. Your brother has been arrested for passing illegal information—"

"*What!*" said Moril.

"—and I want to know where he got it," said the Justice. "That surprises you?"

"I should just say it does!" said Moril. "He couldn't have done! You must have made a mistake."

"Our agents are very reliable," said the Justice. "What makes you think it's a mistake?"

"Because Dagner wouldn't. He's just not interested. He's only interested in making songs. Besides, there's nowhere he *could* have got information," Moril said frantically.

"That sort of assertion is not at all helpful," said the Justice. "I fancy both you brothers are concealing something. You say you last performed in Fledden. That must have been a week ago. Where have you been since?"

"Markind," said Moril, wondering why on earth

Dagner had not mentioned it. "Then we came here by Cindow."

The Justice and the younger man looked at one another, and seemed incredulous. It was clear that they thought Markind the last place where anyone could obtain illegal information. Moril took heart a little. "Why Markind?" snapped the younger man.

"My father was killed," Moril explained, his voice wobbling a little.

"We know. At Medmere. Why did you go to Markind?" said the younger man.

"My mother went to marry Ganner," said Moril.

"*Ganner!*" they both exclaimed, and both looked at Moril in flat disbelief. "Ganner is Lord of Markind," the Justice said, as if he thought Moril did not know.

"I know," said Moril. "Mother was betrothed to him before she married Father, and she went back there."

"Very likely," the Justice said cynically. "In that case, why did you and your brother leave?"

Angry tears came into Moril's eyes. "Because I saw one of the men who killed Father there, if you must know! And if you don't believe me, ask Ganner!"

"I most certainly shall," said the Justice. The other man murmured something to him and they looked at one another, the wrinkles of the Justice smocked into a tight yellow bunch. Moril saw Brid had been right after all to tell him to mention Ganner. But like Brid, the Justice had jumped to the conclusion that Ganner had had Clennen killed, and the younger man was wagging his eyebrows at him to warn him that Ganner was far too important to be accused. The Justice showed himself neither very nice nor very just by giving a cynical little laugh, smiling and shrugging. Moril supposed he should be glad, if, as Kialan had said, Ganner really had nothing to do with Clennen's death. Then the Justice turned to Moril again and Moril saw, sadly and rather bitterly, that there was one law for Ganner and quite another for himself and Dagner. "Did your brother talk to any strangers in Markind?"

"No," said Moril. "Only Ganner's household."

"Then who did he talk to between Markind and here?"

"Only us," said Moril.

"Listen, my boy," said the Justice, "you're not being very helpful, are you? Perhaps it will jog your memory if I remind you that your brother's crime is one for which he will be hanged in due course. Therefore, I can put you in prison for withholding information."

Moril felt sick. "I *am* being helpful," he said. "I've *told* you it's a mistake. But if you're only going to believe me

132

if I tell you Dagner's guilty, then it's no use asking me questions. Because he didn't do it!"

The younger man half stood up, looking savage. Moril blinked and waited for them to hit him, or clap him in a cell, or both. But they did neither. The younger man, after a dreadful pause, told Moril coldly to go and sit down at the other end of the long room. Moril did so. He sat on a hard shiny stool near the door and watched the two conferring together in low voices. There were footsteps beyond the door, so that he was unable to hear anything that was said, though he thought he caught Ganner's name more than once. Then they called him back to the table.

"We're going to let you go, boy," said the younger one. "We've come to the conclusion you know nothing about this matter."

"Thank you," said Moril. "Can I see my brother now?"

The younger man glared at him and was obviously going to refuse. But the Justice said irritably, "Oh, very well, very well. I said you should if you answered my questions. I wouldn't like you to go away thinking we're unjust here."

Moril thought Brid would have made the obvious answer to this. He held his tongue, with a bit of an effort.

CHAPTER EIGHT

THE MAN WHO had fetched Moril before came back. He took Moril downstairs to a great gloomy room with guards at the door. In the middle of this room were two rows of benches about three feet apart. People were sitting facing one another at intervals along these benches. Those on the further bench were all prisoners. Moril could see they were, because they all had a dingy, sullen, dejected look and held their heads hunched forwards. He had once seen a dancing bear with the same look. And the people on the nearer bench were plainly visitors, from not having that look, and being brisker and more nervous. There seemed to be guards everywhere, standing about in a bored way, and the nervous looks of the visitors were mostly directed at the guards. The room rang and whispered with shuffling feet and sad conversations.

The man told Moril to sit on the nearest bench. After a while two guards led Dagner through a door at the other end. Dagner had the same dingy, dejected look already. He looked unexpectedly small between the guards. Moril was sure he remembered him bigger.

They sat Dagner down on the bench opposite Moril. "You can have ten minutes," they told Moril. Then they left them to talk. Moril swallowed and could not think what to say.

"Just a moment," said Dagner. "Look at the room behind me, will you, and tell me if there's anyone you think can hear what we say."

Moril looked. The nearest guard was a good way off, talking to another. "No. They're two cart-lengths away at least." He was about to turn round and see if there was anyone behind him.

"Don't move, you fool!" said Dagner. "I can see it's all right behind you."

"Then that's all right," said Moril. "I saw the Justice and I told them it's all a mistake. They can't really think you were passing information, can they? It's just not true."

"Yes, it is," said Dagner. "I did."

Moril stared at him.

"Father asked me to," Dagner explained. "I had to give a message and some money to one of our men here. I didn't manage very well," he said sadly. "I wasn't sure – anyway, I think the one I gave it to must have been the spy. And when I think how relieved I was once I'd got rid of them, I – well, it's no use thinking of that, I suppose."

"But, Dagner!" Moril said, quite horrified. "They'll hang you for that!"

"You don't think I don't know that, do you?" Dagner said irritably. "Is there still no one near?"

"No," said Moril. "Dagner, it isn't true, is it? You're joking."

"I'm not joking," said Dagner. "If you don't believe me, take a look at that wine jar – unless they've searched the cart by now. But that's not important. What *is* important is that you've got to get Kialan into the North. You and Brid just have to go on and get him to Hannart if you can. Can you do that, Moril?"

"I suppose so," said Moril. "But I think he sloped off when they arrested you."

"No, he didn't," said Dagner. "He'll be waiting outside

Neathdale, like he said."

"If you think so – Dagner, *why* is it so important?"

"Ask Kialan," said Dagner, with his eyes on someone behind Moril. "I ordered some flour and some more oats," he went on, rather artificially. "And there was a friend of Father's letting me have a side of bacon cheap. And onions. You can get bread on the way."

"And eggs," agreed Moril. "And I'll polish your cwidder for you, I promise."

"You needn't bother," said Dagner. "Right, he's gone. Now, listen. There are two things I want you to tell Kialan. One is that Henda *has* asked a ransom for him—"

"Ransom for Kialan?" said Moril. "But he's—"

"Never mind. Just tell him," said Dagner. "And the other thing is far more important. Earl Tholian is gathering an army and—"

"Tholian? He's dead," Moril objected, and he had a muddled and upsetting notion of an army of ghosts.

"This is the new Earl. He's called Tholian too. Don't keep interrupting. There's someone on his way over behind you," said Dagner. "The point is that nobody in the North knows, and there's nobody going through but you and Kialan. Have you got those two things?"

"Ransom and Tholian," said Moril. "There's somebody

coming behind *you* now."

The guards behind Dagner came right up to him. "Come on. Time's up."

"We haven't had anything like ten minutes," Moril pointed out.

"Too bad. The Justice wants to see him. On your feet, fellow," said the guard.

Dagner got up and climbed back over the bench. He made Moril a face as he was marched off, which Moril thought was intended for a smile. Moril himself, feeling utterly crushed, wandered to the door and was shown briskly through to the entrance again.

"You're out again, are you?" said the man on duty. "You've been lucky."

Moril had not the heart to reply. He did not think he was lucky, particularly as the first thing that met his eyes outside was the two dangling feet of the hanged man.

Beyond the dangling feet, Brid was sitting in the cart looking haughty and impatient. The cart was still in a clear space, and the sack of oats had been joined by a number of other sacks and bundles, all of them too heavy for Brid to lift by herself.

"Where have you *been*?" she demanded, as soon as Moril was near enough. "I thought you were never coming back! What's the matter? You look like a jug of spilt milk."

Moril was feeling so lost and peculiar that all he could do was to go to Olob. He put his arms round Olob's neck and rubbed his forehead on Olob's nose.

"Well, tell me!" said Brid. "Have you seen Dagner?"

"Yes," said Moril.

"Did you tell him to say what I told you?"

"No," said Moril.

"Why *not*? Moril, I shall hit you in a moment if you don't tell me sensibly what happened!"

"I can't," said Moril. "Not here."

"Why *not*?" Brid almost shouted.

Moril realised that he must stop her attracting attention to them. "Please, Brid. Shut up," he said, looking at her as meaningly as he could from beside Olob's nose. "Let's get these sacks loaded and get on."

Brid began to see that something terrible might have happened. "Without Dagner?" she said, in a more subdued voice. Moril nodded, tore himself away from warm, soft, friendly Olob, and began to heave at the nearest sack. Brid came down and joined him. "Moril, for goodness' sake!" she whispered angrily. "It can't be that bad! You're behaving as if they're going to *hang* Dagner."

"They are," said Moril.

Brid went white, but she did not really believe him. "Oh no!" she said. "Not on top of everything! Why?"

"Get these things in, and I'll tell you when we're moving," Moril said.

They loaded the cart, and Brid drove out of the square. When they came into the cobbled streets, where the cart made sufficient clatter to cover up whispers. Moril told Brid what had happened. It turned Brid so sick and weak that had Olob been that kind of horse, he could easily have got out of control.

"I can't believe it!" she kept saying.

She was still saying it when half a mile out of Neathdale, Kialan pushed his way out of a hedge and came to join them. When he first looked at them, he was smiling, as if he were relieved. Then he saw there were only two of them, and his smile vanished. He looked along the cart to make sure Dagner was not there, and then at their faces. When he climbed up to join them, his brown face was tired and yellowish. "What happened?" he said. "Better drive on."

"Moril says they're going to hang Dagner for passing information," said Brid. "He says Father told Dagner to do it. And I can't believe it! I just can't believe it!"

"Oh," said Kialan. "They got him for that, did they?

I thought that was too much of a risk on top of everything else."

"You're mighty cool, aren't you?" said Brid. "But I suppose Dagner's not your brother!"

There was a pause, in which Kialan tried to control his feelings. But his natural outspokenness won. "All right," he said. "So he's not my brother. So you think I don't know how you feel. You just thank your stars, my girl, that you don't have to stand there and watch them hang Dagner, like I had to with *my* brother!" Brid and Moril turned round in the driving seat to stare at Kialan. But they turned back, because there were large, angry tears running past Kialan's high-bridged nose, and more tears filling and reddening his light blue eyes. "I always thought the world of Dagner, anyway," he said. "I remember him quite well from when we were small."

There was silence, except for horse and cart noises. Brid encouraged Olob to make the best speed he could up the first steep hill to the Uplands. It was horrible to be urging Olob away from Dagner. There were tears in Brid's eyes too.

"Why did they hang your brother?" Moril asked at length.

"No reason," Kialan said angrily. "It was Tholian's

idea – that pale-eyed murdering swine who killed your father – but I didn't hear Hadd or Henda or any of the others making much objection. They just had us put on trial first, to make it seem respectable. And then it came out that I was only fourteen—"

"Oh! I thought you were older!" said Brid.

"People do," said Kialan. "But I was fourteen in March. Tholian was furious, because the rest of the earls said it was against the law to hang me for another year. But they hanged poor Konian, and the ship's captain, and all the crew they could catch, and they made me watch. It was just like our luck to land when all the earls had got together to invest that brute Tholian! His grandfather died the week before."

They were now high enough above Neathdale to have, at that moment, an excellent view of the same Tholian's mansion. Moril looked down at its long white front, peaceful and pompous and bowered among trees, and felt like a mouse running over the paws of a cat. He wished the cart was not so very pink and noticeable.

"I'm beginning to think," Kialan said miserably, "that I bring bad luck on people. First Konian, then your father, now Dagner – and goodness knows what happened to the people who helped me escape from Hadd!"

"If you don't mind my asking," Brid said cautiously, "who are you exactly?"

"My father's the Earl of Hannart," said Kialan. "And if you want to dump me out and drive off, I won't blame you."

Moril looked round for Tholian's mansion again. To his relief, it was now hidden by a bend in the road. He was glad. He felt as if this piece of news had put them suddenly in great danger. He was limp with terror, although he knew that they must have been in exactly the same danger from the moment Kialan joined them. Any earl of the South – not only Tholian – would have been overjoyed to get his hands on Kialan. His father was their chief enemy. Anyone found helping Kialan was bound to be savagely punished. Moril thought back, terrified, to Kialan walking through towns so as not to seem to belong to them, sharing the cart in full view of travellers on the road, and even being introduced to Ganner as one of them. And if that was Tholian he had seen in Markind, Moril could hardly bear to think what a risk it had been. Clennen could not have known who Kialan was. He would never have done it for the son of someone he had quarrelled with. But it looked as if Lenina had known.

"I should have known you were from the North," Brid said ruefully, "when you said your name was spelt with a K. They don't use K's in the South, do they? I wondered why Mother told Ganner your name was Collen."

Kialan chuckled slightly. "Your mother's a cool one, isn't she?"

"I suppose she is. But look here, " said Brid. "What were you and your brother doing in the South? Didn't you know what would happen?"

"It was an accident," said Kialan. "Do you remember that storm at the end of April?"

"Yes. We nearly lost the big tent. Remember, Moril?" asked Brid. Moril nodded.

"Well, we nearly got drowned," said Kialan. "We'd been to our aunt on Tulfer Island, and the storm hit us on the way home. We were blown all over the place, and the boat was sitting half under water with sea pouring in, and I don't think the captain knew where we were any more than I did. He said we'd have to get to the nearest haven before we sank. And we did. And it turned out to be Holand. And there were all the earls of the South, smacking their lips at us. To tell you the truth," Kialan said, "I didn't even feel frightened at first. I was so glad to be on land again."

"We were near Holand then," said Brid. "But we never heard— Oh, yes, Father gave it out as news, didn't he? Is that how Father came into it?"

"Don't you think he was bound to be in on it?" asked Kialan. "He didn't tell me much, but I'm sure he arranged it all. I know the people who helped me escape seemed to spend all the time waiting for messages from the Porter to know what to do next."

"What? Father?" Moril said, puzzled.

"Yes. Your father," said Kialan. "You don't mean to tell me you didn't know he was the Porter?"

"He was *not*!" Brid said angrily. "The Porter's a spy with a price on his head."

"Yes, of course, in the South," said Kialan. "They were mad to catch him here, because he was the main agent for the North. You must have known! He brought all the important messages and most of the refugees. They must have come in this cart. And he organised people here against the earls – I know that, because Konian told me. Konian sent a message to your father for help, during the trial, but it didn't get to him quick enough."

There was a sombre pause. Olob clopped patiently upwards, zigzagging with the road across the steep hillside, while Brid and Moril tried to take in what Kialan had said.

"I thought," Moril said, "that your father had quarrelled with ours?"

"So did I," said Kialan. "But I think that was a pretence. I found out last year – I wish people told me things! – because my father vanished and I needed him for something. And Konian told me to shut up, because he'd gone to meet Clennen the Singer like he always did, but no one was supposed to know. I think they arranged what to do next then."

"I refuse to believe that my father was a common spy!" said Brid. "Why didn't he *tell* me? He ought to have told me! It's so sneaky, somehow!"

"Don't *shout*!" Moril said, with an anxious look round at Tholian's mansion, which had come into view again, lower down and further off.

Kialan laughed outright. "But he wasn't sneaky! That was the splendid thing about him! I couldn't believe he really was the Porter at first. I saw this fat man with a great big voice, who spent all his time trying to impress people, and I thought there'd been an awful mistake. Then I saw him go into towns, in this shocking bright cart, in a scarlet suit just to make sure people didn't miss him, and sing his head off, and call out at the top of his voice that the price on the Porter's head was two thousand in gold. It was incredible! Then he and your mother would call out messages and hand out notes, right in front of everyone, and I knew half of them were illegal. But no one would believe it, because it was all done so openly. Nobody thought he was anything more than a very good singer. And I really think Clennen thought that was the best joke about it."

Moril blinked a little at this view of his father. But Kialan had hit Clennen off in a way. Clennen *had* treated their shows as a rather serious joke. If he was really the Porter all along, then that would be why. "I suppose that's where Dagner went wrong," he said sadly. "Trying to be secret."

"Dagner was awfully stupid to think he could carry on where Father left off, anyway," said Brid.

"He didn't," said Kialan. "Dagner wasn't trying to do that for a moment. But Clennen asked him to finish off the important things if he could. Then he was to go North and stay there. And the message to Neathdale was important because it was about a spy who'd got in among them there."

Moril sighed. He did not say that Dagner thought he had given the message to that very spy. There seemed no point. He said, "Dagner said I was to tell you Henda has asked for a ransom for you. And Tholian is gathering an army."

"Oh damn!" Kialan said wearily. "Then I'll *have* to get through somehow, won't I? You saw Dagner? Tell me."

Moril told Kialan all that happened to him in the jail. He could not help speaking low and looking nervously at Tholian's mansion each time it came into view. He was relieved when they crossed the brow of the first hill and could not see it any more.

"You were lucky, Moril," said Brid. "If you'd known all the things Kialan's just told us, we might be in jail at this moment." Moril nodded soberly. He certainly could not have acted the surprise he felt when they told him what Dagner had been arrested for. But he knew it had been the merest good luck that he had not happened to mention Kialan.

"I couldn't think," said Kialan, "why Clennen made such a point of not telling you two anything. He wouldn't let me say who I was, and neither would Dagner. But I think it saved our skins. I wish it could have saved Dagner's."

"You don't think Dagner was really arrested because of you?" Moril asked.

"I did at first," said Kialan. "I thought we'd all had

it, all the time I was sitting in the hedge. I could hardly believe it when I saw the cart coming. No. I think Dagner's trouble is separate, and thanks to you, Moril, they think he just did a bit of freedom-fighting on the side. But I hope it doesn't get round to the Earl. Tholian will put two and two together all right."

"Why did Tholian kill Father?" said Moril.

"He was looking for me," said Kialan, "and he didn't want anyone to know, because I'm supposed to be Hadd's prisoner – or Henda's, only they were still arguing about that when I escaped. Dagner thought that maybe the Neathdale spy – or perhaps it was the fellow they hanged – might have given Tholian a hint about your father. But he couldn't have known much, or we'd all have been arrested. Tholian's the sort who says dead men tell no tales, so he kills Clennen and then beats the woods for me."

"If only we'd known!" said Brid. "Where were you all that time?"

"Up a tree," said Kialan, "rabbits and all. They were crashing about searching all the time you were playing that cwidder, Moril, and it worried them like anything. They kept saying that blessed boy and his music made their heads go round. Tholian suggested going back and killing you too, but none of them could quite be bothered to. And when you left off, they'd had enough and they went."

"Could you pass it me?" said Moril. Kialan obligingly crawled back to the instrument rack and reached the big cwidder over to the driving seat. Moril took it and clutched it to him. It felt fat and hard and comforting. Apart from the fact that it seemed to have saved both his life and Kialan's, it was in its rather more awesome way as good as Olob's nose. He felt he needed it, somehow, after the events of today.

"Play something," suggested Kialan.

"No, don't," said Brid. "Not until we've decided what to do. We're slap bang in the middle of Tholian's earldom, and we've obviously got to get North, and everyone knows this cart. And we've no money. I daresay Father meant to go this way because it would have looked suspicious if he didn't, but I vote we turn east and try to get North through the Marshes."

Kialan fetched the map out and scowled at its sketchiness. "I suppose we could try the sea," said Moril. "We might find a boat that wants a singer."

Kialan glared at the map. "We'd take ages, either way. And we can't be more than four days off Flennpass here. Don't either of you understand? Tholian's getting an army together to invade the North, and Henda's sent to my father to say he'll ransom me, so my father thinks I'm a prisoner and daren't do a thing! And I suppose," he added, "Henda's message is the first news my father gets that we're not both drowned. If you don't mind, I'd like to get North as quickly as I can – but it's your cart, of course."

Moril glanced at Kialan and decided that his hectoring tone had much to do with the tears in his eyes. Brid did not notice. "Oh, *is* it our cart?" she said. The result was that Kialan managed to laugh, rather sheepishly.

"We'll go straight on," Moril said, suddenly deciding. "We'll do it Father's way and be quite open about it. It worked for him, and it worked for me in the jail."

Brid and Kialan seemed to be relieved that Moril had taken the lead. But as Olob dragged the cart into the level ground of the first Upland, they began to make nervous objections.

"Innocent little children is all very well," said Brid. "What about when the Earl hears of Dagner doing the Porter's business?"

Moril looked round on fields with green corn showing and sheep grazing. The hills of the North towered against the sky, so high and blue-grey with distance that, on first glance, Moril took them for a bank of cloud.

"A certain pink cart will be looked for," said Kialan. "Could you paint it?"

"Dark green would be best," said Brid. "But we've no money."

A village came in sight, looking very small against the hills of the North. Moril roused himself before Kialan and Brid could have any wilder ideas. "Tholian knows me," he said. "He recognised me up a ladder in Markind. That's the trouble with having red hair."

"Wear a hat," said Kialan.

Moril turned round to quell Kialan. "What about this village?" As he said it, he realised that Kialan was tired out. His face was as white as such a brown complexion could be, and there were dark rings under his eyes. All the watching at night and the suspense in Neathdale had been rather too much for him. "Get down in the cart," Moril said, taking pity on him. "I'll put the cover half up."

Kialan lay thankfully down beside the wine jar, and Moril pulled the canvas forwards until it hid him. They drove straight through the village, Brid holding the reins and Moril sitting beside her, gently strumming the cwidder. On the heights above the village there was an odd little grey tower, belonging to the Lord of the Uplands. Brid looked at it and quivered with terror, knowing as she did that the Earl of Hannart's son was hidden in the cart. But Moril knew it was no different from any other risk they had run without knowing. The tower and the mountains made him think of his imaginary Hannart. He felt soothed and peaceful.

Several people looked up, or out at doors, hearing the cart and the cwidder. When they saw what it was, they smiled and waved. Brid did her best to smile and nod back. Then a woman came out of a house and walked beside them.

"Have you been through Neathdale today?"

"Yes," said Moril.

"They tell me there was to have been a man hanged."

"Yes," said Moril. "He was. We saw him."

"I knew it!" the woman said, smiling. "He was bound to come to it!" She seemed so gleeful that Moril thought she must have hated the hanged man, until he noticed the tears in her eyes. Then he saw she was just trying to hide her feelings. He wanted to say something kind to her, but she left the cart and went back into her house. Moril wondered whether Clennen had known her, and what her connection was with the hanged man.

CHAPTER NINE

A MILE OR SO beyond the village, Olob looked at the
sun moving into the blue mountains and turned
towards a cart track which led away to the left. Brid tried
to stop him. "No, Olob. We must get on."

"Let him find a place," said Moril. "I told you. It's no
good looking guilty. Besides, we haven't eaten a thing
since this morning."

"You had a pie, you lucky pig!" snapped Brid, but she
gave in and let Olob pull the cart into a secluded grassy
space under a cliff. A stream ran in a trickle of green
mosses down the rock face. Moril came down from the

cart, feeling shaky at the knees.

"If we're going to camp this near the village," said Kialan, emerging from hiding, "then we'd better set a watch tonight."

"What for?" said Moril. "Nobody's going to bother to come at night, not after three children. And if they come while we're awake, we'll hear them."

"I'm going to watch, all the same," said Kialan.

"No, you're not," said Moril. "There's no point."

"Bossy, aren't you, all of a sudden!" Brid snapped. Then she rounded on Kialan. "And if you make yourself ill staying awake every night, what are we supposed to do with you?"

Moril realised that Brid was angry because she was tired and miserable. So he said nothing and simply began to get Olob out of the shafts. Kialan must have realised it too, because he said wearily, "Oh, all right. I give in," and started collecting firewood.

Brid investigated the provisions Dagner had bought. "What am I supposed to do with all this flour?" she demanded. "And no eggs!"

It looked as if Dagner's idea had been to stock the cart with enough food to last them until they reached the North. But as Brid said mournfully, his mind must have been on that message, for the only useful things he had bought were the bacon and a large cheese. Among the less useful things were lentils, candles and a big bunch of rhubarb.

"Look at this!" said Brid, wagging the rhubarb about. "What was he *thinking* of?"

"Waste of money," agreed Kialan. "Did he use all you earned?"

"Yes," said Brid. "Every penny. And there's not even any bread."

They had a rather strange supper of fried bacon, cheese and experimental pancakes made out of flour and water. Brid, after nibbling one, promptly put them in the frying pan that held the bacon, and Kialan thought of melting cheese over them to improve the taste. This left them still so empty that they finished the meal with about a quart each of stewed rhubarb; luckily, Lenina had left some sugar in the cart.

Moril felt better after that. He got up, fetched the bucket and carefully cleaned the cart. It was looking very dusty and uncared for, and to his mind, it had a furtive, illegal look. He thought about Dagner as he worked. He wondered what he had to eat in prison and how soon he would be tried and hanged. Or did the questioning by the Justice count as a trial? Moril feared that it did. He wondered again what Dagner had said when they questioned him. Then he thought of Dagner trying to carry on Clennen's work in Dagner's way. It had not seemed wise. Dagner had been nervous and secretive, and he had made a fatal mistake. But on the other hand, Dagner was so unlike Clennen that it was probably the only thing he could do. Moril thought about himself going back to Clennen's way and wondered if that was wise. He was not like Clennen either. But he did not know what he was like. He supposed that sooner or later he would have to find out, and then do things in the way best suited to what he found.

Brid and Kialan were washing the pans. Kialan was looking exhausted. Tears kept coming into Brid's eyes, and she angrily wiped them away with the back of her greasy hand. And they were both pretending they were cheerful.

"Do you think if we mixed the cheese in with the flour, they'd taste better?" Brid said.

"What about rhubarb? Sort of fritters?" said Kialan.

"Ugh!" said Brid. "When I see Dagner, I'll—" She wiped off another set of tears and said brightly, "He must have had his reasons, I suppose."

Moril tipped away the dirty water, wondering if there could be three more unhappy people in Dalemark. Kialan must know he was a danger to himself and his companions. His landfall in Holand must have been horrible. And since then, Moril realised, Kialan's life had been one long, tense escape, which was not over yet. As for himself and Brid, they had seen their family simply dwindle away, until it was down to their two selves. And Kialan had been fond of Dagner too – fonder than he had realised.

Moril stopped himself in the midst of a snuffle of self-pity. No. Last year, as soon as they were safely in the North, Clennen had told them some of the other things that happened in the South. Whole families had been arrested. The older ones had been hanged, and children younger than Moril had been left with nothing in the world, and nobody dared help them for fear of being arrested too. Clennen had told them how Henda had calmly doubled his taxes last year and turned those who could not pay out to starve, and how old Tholian had hunted an old man with dogs for not raising his hat to him fast enough. Moril knew there must be hundreds of people in the South even worse off than he was. They had a horse and cart, and Clennen had left them with a means of earning a living and a licence to do it. If it came to the worst, they could go back to Markind. Moril did not like the idea. He tried to tell himself that they could not go back, because of Kialan. But he knew that was not it. Lenina would help Kialan. The reason for his not liking it, he was forced to admit, was that he was not at all clear whether they had deserted Lenina, or she them. And it made him uncomfortable.

"We'll give more shows," he said, putting Lenina out of his mind. He went to the cart to polish the instruments and stopped at the sight of the wine jar taking up so much room inside. "Do you know anything about this wine jar?" he called to Kialan.

"No— Oh, you mean the papers?" Kialan said, coming over to the cart. "Dagner had a look in Markind, because he had to find the message for Neathdale. They're down inside its basket."

Moril scrambled up to look. Kialan took down the tailgate and told him where to put his hand down between bottle and basket. Brid hurried over and watched Moril fish about, feel paper and pull it out. "What are these?"

"Messages that weren't so important," said Kialan. "Lucky they didn't search the cart, wasn't it?"

Brid and Moril held the papers into the sinking sun and

spelt out, in Clennen's writing: *For Mattrick. Someone in Neathdale – I think Halain – smells of lavender. Dirty washing through Pali and Fander in future.*

"Lavender!" said Brid. "Really, Father!"

The other notes said the same, and were marked to be delivered to places between Markind and Neathdale.

"Go and put those all on the fire," Moril said, handing them to Kialan. "Now do you believe we can read?"

Kialan grinned and took the papers. While he was stuffing them under the embers and the air was filling with the strong smell of burning paper, Moril busily worked his hand on round the wine jar. Halfway round, he felt more papers. He pulled them out and unfolded them.

These were all in different people's writing. Some of them seemed to have come from parts of the South they had not visited in years. Others concerned the places they had passed through, and these were mostly in Lenina's writing. Moril felt oddly glad to see his mother's small, bold writing. He could see that whatever Lenina had thought, privately, of Clennen's freedom-fighting, she had most scrupulously done what Clennen wanted while he was alive – even at the risk of being hanged for spying. It was queer to find her so honourable, but

Moril liked it. Among other things, she had written: *Crady – 169 taken north to Neathdale* and *Fledden – 24 pressed yesterday, with horses.* The other notes said much the same.

"What do you think this means?" said Brid.

Kialan came over to look. "Do you think," he said, after some puzzling, "those might be for my father or someone in the North? It could be about the army Tholian's gathering."

"You know, I do believe that's it!" said Brid. "They mean how many men went for soldiers from each place. Don't you agree, Moril?"

"Probably," said Moril. It seemed a bit boring to him. "We'd better take them North, then." He put them back and, just to be on the safe side, went on working his hand round the other side of the jar. There were cold, hard things. He gripped one and pulled it out. "I say!" It was a gold piece. "Whose is this?"

They were all mystified. Brid suggested that it was payment for taking Kialan North, but, as Moril and Kialan rather scornfully pointed out, if Clennen had organised that, he would have been paying himself. No other explanation seemed likely, either.

"Anyway, that means we can buy food tomorrow,"

Brid said. "Father couldn't mind that."

"Don't be a big idiot!" said Moril. "When did we ever have a gold piece before? Someone's going to think we stole it, and if *we* get arrested, the whole thing's going to come out." Carefully he slipped the coin back behind the basket again.

Brid sighed. "A whole bottleful of gold! Oh, all right. I suppose you're right and it would look odd. I'm going to bed. Get out of the cart."

Moril helped Kialan put up the tent. By then Kialan was so tired that he dragged a blanket into it and fell asleep before the sun set. Moril felt too agitated to go to sleep straight away. He sat against the cliff, with Olob companionably cropping grass nearby, and strummed on the cwidder for comfort. He did not play any particular song, just snatches of this and a bar or so of that. It seemed to express the state of his feelings. He still found it hard to believe that his father had been a notorious agent. Of all the discoveries of the last few days, that one was hardest to take. He had thought he knew Clennen. Now he saw he had not. He wondered when Dagner had found out and how he had felt. And he made an effort to think of Clennen in this new light.

But somehow, he did not want to think of his father.

He wanted to forget the blood gushing into the lake, and he did not want to consider how Clennen could be so public and so private at one and the same time. Instead, by degrees, Moril took refuge in hazy memories from much earlier. He thought of the cart rolling down a green road in the North. Clennen was singing in the driving seat, Lenina doing some mending beside him and the three children were playing happily on the lockers. The sun shone – and, somewhat to his surprise, the cwidder began to produce a muzzy sound. It was a very queer noise. Moril did not like it, and Olob looked round at it disapprovingly.

"Time for bed," Moril said to Olob. He got up and went to put the cwidder back in the cart.

Inside, the cart was hot, and Brid and the wine jar seemed to fill it. Moril hesitated, thinking of the active elbows and knees of Kialan. But he could not bear the heat, so he took a blanket and wriggled into the tent with Kialan.

Luckily Kialan was so exhausted that he did not move in his sleep. Both he and Moril woke feeling fresher and happier. Brid was the sombre one, but she improved after a breakfast of bacon steaks fried by Kialan. Then Moril fetched Olob's harness to clean. He was determined that their turnout should be as spruce and innocent as he could get it. Kialan, without being asked, went to groom Olob. And Moril realised that not only had Kialan done his full share of the chores ever since they left Markind, but nobody had either noticed or thanked him.

"You don't have to do Olob," he said. "I'll do him."

"Am I supposed to stand around and watch you wear yourself out, or something?" said Kialan. "Move, Olob, you lazy lump."

"Well, you used to," said Brid, scrubbing the frying pan. "And you're an earl's son."

"I thought I'd get that sooner or later!" Kialan said with his most fed-up look. "I didn't know what needed doing at first, and there always seemed loads of you to do it, anyway. But if you two are having to earn money now, it's only fair you don't do everything else."

"Moril," said Brid, going very sombre again, "do you think we really *can* earn money? I mean, even with Dagner, we sounded so – so thin and pale, didn't we?"

"No, you didn't," said Kialan, at work on the further side of Olob. "You just gave a different kind of show. Only I think you made a mistake in not building it round Dagner more. You should have got him to sing again, Brid. He'd have done it in short bursts, and his songs are really good."

"They are, aren't they?" Brid said sadly. "And now—"

"Moril," said Kialan, appearing under Olob's nose, "you can't happen to remember Dagner's songs, can you? Enough to play them yourself?"

"I never thought of that!" said Moril. As soon as he had finished the harness, he fetched out the instruments. While Brid set to work polishing them, Moril took up the big cwidder and tried out the first song of Dagner's that came into his head. For some reason, it was the song Dagner had never finished, the one Clennen had forbidden him to sing until they were in the North. Moril stopped after the first few notes, to make sure nobody was about. There seemed to be no one, so he went on. He found he wanted to finish it for Dagner. It seemed the only thing he could do for him.

Dagner had only sketched out part of the tune. Since Moril had no idea what Dagner intended, he let the words take him, this way and that, through a melting blackbird phrase:

"*Come to me, come with me.*
The blackbird asks you, 'Follow me.'"

– and then to a kind of birdsong triumph in

"Wherever you go, I will go."

Kialan seemed almost awestruck. But Brid, as soon as she realised what song it was, looked up the cliff and down the slope to make sure they were not overheard. Moril knew he was breaking the law. But he wanted to finish the song, so he went, rather defiantly, on to *The sun is up.*

The cwidder produced a shrill and defiant sound. Moril, cross with himself for being scared, tried to recapture the first melting tone and only succeeded in making a scratchy, bad-tempered tinkle. Dagner would have hated it. Moril thought of Dagner and put in the first four lines again at the end, as Dagner had suggested he might. But he was not thinking very clearly of Dagner himself – more of Dagner as part of that happy family on a green road in the North that he had pictured the night before. And just as he had last night, he heard the cwidder making that odd, muzzy noise.

Moril sprang up and sprang back. He could not help it. The cwidder fell on the turf with a melodious thump.

"Moril!" said Brid. "You'll break it!"

"It was splendid!" said Kialan. "Don't stop."

"I don't care!" Moril said hysterically. "I've a good mind to jump on it! The blessed thing was playing my *thoughts*! It played the way I was thinking!"

Brid and Kialan looked at one another, then at Moril. "Don't you think," Kialan said, "that that's the way it works? It's your thoughts that bring out the power."

"But it never did that for Father!" said Moril. "He told me! He said it only did it once."

"Well," Kialan said, rather awkwardly, "he couldn't really use it, could he? It wasn't his kind of thing."

"Except just that one time," said Brid. "Which proves it, Moril. Because it must have been when Father saw Mother in Ganner's hall. And he wanted her to love him instead of Ganner so much that he managed to make the cwidder work, and she did love him enough to come away with him."

After that Moril went and put the cwidder away. Brid got it out again and polished it for him, but he pretended not to notice. When Olob, the cart and all the instruments were gleaming with care, they set off again through the first Upland, towards the steep hill to the second. Brid drove. Moril sat beside her, trying out another of Dagner's songs on his small treble cwidder. But it was no good. The treble cwidder just felt foolish and flimsy and shrill, and it sounded terribly ordinary. As Olob settled into a slow, heaving walk up the steep hill into the next Upland, Moril was forced to turn and ask Kialan to put the little cwidder away and pass him the big one.

The matter-of-fact way Kialan handed it to him made Moril feel much better about it. Moril took the cwidder thankfully. It felt right. He was not sure now whether it was a comfort or a burden, but if Kialan could accept so easily that it was a powerful and mysterious thing, so could he. But he knew he was going to have to learn to control the thing. You could not earn your living with a cwidder that whined if you were miserable and croaked if you were cross. "How should I start?" he asked Kialan over his shoulder.

Kialan hesitated, not because he did not understand Moril, but because he was not sure how Moril should start. "Understanding yourself, perhaps?" he asked. "I mean, I've no idea either, but try that. Er – why didn't you stay in Markind, for instance? Was it just seeing Tholian there?"

Moril, by this time, was sure that it was not. "Why didn't *you* want to stay?" he asked Brid, as a start. "Duty to Father?"

"Like Mother, you mean?" said Brid. "N—no. A bit

of that. I do prefer Father's outlook to Mother's, but it was really almost more like the way Mother went back to Ganner. It's what I'm used to – this – and nothing else felt right."

Moril felt that went for him too. But there was more to it than that. He could have persuaded Brid to go back to Markind after Dagner was arrested, but he had not thought of it, even. He had not wanted to go back when he had found out how dangerous their journey North really was. And he was still going North, as if it was a matter of course. Why?

"Why, Moril?" asked Brid.

"I was born in the North," Moril answered, rather slowly. "When I – er – dream of things, it's always the North. And the North is right and the South is wrong."

"Bravo!" said Kialan.

Moril turned to smile at him. He found himself turning from the towering unseeable hills of the North to a low, blue vision of the South, beyond Kialan's head. "But I still don't understand," he said.

At the top of the hill there was a village, a very small place, simply ten houses and an alehouse, clinging to the steep brow of the hill.

"Don't let's perform here," said Brid. "There's a bigger

place further on, I know."

They went past the village into a wider Upland, full of grazing sheep. By the middle of the morning Moril's cwidder was sounding melancholy. "I can't see us getting much," he said. "Not just the two of us."

"Would it help at all," said Kialan, "if I were to pretend to be Dagner?"

Both their heads whipped round his way. It was almost a marvellous idea.

"Would they remember Dagner from last year?" said Kialan.

"We didn't perform in the Uplands at all last year," said Brid. "But—"

"I've been thinking," said Kialan. "No one but the earls knows I'm in the South. And it's so out of the way here that no one's going to know Dagner was arrested unless we tell them. I think it would be safe enough – and a bit in your father's style too."

Moril made the obvious objection. "You can't sing." They looked at one another for a moment. Moril remembered Kialan listening in to his lessons with Clennen, appearing in the crowd whenever they gave a show, and seeming so knowledgeable the time the big cwidder went out of tune. "Or can you?" said Moril.

"Not as well as you," said Kialan, "but – may I borrow one of these cwidders for a moment?"

"Go ahead," said Brid.

Kialan took up Dagner's cwidder and tuned it without needing to be given a note. Moril and Brid looked at one another. Neither of them could do that. And from the moment Kialan started to play, they knew they were listening to a gifted person very much out of practice. If he did not sing as well as he played, it was merely because he was the age when his voice still moved troublesomely from low to high. Moril vividly remembered the trouble Dagner had had at the same age.

What Kialan sang was a song of the Adon's, one that Clennen never sang in the South.

"Unbounded truth is not a thing
Cramped to time and bound in place—"

"Ooh!" said Brid, looking nervously round.

"No one about. Shut up!" said Moril.

Kialan did that part meticulously in the right old style. But then he gave Moril a bit of a wink and dropped into the same kind of different fingering Moril had used in Neathdale. The song seemed to come alive.

"Truth strangely changes space,
By right of its reality.
It moves the hills containing me
Wider than the world, or small
As in a nut. Truth is free
And laws are stones, or not at all,
And men without it nothing."

"Oh, I liked that!" said Moril.

"I took a leaf out of your book," Kialan said, rather apologetically. "I don't like the old style either, and I don't see why old things should be sacred. Wow! I'm out of practice, though! Do you think I'll be any use to you?"

"You know you will," said Brid. "You big fraud. If you're that good, why on earth didn't you say so before? Father would have put you in the show, instead of making you walk through all the towns."

"I know he would!" Kialan said feelingly. "He'd have dressed me in scarlet and flaunted me. I didn't quite like to say anything at first – you were all so excellent – and as soon as I realised what your father was like, I'd have died rather than tell him. It was frightening enough walking."

The upshot of this was that Olob quietly pulled the

gleaming cart on to the green of the village a mile or so on, and three people stood up to sing and play. Moril and Kialan were nervous, Brid, as usual, as confident as a queen. Moril did one or two of Dagner's songs, but mostly they sang ballads, since those were Brid's speciality and Kialan's voice was not equal to anything more difficult. A scattering of people listened and clapped. Someone asked for an encore, and Brid gave them *Cow-Calling*. They got a little money, enough to buy eggs, milk and butter, and a woman gave Brid a basket of somewhat withered apples. It was not a raving success, but it was no failure either.

"We can do it!" said Brid.

Moril smiled, and strummed his cwidder as they took to the road again. Every so often he played a tune in earnest, and Kialan would come in too, on Dagner's cwidder. Kialan was getting more in practice every moment. They experimented, and tried for effects and new settings. Moril had seldom enjoyed making music so much. He almost wished the distance to Hannart were twice as long.

CHAPTER TEN

They had a sort of cheese omelette for lunch, sitting on a point of green land between two brisk streams. Kialan would have it that what they were eating was scrambled eggs. Brid disagreed. Moril did not join in the argument because he was listening to the sound of the water. It made him think of the North. The sound of water running was never far away in the North. He was dreamily considering whether one could make a tune that captured the noise when Brid shook him sharply and told him they were moving.

"You didn't have to do that!" said Kialan.

"Why not? You know how maddening he is when he goes into a dream," Brid retorted.

"Yes, but it's just his way," said Kialan. "He's about six times as awake as most people, really. I bet he heard every word we said – didn't you, Moril?"

"I suppose I did," Moril said, in some surprise.

"Can I drive this next stretch?" Kialan asked.

Neither Brid nor Moril objected. Letting Kialan drive Olob seemed the best way to show he was a full member of the company now and not a passenger any longer. So Kialan held the reins, and Olob clopped onwards through the lonely Upland. Moril sat beside him, still strumming the cwidder, looking dreamily around at the hills, the flocks of sheep and the occasional shepherd in the distance.

They came to a steep rise to the third and last Upland. It was the highest and also the most beautiful of the three climbs, because it was clothed in trees the whole way up. The road, though it was the main road, dwindled to a rutty lane, damp and stony, boring its way upwards through the woods. The sunlight fell in gay splashes through the bright leaves of springtime. All three of them looked upwards and grinned at the way their faces became speckled and greenish.

But Olob, whether he objected to Kialan's holding the reins or to having to climb two steep hills in one day, became steadily more restive. At first it was simply tossing his head and stopping. Kialan persuaded him to move again, each time with more difficulty. But, as they went on upwards, Olob took to trampling this way and that, so that the cart wheels caught in the hawthorns at the side of the road. Kialan grew exasperated. The fourth time Olob did it, Kialan lost his temper and swore at Olob. Olob promptly turned right across the road and seemed to be trying to climb the sheer bank into the woods. Moril thought the cart would overturn. The wine jar fell over and knocked Brid sideways, with a dreadful twanging of cwidders.

"Let me take him," said Moril.

Kialan crossly handed him the reins. Moril propped the cwidder across his knees and worked with both hands and some shouting to persuade Olob back on to the road again. Olob refused to come out of the bushes.

"What's got into him?" said Kialan.

"No idea," said Moril. As he said it, two memories came to him. One was of almost exactly the same conversation, between himself and Lenina, just before Tholian came out of the wood and killed Clennen. The other was of Olob behaving like a colt in Neathdale, just before Dagner was arrested. "Quick!" he said to Kialan. "There are enemies near, and Olob knows. Get out and go through the woods until we've passed them."

"How *can* he know?" said Kialan, with his most fed-up look.

"I don't know, but he does. Father always said he wouldn't part with Olob for an earldom, and I think that's why. Get *out*, I said!" Moril said urgently.

"Do as you're told, Kialan!" said Brid from the tilted bottom of the cart.

Kialan, entirely unconvinced, swung himself grudgingly down from the cart. As Olob was halfway through a bush, up the right bank of the road, Kialan went up beside him by the space he had cleared, and vanished among the trees higher up. Moril could hear his cross footsteps swishing along the steep hillside.

"Go quietly!" he said, but he could tell Kialan took no notice. Moril dumped the cwidder in the canted cart and went to Olob's head. Olob was most unwilling to leave the bush. "I know, old fellow, but we've got to go on and look innocent," Moril said. "*Come* on, now!"

It took some time to get Olob back on the road. When he did consent to come, Brid had to lean on the cart to keep it upright. Then she climbed in and tried to set the wine jar and the instruments to rights. Olob reluctantly climbed onwards. Above them in the woods, Kialan's feet kept pace with the cart, swishing loudly and cracking twigs. Moril wished he would not make so much noise.

Olob toiled round three corners and Brid still seemed to be busy in the cart. "What are you doing?" Moril asked.

"Putting my boots on," said Brid. "If there *are* enemies near, I'm going to look respectable. And I'm putting the sharp knife down the right boot." She joined him shortly, looking flushed and determined, firmly booted. "I'll drive," she said.

Moril gave her the reins and hung the cwidder round his neck by its strap, which, he supposed, was his way of looking respectable. His boots, by this time, were nothing like as new and smart as Brid's. Brid was better at managing Olob. Olob put on a great act of this being the most difficult climb of his life and did everything in his power to suggest that they turn back, but Brid kept him going. Beyond the protesting clatter of his hooves, Moril listened for Kialan, but he could not hear him any longer. By this time they were near the top of the climb. They rounded what must have been the last corner, and Olob shied.

"Clever Olob," Brid remarked.

There was a stout wooden trestle in the road. It did not fill the road, but it was placed so that there was no room for a cart to pass on either side. There were a number of men with it, one of them sitting on the trestle. To Moril's dismay, they were all in full war gear. Each of them wore a steel cap and a steel breastplate with a pointed front – which gave them all chests like pigeons – over jackets and trousers of tough leather. They wore great black boots and long swords in black leather scabbards.

Brid drew the alarmed Olob up. "Would you mind moving the trestle? We need to get by," she said haughtily. She was frightened and daunted, but there were enough soldiers to make her feel as if she had an audience.

Three of the men strolled forwards. None of them made any effort to move the trestle. "What's your business?" said one. The other two strolled on and looked over the sides of the cart to see what was in it.

"Drunkards, by the look of this wine," one said, and both of them sniggered a little.

"We're singers," said Brid. "Can't you see?"

"In that case, let's see your licence," said the first man, and held out his hand for it. Brid, after a moment's hesitation, fetched the licence out of the locker under the seat and handed it to him. He looked at it casually. "Which of you is Clennen?"

"That's my father," said Brid. "He was killed four days ago."

"Then you haven't got a licence," said the man. "Have you?"

"Yes, we have," said Brid. "We're entitled to sing under that licence for six months. That's the law, and you can't tell me it isn't."

"That may be the law in the other earldoms, but not in the South Dales," the man said, grinning. "You haven't read the small print." He unrolled the parchment and pointed vaguely to the bottom of it. When Brid leant over to look, he took it out of reach and let it roll up again. "Too bad," he said. "You'd better come and explain yourselves."

"It doesn't say that at all!" Brid said furiously. "You're just using it as an excuse. That licence is perfectly in order, and you know it!"

The man stopped grinning. "You'll do as you're told," he said. He nodded to one of the other men, who took hold of Olob's bridle. The rest moved the trestle aside. The one holding Olob hauled on him and Olob, passively resisting for all he was worth, was forced to move reluctantly on. Brid and Moril were towed after him, feeling quite helpless. It was clear that someone – Tholian, probably – had given orders that all travellers were to be stopped. Moril looked back to see the soldiers putting the trestle across the road again and sitting on it to wait for any other comers. He wondered about jumping off the cart and running. But there was a soldier walking on either side of it and it did not seem worth trying. Their only hope seemed to be to use Clennen's method and appear as open and innocent as they knew how.

They went fifty yards or so – a difficult jerky fifty yards, because Olob was extremely frightened and did not want to move, in spite of the names the soldier called him – and came to a steep road branching to the right. The soldier dragged Olob into it. Moril had forgotten this road. It worried him that Kialan would have to cross it on his way to the last Upland.

"Where does this road go?" he asked Brid.

"To a sort of extra valley at one side," Brid said. "We camped here the year before last. Don't you remember? Moril, they will let us go, won't they?"

Moril glanced down at the soldiers. "We haven't done anything wrong," he said carefully. But the wine jar came into his mind as he said it, and he wondered why on earth he had not left it behind somewhere.

A twig snapped in the wood up to the right. Moril looked up. And looked away quickly, in case the soldiers noticed. He had a very clear sight of Kialan staring down at the cart, alarmed and rather puzzled, as if he had not gathered what was going on. Moril stared at the steep road ahead and tried to will Kialan to cross the road while he had the chance and go on North. But he was very much afraid Kialan intended to follow the cart.

The trees opened like the end of a tunnel, and they came out into the valley. Brid gave a little moan. Beyond two groups of soldiers, evidently on guard, were tents, weapons, horses and many more soldiers, as far as they could see. It was a long, thin valley, and winding, so that half of it was out of sight. But they had no doubt that the part of it they could not see was also full of soldiers and weapons and tents.

The nearest tent was a very large one. There was a chair outside it, and in that chair sat Tholian. His head turned as the cart came out from among the trees. As far as he could tell from this distance, Moril thought Tholian smiled. And he saw that Clennen's method was not going to help them here. In fact, he doubted if any method was going to be much use.

"Get down," one of the soldiers said to Brid and Moril.

They climbed down, Brid a little awkward in her boots, Moril clutching the cwidder, and stood where they had a lower and even busier view of the teeming valley ahead. Moril dimly remembered that the year before last there had been fields and crops growing here. There was no sign of them now. As they were taken towards Tholian, he saw nothing but men drilling and training, all down the valley. It was filled with orders and curses, and the thick warm smell of many people and horses. The grass, and any crops there might have been, were trampled to earth, except for a green stretch round the large tent where Tholian sat.

Tholian signalled to the soldiers to make Brid and Moril stand to one side of the patch of grass, and turned his pale eyes from them to the soldiers. "Just these two in the cart?" he asked.

Moril seized the opportunity to look over his shoulder to see what had become of Olob and the cart. He was glad to find one of the soldiers struggling to tie the unwilling Olob to a tree beside the road.

"Could I have your attention, cousin?" he heard Tholian say, and he turned back hurriedly. Tholian sounded irritated. But when Moril looked at him, he was smiling. He could have been friendly in spite of his queer, shallow eyes. "We are related, aren't we?" he said.

Moril thought about it. "I suppose so. But it's Mother who's your cousin."

"Once removed," said Tholian. "Which makes us twice removed, I believe."

"I'm surprised you acknowledge it at all," said Brid. "Considering—"

"Why not?" said Tholian. "It doesn't hurt you. But don't deceive yourselves into thinking your mother's going to get a penny of dowry out of me. I'm content to do as my grandfather wanted. Ganner's a fool if he thinks I'm going to make him rich on Lenina's account."

This seemed a very odd thing for Tholian to start talking about. Moril wondered if he was a trifle mad. "I shouldn't think Ganner does think that," he said.

"He's fond of Mother, you see," explained Brid.

Tholian laughed. "Fool, isn't he?" He was so contemptuous that Brid all but sprang to Ganner's defence. "But I stayed for the wedding," Tholian said, before Brid could speak, "which was more than you did. You threw Ganner into a fine old fuss by leaving like that, you know. Your mother took it much more calmly. So I promised them I'd look out for you on the road and send you back to Markind when I found you."

"That was kind of you," Brid said coldly. Nevertheless, both she and Moril were beginning to feel distinctly easier. If Tholian were regarding them simply as silly young relations and himself as doing Ganner a favour, then the position was nothing like as bad as they had feared. It would be exasperating to be sent back to Markind, but at least Kialan, with luck, could get North on foot from here.

"Didn't Mother recognise you?" Moril said slowly, rather puzzled at the way Tholian was now being a friend of the family.

"Of course," Tholian said, not at all disconcerted. "But as I'm Ganner's overlord, there wasn't much she could say. Not that she would. She has a way of saying things in silence, your mother. By the way, what became of your brothers?"

They saw he had just been showing them how much he knew. It gave them both a jolt. Moril reacted best, because he was able to rely on his habitual sleepy look. He went on staring at Tholian in a vague, friendly way, though he had never felt less vague or less friendly in his life. But Brid was so shaken that she had to put on an act.

"Funny you should ask," she said, with artificial

brightness. "We don't quite know—"

"Yes, we do, Brid," Moril said, fearing she was going to babble herself into trouble. "Dagner went back to Markind." It was a risky thing to say, but Moril knew that if Tholian already knew that Dagner had been arrested and why, it did not matter what he said anyway.

"Did he, indeed?" said Tholian, and there was no telling whether he had heard about Dagner or not. "And what about the other brother – er – Collen, was it?"

Moril knew Tholian had not seen Kialan in Markind. If he had, none of them would have been allowed to leave. He must have heard Ganner talk about him later. And no one would be surprised to find Ganner had got something wrong. Moril opened his mouth to say they had not got another brother, but Brid, to his annoyance, came in first, with tremendous verve: "Oh, Collen! He's so stupid you never know *what* he'll do! But we think he went with Dagner."

"Curious," said Tholian. His untrustworthy eyes slid over Brid, and over her again. "Now I thought I was reliably informed that there were three of you giving a show in Updale this morning."

That had obviously been a fatal mistake. But how could they have known Tholian was so near? The only thing to do was to say that the third one had been Dagner. Moril drew a breath to say it, but once more, Brid rushed in. "Yes, of course. But that's what I was telling you. Collen went back after that. He said he was going to Neathdale and he – er – he got a lift in a farm wagon."

Moril sadly wished that Brid would let him do the talking. Brid was not as clever as she thought she was. No doubt she had thought she was doing very well, but she had first admitted Kialan's existence and now that he was quite near, and Moril knew there was no need to have done either. Tholian had never seen Kialan in their company. He was only going by guess. But now he was almost certain. He was looking at Brid, worrying her by just looking, and obviously enjoying the way he was worrying her.

"I don't think you quite understand the position," Tholian said when Brid, flushed and alarmed, had dropped her eyes from his pale ones to her boots. "I'm ready to send you both back to Markind safely, in exchange for Kialan Kerilsson. Not otherwise. Is that understood now?"

"I don't understand you at all," Brid said valiantly.

Tholian looked at Moril. "Do you?"

Moril tried to repair some of the damage Brid had

done by saying, "Not really. Who's this person you're talking about?"

The only result of this was that Tholian turned his eyes back to Brid. "Keril," he said, "as I'm sure you know, is Earl of Hannart." Without bothering to turn round, he snapped his fingers to some of the men near. They came hurrying up. "Listen," said Tholian. "Kialan Kerilsson is about five feet seven, solidly built, with a dark complexion and fair hair. His nose is aquiline and his eyes are much the same colour as mine. Start searching the woods for a boy of that description."

The men at once turned and went hurrying further into the thronged valley. Brid, as Moril knew she would, showed her consternation by saying, with horrible brightness, "What a queer kind of person that sounds!"

"No, no," said Tholian. "Just a typical Northerner." Beyond him, captains waved their arms and shouted orders. In a matter of seconds, quite a surprising number of soldiers left off drilling and moved at a run towards the woods behind Moril and Brid. Moril could only hope that Kialan had had the sense to cross the road and go North as fast as he could. Tholian's eyes moved sideways to make sure his orders were being carried out and then turned back to Brid. "You seem worried," he said, and laughed at her.

"Not in the least," Brid lied haughtily.

"But you don't," said Tholian, looking at Moril. "Why not?"

Moril did not see why Tholian should make a game of him. "Why did you kill my father?" he said.

Tholian was not in the least discomposed. The cool way he took the question upset Moril more than a little. It reminded him of Lenina. "Now, why was it?" Tholian said, pretending to remember. Moril thought of Lenina coolly stopping Clennen's bleeding and saw an actual family likeness to Lenina in Tholian's calm face. He wished he had not seen it. "I was having a little trouble finding Kialan," said Tholian, "as I recall. But I think the main reason I killed him was that it was probable he was the Porter."

Brid gasped, which amused Tholian. Moril felt hopeless, though he managed not to show it. "If you thought that, why didn't you have him arrested?" he said.

"Legally, instead of murdering him," said Brid, who was in such despair that she no longer cared what she said.

"But that would have been a silly thing to do," Tholian said laughingly. "A man arrested and tried for crimes like the Porter's very easily becomes a hero. You hang him, and people take his side or even rebel in his memory. Besides, I've seen Clennen give his shows in Neathdale. And I really didn't see why he should be given the chance to put on the biggest performance of his life. He'd have enjoyed it too much."

"You—" Brid hunted for the nastiest word she knew. "Fiend!" she said. Tholian, of course, laughed.

Moril said nothing. Up till then he had disliked Tholian, and he was afraid of him, because he was powerful and had such queer eyes. But after that he hated him, violently and personally. He should have hated him before, he supposed, but the fact was that in an odd way, he had thought of Clennen's death almost as if it were an accident, unfair in the way accidents were. Now he knew Tholian had intended it to be unfair, he hated Tholian for it.

"And how did you find Father?" Brid said. "Did Ganner tell you, you murdering beast!"

Tholian, luckily for Brid, still seemed to find her funny. "Ganner? Oh no," he said. "I don't have to rely on Ganner for information. Though I must say, Ganner didn't seem to be breaking his heart over Clennen when I told him he was dead." He laughed. "I suppose we put Ganner in a bit of a spot," he said, "all turning up in

Markind almost together that day." He looked at Brid, to see how she took that. Brid realised Tholian was trying to torment her. She stared haughtily away at the busy soldiers in the valley. Tholian's eyes looked past her, at something behind them. "One last thing," he said. "Never try to carry on like your father. It's stupid, and it never pays. If I'd copied my father, I wouldn't be here with an army."

There was a nasty reasonableness about this that annoyed Moril. "Yes, but you see," he said, "it was something that needed doing."

Tholian was not interested any longer. He stood up. "Bring him here," he said. "Move, can't you!"

A group of soldiers hurried up, dragging Kialan. Kialan was dishevelled and red in the face. Twigs were clinging to his clothes. He was resisting, rather, but he also had his head bowed in the sullen way Moril had seen among the prisoners in Neathdale. It was the way you looked, Moril realised, when you were caught. You had it whether you were guilty or innocent. It did not surprise him that Kialan was caught. He had made the mistake of staying near the cart. No doubt he had hoped to help Brid and Moril. Perhaps, since he was now the eldest, he had felt responsible for them. But Moril did not feel one twinge of gratitude. He just felt sad. Kialan had hung about, and Brid had made sure Tholian guessed he was near. That was the trouble with people who thought too well of themselves.

CHAPTER ELEVEN

"AH! KIALAN!" SAID Tholian. "Nice to see you where there aren't any other earls to interfere."

Kialan looked up at Tholian from among the soldiers, with his head still a little bowed, but did not answer. Moril noticed that it was indeed true as Tholian had said, that Kialan's eyes were almost the same colour as Tholian's. It made him see the difference between them. For Kialan, scared and sullen though he was, had a direct and living look, and Tholian's eyes were blank and strange. It was clear that while Tholian thought of Brid and Moril as rather funny and not at all important, he thought of

Kialan as quite another matter.

"I thought you'd appear on this road sooner or later," Tholian said. "But we were watching the Marshes too, in case. I'm hoping to let your father know you really are our prisoner. You'll have to write him a letter."

"I'm blowed if I shall!" said Kialan. "Write it yourself."

"Very well. I will," agreed Tholian. "I suppose he'll recognise one of your ears if I send it with the letter. Hold him tightly," he said to the soldiers. He took a knife from a sheath at his belt and walked towards Kialan.

Kialan tried to back away and was held in place by two soldiers. "All right," he said hurriedly. "I'll write you a letter if you want." Moril did not blame him.

But Tholian took no notice. The blank look in his eyes did not alter. The soldiers screwed up their faces. Moril, sickened and terrified, realised that Tholian just wanted an excuse to hurt Kialan. He clutched the cwidder and wondered what he could do. Kialan, even more frightened, tried to duck his head away from the knife. "Hold him, I said!" said Tholian.

One of the soldiers took a handful of Kialan's hair. Brid, without really thinking what she was doing, plunged forwards and tried to catch hold of Tholian's arm. She got no further than the nearest soldier, who pushed her sharply away. Brid staggered back and bumped into Moril, jolting his right hand on the cwidder, so that he accidentally struck a long humming note from the deepest string.

An extraordinary buzzing numbness filled the air and seemed to be eating up Moril's brain. He could do nothing, and barely think. The noise pressed into his head and forced him down on his knees. Everything outside his head was grey and pulsating, burring and blurred, and the feeling went on and on and on. He thought he saw Tholian, looking a little bewildered, stand still and slowly sheathe his knife, while Kialan and the soldiers all shook their heads like people who have been hit. Brid pressed both hands to her eyes. Their movements made Moril feel sick. He knelt with his head bent, looking at the pulsing earth, and wondered if he was going to die.

Brid knelt down beside him. "Moril, are you all right? It was the cwidder, wasn't it?" Moril shook his humming head at her, wanting her to be quiet.

Everyone except Moril seemed to have quite recovered, except that Tholian looked puzzled, as if he had forgotten a word that was on the tip of his tongue. "Tie him up for now," he said to the soldiers, in a rather irritated way. "Get some rope, one of you."

"You made Tholian forget!" Brid whispered. "Do attend, Moril. You might be able to do it again." But Moril could not attend. His face was so white that Brid became worried, which meant that she was very cross with him in a harsh, snapping whisper which hurt Moril's numbed head. Then Brid suddenly jumped to her feet and dashed away from him. "You can't do that!" she shouted. "It's cruel!"

That jerked Moril to his senses. He looked up and saw Kialan had been tied with his hands behind him to one of the stakes that carried the tent ropes. The reason for Brid's outcry was that Tholian, not satisfied with merely tying him, had put a noose round Kialan's tied hands and was hoisting them up his back. The effect must have been like having both arms twisted at once. Moril could see Kialan was in agony.

Tholian turned to Brid as soon as he had made the rope fast. "Can't?" he said. "Go back to your brother." When Brid did not move at once, Tholian advanced on her, with his strange eyes blank. "Are you going to do as I said?"

Brid was frightened enough to turn and run back to Moril. As she came, she mouthed, *"Do something!"*

Tholian started off towards where several captains were hovering, wanting to speak to him. "Those two are

196

not to move from there," he said over his shoulder to the soldiers round Kialan.

"Moril," whispered Brid. "The cwidder. Make it undo the rope."

Moril wished he could. He was sure the cwidder was quite capable of releasing Kialan, if only he knew how to work it. Osfameron had made it move mountains. But Moril had not the slightest idea how to begin and was very much afraid of making a mistake and bringing that awful humming into his own brain again. Kialan tried to give him a brave look although he was grinning with pain. Moril could see him struggling to get into a more comfortable position when there was no way of doing so. And Tholian might leave him like that for hours. It was worth a try.

Remembering the way the cwidder seemed to play his thoughts, Moril set himself to imagine Tholian's noose pulling and twisting Kialan into that unnatural position. It was horrible. His arms ached and sweat dropped out from under his hair. He thought fiercely, This must *stop!* and gently touched the slack bottom string.

It chimed like a soft, deep bell. Moril braced himself against the humming, but it did not come. Its effect, though it was not at all what he expected, was on Kialan alone. He saw Kialan's head suddenly drop and his knees give. He did not move, and it was clear that only the ropes were holding him up. Terrified, Moril clapped his hand across the string and stopped it vibrating.

Brid rounded on Moril with tears whisking down her cheeks. "You stupid idiot! You've killed him!"

"Shut up!" Moril whispered, anxiously watching both Kialan and the soldiers just beyond him. "They'll realise. Look. He's breathing. He's only passed out."

"But what about the ropes?" Brid whispered.

Moril shook his head. "I can't. I was trying to. I think I can only make it work on people."

One of the soldiers turned and saw Kialan sagging. When Tholian came back from talking to the captains, they pointed Kialan out to him. Tholian simply shrugged and passed by on his way somewhere else.

"I *hate* Tholian!" said Brid.

Moril said nothing. He knelt on the ground, nursing his cwidder, thinking as he had never thought in his life before. The soldiers, meanwhile, looked at one another, looked around to see how far away Tholian was, and undid the noose from Kialan's hands, so that Kialan slid to his knees with his head hanging almost upside down.

"Look, Moril," Brid whispered. "You did undo the

ropes, sort of."

Moril had seen perfectly well, though he gave no sign of it. He was as alert as he had been in the jail in Neathdale. He could have told Brid exactly how many captains, troops and horsemen there were in the part of the valley they could see. He was aware of every time a group of new recruits came marching in, and how many came in each group. Four groups arrived while he knelt and thought and while Kialan hung in a heap, head downwards. Moril saw that they did not come by the road, but down through the woods, to keep their mustering secret. He also saw that almost every new arrival was miserable. They trailed their feet and held their heads at that sullen angle Kialan and Dagner had both held theirs when they knew they were caught. He could see that few of them had joined Tholian's army willingly. But he was thinking, thinking. For he was sure that the cwidder he was hugging on his knees was capable of saving all three of them and getting them North with news of Tholian's army. He knew how it could be done. The only thing he did not know was how to call up the power in the cwidder to do it.

Since it was his thoughts the cwidder responded to, Moril tried to understand how he might feed his entire self through it into the enormous power he knew was needed. His father had said Moril was in two halves. "Come together," Clennen had said, "and there's no knowing what you might do." Moril supposed Clennen had meant the way Moril was incorrigibly dreamy and also unbelievably alert at times, just as he was now. But as Kialan had noticed, he was often both at the same time, unless he went vague in self-defence. Moril thought that could not quite be it.

But there was another way he was in two halves. His mother was a Southern aristocrat, and his father a freedom-fighting singer from the North. As Dagner had said, there was no doubt it was a weird mixture. It was cold and hot, strict and free, restrained and outspoken, all at once. The trouble was, this did not quite add up to Moril. He did not think he had inherited much from his Southern ancestry – certainly none of the unfeeling tyranny that made his distant cousin Tholian so detestable.

But Tholian's calm cruelty had, in a horrible way, reminded him of Lenina. Moril remembered Kialan saying, "Your mother's a cool one." And that was it, of course. Lenina never lost her head, and neither did Moril. He knew that, if Brid had only let him, he could coolly have led Tholian to believe that none of them had ever set eyes on Kialan, just as Lenina might have done. Keeping your head was part of the strict standard of the South. It was the same strict standard that had kept Lenina so loyal to Clennen, even though she hated life in the cart and disagreed with the freedom fighting. And Moril saw that it was the same kind of strict loyalty that had brought him North – only, with him, it was loyalty to the North.

After this followed something very uncomfortable, which Moril would not have faced if he had not had such a pressing need to use the cwidder. He had to admit he had deserted Lenina. He had gone off and left her when she had been trying to make them happy. He hoped he had not made her too unhappy, because he knew that seeing Tholian in Markind had only given him the excuse he had been looking for to go North. And going off like that, he had been trying to deny the Southern part of him – all the strict, honourable things which were the good aspect of the South. It did not do to deny them, even though he thought he had been doing it out of loyalty to Clennen.

Then he tried to find out what he had got from Clennen. Goodness knew what strange blood the singers came from. They could all sing and play. They saw a little more than most people, and some of them dreamed dreams. But Moril knew that all he had got from Clennen himself were ideas of freedom and his love of the North. The rest was the common stock of the singers.

The puzzling part was that these two halves added up to three quite different people: Brid, Dagner and Moril. Brid had Lenina's sharpness and some of Lenina's efficiency, and she had Clennen's love of an audience, without Clennen's gifts – though she thought she had them. Dagner had far more of the gifts, but he had all Lenina's reserve, and more. In fact, it had been very much in Lenina's manner that Dagner had set off North to finish Clennen's work for him, knowing he had not the personality to do it. None of them had inherited the largeness that made Clennen what he was. And why had Clennen not told Brid or Dagner they were in two halves?

Moril found himself suddenly at a dead end. He saw he would have to get at the cwidder's power some other way. He had to. The third batch of recruits had just arrived. The valley was filling with soldiers, and the North did not know. And the Earl of Hannart would not dare move because of Kialan. And Moril knew Kialan was actively in danger from Tholian. Tholian passed several times, and each time he looked at Kialan's hanging body as if he wanted it awake and writhing.

Moril thought of the cwidder itself. Though Osfameron could use it on things, it seemed that Moril was only going to make it have an effect on people. That was right for music, in a way. You performed, and people listened and were affected by it. So what did you put into a performance to bring out the power?

Moril did not know. He had only the vaguest idea what he had done to make Kialan unconscious. *All right*, he thought. *What* didn't *my father do, that he could never use the power more than once?* And he thought of Clennen, from day to day, as he had known him, huge, genial and sociable – and boring Kialan stiff by telling the same story three times over. He thought of the way Clennen had been the Porter, quite openly, enjoying deceiving people by the simple fact that he did it all in public, as obviously as possible. Kialan had been positive that this was what Clennen enjoyed particularly. Then Moril thought of Clennen saying "Remember that" so often – almost as if he hoped one of them might write all his sayings down one day. Perhaps Brid would, Moril thought, smiling a little. Then he remembered a particular saying of Clennen's, the day they picked Kialan up. Clennen had said the cart was like life. "You may wonder what goes on inside, but what matters is the look of it and the kind of performance we give." Later on Clennen had asked Dagner about another saying, and Dagner had got this one wrong. "Something about life being only a performance," Dagner had said.

And that was it, Moril thought. Clennen was all performance. Layers of performance. He was the best singer in Dalemark and he used it to play the Porter, and he was the Porter because he was using his sincere feelings about freedom to play the singer – to and fro, over and under, Clennen had performed, even to his own family. His whole life had said, "Look at me!" He had known he was a performer, and he had used that knowledge, just as Brid had used her real sorrow to perform with in Neathdale. But he could not use the cwidder. It was not going to say, "Look at me!" It did not work like that.

If you did not say, "Look at me!" what was the right way? With a joyous feeling of being on the right track, Moril thought of Dagner next. Kialan had called what was really Dagner's performance "a different kind of show". Moril felt warmly grateful to Kialan. Kialan pointed things out. If only because of this, Kialan deserved to be rescued and taken back to the warm-hearted, cocksure, outspoken North where he belonged.

But Dagner – Dagner had been diffident. He had never

said, "Look at me!" because he was shy when people did. What he did was to show people his thoughts – a little – in his songs. "Look here," he seemed to say. "Excuse me. This is what I think. I hope you like it." And people did like it – not in the way they appreciated Clennen but as if they had been told something new.

Moril knew he was unable – at least for the present – to make something new, just as he was unable to use his real feelings for show, like Brid. That left the old songs, Moril's own speciality. Did they help? Yes, they did – thanks to Kialan again. Kialan, just this morning, had sung that song of the Adon's, and it might have been made about this very cwidder! *Unbounded truth!* Moril thought, in rising excitement. *Not a thing cramped to time and bound in place!* Neither was the cwidder when its power was used.

He had it, then. You performed. But you did not say "Look at me!" Nor could you say, like Dagner, "This is what I think." If Dagner's diffident way had been right, Clennen would have given the cwidder to Dagner. No. You had to stand up and come straight out with it. "This is *true*," you had to say. "*This is the truth*. And, though I may not get it over very well, it just *is*." And it was horribly difficult to do.

Moril blinked a little, nerving himself up. The fourth group of new recruits was shuffling its way through the valley, and Tholian was coming back again. With him were the same hearthmen who had been with him by the lake. They all had the same unpleasant look of purpose too. When they reached Kialan, Tholian jabbed at him with the toe of his boot. Kialan flopped.

"Bring him round," he said. "He's going to write me a letter presently." Then he looked across at Brid and Moril, and his eyes were like an owl's caught in a strong light at night. They knew he had no intention of sending them back to Markind.

"Moril," Brid said humbly, "do you think you can do anything?"

Moril scrambled stiffly to his feet, carefully not bumping the cwidder. "I'm going to try," he said, and began to play.

He started with a little sequence of chords, repeated over and over, in a rocking rhythm. He had to start slowly, while he found the thought the cwidder would respond to. He was terrified that Tholian would realise what he was trying to do and stop him, but, though all the men round Kialan glanced irritably at Moril, they obviously had no idea that he was doing anything important. Moril's fear faded. "Not all of you are bad," he told them through the cwidder. "Some are just afraid, others are not good and you are doing wrong." Over and over, he told it.

And to his relief, the cwidder began to hum under his hands. He had got it right. Moril could feel the power gather in it and then, slowly, go humming out over Tholian and his men, right off down the valley, and turn the corner to the part out of sight. The movements of everyone he could see grew slack and a little aimless, and Tholian yawned. Moril thrummed on. He would have rejoiced, except that he knew he was going to have to bring the lowest string in soon, and he was afraid of it. If its power ate into his own head this time, that was the end of his plan. Cautiously he struck it. *Sleep*, it sang, heavily sweet, off down the valley, following the humming path of the power he had already built up. *Sleep*. Tholian's head turned slowly, and he looked at Moril, mistily puzzled. Moril himself was wide awake. He knew it was all right. He had been caught in the power before because he had simply been thinking *No, no, no!* without meaning anything else. Now he meant *Sleep, all you out there.*

Tholian seemed to understand what Moril was doing. He came slowly towards Moril, lurching as if he was very tired. "Break that blessed thing!" he said. His voice was slurred, but he was fighting the cwidder's power for all he was worth.

Quickly Moril passed into a proper tune, a lullaby.

"Go back to the time
When your feelings were blind
When they rocked you and sang
Go to sleep."

If Moril had thought about it, he would have realised he was in fact making up something new. But he did not notice, because all he wanted to do was to put Tholian to sleep. The lullaby was like a gust of power. It held Tholian to the spot. Tholian knew what was happening, but he was helpless. Moril played the tune again, louder, and took pleasure in holding Tholian in place while the tune swept beyond him, out into the valley.

Tholian rubbed his eyes and tried to take a grip on himself. Beyond him, the men round Kialan yawned and the marching and cursing in the valley faded away. The air was clear for the full force of the song, and Moril gave it to them. *Go to sleep.* It went down the valley in slow waves, washing first over Tholian, then on and out.

Tholian's eyelids drooped, his knees bent and he dropped forwards on to the trampled ground with his head in his arms. There he made one final movement of resistance and fell asleep. After him, the other people dropped down too, back and back into the valley. Horses stood still and men keeled over beside them and lay sleeping. Beside Moril, Brid fell sideways and slept curled up as if she was still kneeling. That was a pity, but Moril did not see how he could have excluded her. He played on, sending out wave after wave of sleep-song, until the valley seemed thick with it, and he could almost see it hanging in the air and pulsing gently. Under it every soul was dead to the world.

At last, a little apprehensively, Moril left the cwidder still humming, hoping like that to make the power last, and went through the heavy, silent air to Kialan. He was still tied up. Tholian's friends had not untied him, though they had been about to. Moril went back through the humming silence and fetched the knife out of Brid's boot. "Thanks," he whispered, and he thought Brid stirred a little. With the knife he hacked through rope after tough rope, until Kialan rolled loose on the grass. He was still unconscious.

Moril bent down and shook him. "Kialan!" he said.

Kialan came round as he heard his name. Moril was almost sorry, because Kialan's face was suddenly full of pain and misery.

"It's all right," Moril whispered. "Everyone's asleep. Quick. I don't know how long it'll last."

Kialan climbed to his feet. He was very stiff and winced with every movement. He stared at Tholian, lying on the earth with his head in his arms, at Brid, and out at the silent, humming valley, full of a sleeping army. "Ye gods!" he said. "Was that the cwidder?"

"Yes," said Moril. "Quick." He ran back to Brid and shook her. Brid rolled about, but she did not wake.

Kialan came limping after him. "Suppose you leave her asleep?" he suggested. "Then when she wakes up, you'll know it's worn off."

Moril saw that was an excellent idea. The thing about Kialan, he thought as he raced for the cart, was that he had brains. Olob was dozing too, which was more serious. Moril snapped his fingers under his nose. "*Olob! Barangarolob!*" And Olob shook his head and looked at Moril wonderingly. Moril untied Olob and brought him towards Brid at a run, much though Olob objected to going near even sleeping enemies. As he hauled on the bridle, he thought how queer the valley looked with everyone in it lying asleep except for the lonely upright figure of Kialan. He dragged Olob up to Brid and opened the tailgate of the cart to make it easier to get her in. Then he gently put the cwidder back in its rack. It was still vibrating faintly.

"Throw the wine jar out," said Kialan. "Let's make the cart as light as we can."

Moril heaved out the great jar. It landed with a sploshy thump that ought to have woken the dead, but Brid, who was nearest, did not stir.

Kialan laughed. "Present for Tholian. Information he knows and money he doesn't want. He can drink our health."

Moril gave a muffled giggle at the idea, but he did not speak. He had a feeling that the one thing most likely to wake the sleepers was his voice. He climbed into the cart and threw out most of Dagner's purchases: candles, flour, lentils and the remains of the rhubarb.

"Oh, he'll love those!" panted Kialan. Though he was still very stiff, he managed to lift the head and shoulders of Brid and heave the upper half of her into the cart. Moril took her shoulders and dragged her right in, where she settled with a little sigh. Kialan climbed in beside her. Moril latched the tailgate and got on to the driving seat.

"Now, Olob," he whispered. "Run. Run for your life."

Olob tossed his head and set off. He did not exactly run, but he took the cart briskly across the trampled earth to the road by which they had entered the valley. Moril looked over his shoulder as they went under the trees. Tholian was lying beside their heap of provisions. Beyond him, Moril thought he could see a faint haze vibrating quietly over the whole valley. The cwidder's power still held.

"What about those soldiers by the trestle?" Kialan said, as Olob clattered down the steep road.

"I don't know," Moril said anxiously. He had no idea how far the cwidder's power spread, and the trestle had been behind him as he played. When they came to the main road, Moril held his breath and Kialan craned sideways to get a sight of the trestle.

Those soldiers were asleep too. Most of them were sprawled in the road, pigeon breastplates upwards, snoring. One was asleep with his arms on the trestle, in a most uncomfortable position. Kialan gave a wild little laugh. "He'll be stiff when he wakes up!"

CHAPTER TWELVE

IT WAS A short, steep climb up the last of the hill. Then they came out on to the green spread of the last Upland. They could see Mark Wood in the distance, gay green and bronzed by the afternoon sun, and beyond it, looking deceptively near, the grey bulk of the Northern mountains.

"Now you *must* run, Olob," said Moril.

Olob ran. It could not be called a gallop – Moril had never known Olob to gallop in his life – but he ran, and ran as fast as Moril had ever seen him go. Behind him the lightened cart wove from side to side and bounded in the ruts of the road. Kialan wedged his feet against the side of the cart and tried to hold Brid in one place, but they nevertheless pitched and rolled and bounced until it was a marvel Brid did not wake up. But Brid slept on, stirring once or twice when she hit the side of the cart, but never coming out of her deep sleep. Moril began to hope that it would last until they reached Mark Wood. Once they were there, they could hide the cart among the trees, with a good chance of escaping Tholian.

"How did you work it?" Kialan called jerkily above the rilling of wheels and banging of hooves. "The sleep."

Moril could not explain, any more than Dagner could explain how he made songs. "By thinking," he said. "You said a lot of things that helped me."

They jounced and battered another half mile. "I had a weird dream," Kialan called, "while I was tied up. I dreamt – wow, what a bump! – I dreamt you took me along to your father's grave, by the lake, and opened that board I carved, just as if it was a door. Then you said, 'Do you mind getting in here for a while? I'll call you when it's safe to come out.' And – I say, what happens if we lose a wheel? – and I went in and went to sleep. What do you think of that?"

"I don't know," said Moril. "I might have done.

214

There's no one behind, is there?"

There was no one, though they could hardly believe it. The wide Upland seemed empty. They rattled, wagging this way and that, through a village, and that seemed asleep too. Olob pounded on, blowing now, and Brid still slept. The sun sank, and Mark Wood was nearer. Twilight seemed to come from the trees and soak into the green landscape around them. Big clouds were building up beyond the mountains. The sunset shot them with fierce pink and lakes of moist yellow.

"You know," jerked Kialan, "when I thought – in the valley – that we weren't going to get away this time, I wanted to apologise. I was pretty awful when I first came into the cart, wasn't I?"

"We were too," Moril called over his shoulder. "We didn't know what had been happening to you. Was it horrible in Holand?"

There was a bouncing, battering pause. "Ghastly," said Kialan. "But it wasn't only that. I didn't understand. I thought you were all – beggars or something, and I thought – oh, of fleas and ignorance and so on for the whole way North. And I was fed up."

Moril laughed. "You looked it."

They reached the verge of Mark Wood almost as the

sun set. Olob had not run so far for years. Moril could see steam rising off him in the thickening twilight. His sides were heaving under the scarlet harness, and there were flecks of foam along him. The road went upwards into the trees, under a sloping cliff, and, though it was not a steep rise, Olob slowed down.

"I'll have to let him walk," Moril said, acutely sorry for him. "He's had enough."

So Olob fell to a weary plod, and everything suddenly seemed ten times more peaceful. They could hear birds cawing and calling in the great beech trees above.

"Good gracious!" said Brid, sitting up. "Where are we? Why do I feel so bruised?"

Moril knew it was bound to happen, but he wished it had been further into the wood and not just when Olob was tired out. They explained to Brid. She was rather indignant.

"Using me as a kind of sleep measure! I like that!"

"It was a jolly good idea," said Kialan, "though I says it as shouldn't."

But Brid had realised that Tholian was probably after them by now and changed to being as nervous as a cat. She turned her head back over her shoulder and implored Moril to get in among the trees quickly. Moril looked over his shoulder too. Between the tree trunks, he could see the darkening green of the Upland and a long stretch of the road. It was empty.

"I will when we get to the top of this hill. Olob's tired."

The dark gathered quickly under the trees, but it was still light enough to see. Brid squawked faintly. There were people among the trees on horses, coming slowly down the hill on the cliff side. But Olob gave no sign of alarm. Moril trusted Olob and kept on the road, in spite of Brid's imploring whispers. All the same, it was rather frightening the way that the horsemen, as soon as they saw the cart, turned towards it and increased their pace. They came fairly thudding down on them.

There were three of them. They drew up beside the cart, and Olob stopped walking. Kialan stood up and stared at the foremost rider, and the rider stared back.

"You blinking idiot! What did you have to come South for?" Kialan said, and burst into tears.

Somehow, though they would never have dreamt of addressing Clennen as a blinking idiot, Brid and Moril had no doubt that the rider was Keril. They watched Kialan jump awkwardly down, and the man dismount and hug him, and they were sure of it.

"Konian – they *hanged* him!" Kialan said.

"I know. We heard from a fisherman," said Keril. "It was you I came for. I was hoping Clennen might know— Where *is* Clennen?" he asked.

"He's dead," said Brid, and began to cry too.

Moril sat on the driving seat and felt tears trickling down his face. As far as he knew, he was crying for the whole situation, because he was on his own now, and always would be.

"There's an army," said Kialan. "Tholian's gathered an army to attack the North. In a valley over there. They're probably after us now."

Keril exchanged glances with the two other riders. "We've a small force in the wood. How big is this army?"

"Pretty big," Moril said, sniffing. "There were five hundred men, divided into three troops, and a hundred horsemen in the part of the valley we saw. But that was probably only a quarter of it."

"How do you know?" said Kialan. "Did you count?"

"No. I just know," said Moril. "And recruits came in four batches, while we were there, twenty-three in the first, and thirty-two in—"

"Too many for us, in fact," said Keril. "Thanks, lad. Let's get back to our camp and get fortified."

The Northerners' camp was along the cliff, chosen with an eye to defence. When tired Olob dragged the cart up to it, there was already a bustle of preparation. The campfires were being put out and the two provision wagons dragged across the only place where it could be reached from the wood. These preparations should have made Moril feel alarmed, but in fact, he felt safer and happier than he had been for days. He could see by the light of the few lanterns that the mere fifty or so men bustling about had, many of them, the same dark-fair colouring as Kialan. Moril remembered now that it was something you only saw in the North. Keril was the odd man out, because he was dark, though his nose was the same shape as Kialan's.

They were taken into a tent, where they had the best meal they had had since Markind. While they were eating, Moril gathered that the Earl had been camping here for two days. The night before, he had ridden South almost to Neathdale in hopes of meeting Clennen and hearing news of Kialan, and he had been meaning to do the same that night too. It was Henda's message offering to ransom Kialan that had brought him South. Up till then, everyone in Hannart had supposed that Kialan had been hanged too.

In a tired and muddled way, they told their part, as far as Dagner's arrest. Keril, who had been sad rather than astonished at Clennen's death and not at all surprised to hear of Lenina returning to Markind, broke in angrily when he heard of Dagner. They felt sure he was thinking of Konian too, when he said, "Fancy hanging a boy that age! I wish I could *do* something – er, Moril – is that your name?"

"Not really," said Kialan. "His name's Osfameron. And Brid's Manaliabrid."

Keril forgot his anger and threw back his head and laughed.

"What's so funny?" said Brid. She was sensitive about their names.

"Well, history repeating itself, I suppose," said Keril. "Kialan's the Adon, you see."

"No, he isn't," said Moril. "The Adon lived two hundred years ago. Kialan told me."

"But the heir of Hannart is always called the Adon," Keril explained, and was sad, thinking of Konian.

Moril and Kialan looked at one another by the light of the carefully shaded lantern. Moril was thoroughly put out. If Kialan was the Adon, then he had been living the life of his dearest imaginings for nearly a month without realising it. It had not seemed like that at all. Yet, thinking of the weird dream Kialan had told him of, he suspected that it might have been history repeating itself indeed. "Why didn't you tell me?" he said.

"I didn't sort of think," said Kialan. "I was just me, trying to get home." He was thinking about his dream too. He nodded towards his father. "Tell him about the cwidder."

Moril told Keril how he put Tholian and his army to sleep. Keril marvelled a little, and he asked Kialan to confirm it, but he took it, on the whole, in the same matter-of-course way that Kialan did. "May I see the cwidder?" he said.

Moril felt his way out of the tent to the cart and came back with the cwidder. Keril took it and held it under the light of the lantern. He ran his fingers down the inlay, over the strange patterns. "Yes, this *is* the one," he said. "I used to think Clennen was boasting when he said it was Osfameron's, but I wasn't much of a hand at the old writing in those days." His square, practical-looking finger pointed to a line of swirls and dots made of slivers of mother-of-pearl. "Here it says, *I sing for Osfameron*, and there –" his finger moved to another line of signs – "it says, *I move in more than one world*". He smiled at Moril and handed the cwidder back. "Be careful of it."

Moril fell asleep that night hugging the cwidder, and as far removed as he could from Kialan's knees and elbows. They were a little crowded because Keril had given up his own tent to Brid. Moril had meant to do some more thinking, but he was far too tired. He awoke at dawn, because somebody came to talk to Keril, very annoyed with himself. For he was sure that, by reading the strange writing, Keril had really told him how to use the cwidder as Osfameron had used it.

There was no time for thinking for a while. The man had come to tell Keril that a troop of riders had gone by on the road during the night and that the same troop had just come galloping back, probably on their way to report to Tholian. Both times they had been going too fast to notice the camp.

It was clear the riders had been looking for the cart. Tholian must have assumed that Moril, Brid and Kialan were driving North as fast as they could. Since the riders had not found them, Keril knew Tholian would think Kialan had already reached the North, and his news with him. "And if I were Tholian," he said, "I'd be on the march now, before the North can be ready for war. We'd better hurry."

They broke camp and went. The cart went too, with a strange youthful horse between the shafts, for more speed. Olob looked so disconsolate that Brid said she would ride him. "He'll let me," she said, "if no one puts a saddle on him. I hate him to feel neglected." So she rode Olob bareback with her boots on – for, after all, she was in company with an earl – and Olob did not seem to object. He was just rather slow. Brid had some difficulty keeping up with the cart, where Moril sat with his cwidder, thinking. The cart was being driven by a large slow-spoken Northerner called Egil, and Kialan had borrowed Egil's horse.

"You know," Brid said to Moril, "I do wish Kialan hadn't turned out to be the Adon. I feel embarrassed about liking him."

Moril was very busy thinking, but he chuckled at this. "You'll get used to it."

"You're *hopeless*!" said Brid, not as angry as she meant to be.

Kialan's turning out to be the Adon was important to Moril's thoughts too. It was one of three things he kept trying to put together in his mind. The other two were what the writing said on the cwidder and his own discovery about the way you had to tell the truth with it.

He thought it was odd how easily one got used to new ideas. What had seemed an entirely new thing yesterday was an old idea today, which he could use to take him on somewhere else. He went on trying to put ideas together while the band of Northerners hurried through Mark Wood.

They were not taking the road because Keril dared not risk being seen. There were clearings and villages all along the road and probably enough people in them to hold the small number of Northerners up until Tholian came to wipe them out. So they worked their way North through the trees. It was easy enough for the riders, but heavy going for the cart and the wagons. And everybody was worried about the final stretch, where they would have to come out of the trees in order to get to Flennpass. Once they were in the pass, they would be safe. It was guarded by Fort Flenn, which was the southernmost fort of the North.

Night came before they were out of the wood. Keril was anxious at their slow progress, but they had been travelling all day and they were tired. They had to risk camping for the night. After supper, round a carefully shaded campfire, they told Keril their doings in more detail. Kialan said things which confirmed Moril's feeling that his time in Holand had been more horrible than they had realised. Keril became so angry and sad that Kialan changed the subject and talked about the wine jar.

"I regret leaving Tholian all that gold," he said. "He can have the rhubarb with pleasure, and the papers, but we should have taken the money out."

"Set your mind at rest," said Brid. "I did. I put it in the money locker."

Everyone laughed. Brid wanted indignantly to know what they took her for, leaving a sum like that in a wine jar.

"But I wish I knew whose it was, and where Father got it from," she said.

"I think," said Keril, "that it was probably the remains of what I gave him for expenses. I gave him a hundred gold every year in Dropwater. No," he said when Brid offered to give it back. "Keep it. You deserve it. You can use it as pocket money when you're living in Hannart."

In this way they gathered that Keril intended them to live with him in Hannart.

"That's frightfully nice of you," Brid said awkwardly. "Because I don't know what else we'd do, do you, Moril?"

"It's the least I can do," said Keril. "I owe Clennen a great deal. If it hadn't been for him, we'd have had no news from the South worth having." Then he told them things about Clennen they had not known before. Keril had met Clennen in the South in the days when he was still only the Adon, and they had both helped in the uprising there. But Keril's father died, and he had to go North. Clennen stayed in the South, until soon after he met Lenina. Then, what with old Tholian's fury and the failure of the uprising, Clennen found the South too hot to hold him. He went to Hannart and became singer to the court. Dagner, Brid and Moril had all been born in Hannart. It had been Clennen's idea to go South again when they heard reports of what was going on. The Porter had been his idea too. But Keril had thought of staging the quarrel so that no one would suspect Clennen was Hannart's agent.

Moril sat staring into the fire, dreaming of Hannart.

"What is it, Moril?" Kialan said jokingly. "Dreams coming true?"

Moril looked up and grinned. He did not say anything, but he went to sleep sure that Kialan had just told him the way the cwidder really worked.

He thought it out as he rode in the cart next day. It came to him first as a memory. It had rained in Crady, so Clennen had told one of the stories of the Adon indoors, and Moril had looked up to see Kialan in the audience. He had been annoyed, because he thought of Kialan as part of dreary, everyday life, and he had felt as if he had a foot in two worlds which were spinning apart from one another. Yet Kialan was the Adon – or *an* Adon – all the time. And the cwidder itself said, "I move in more than one world."

It came on to rain just then, though not as heavily as it had rained in Crady. Moril smiled and lifted his face into the wet. They were nearly in the North, and it rained a lot there. His smile became rather rueful as he realised that in none of his dreams of Hannart or hazy imaginings of the cart on green roads had he ever thought of it raining. The cwidder had made a muzzy sound. And that was the point. That kind of dream was not true. There were true dreams, but they had to be part of life as well, just as life, to be good, had to embody dreams, or a good song had to have an idea to it. The Adon's song Kialan had sung had been saying that. But Osfameron's song had gone one further and talked of the other worlds the cwidder moved in.

Moril thought of the way life and dreams had met for him, willy-nilly, on this journey. But he knew they met in him naturally too, when he could be miles away, thinking, and yet count all the soldiers in that valley, or every beech tree they were passing at the moment. He saw that Clennen had not got it quite right. He had been too practical to see. The important thing was that Moril *was* in two halves. Provided he knew what was true in both, he could use the cwidder as it should be used. He could send ideas through it, into reality.

About mid-morning, they came to the end of Mark Wood. Moril looked past Egil's broad back at the mountains at last, vividly close, and the deep V in them that was Flennpass. The rain had stopped, but the clouds over the mountains were heavy with more. It was a grey, threatening scene. Fort Flenn was out of sight, behind a sharp peak, since it was at the North end of the pass, but Moril could see the South's answer to it. The wood had been cleared for a mile or so in front of the pass, so that no one could go in or out of it unseen. He looked at the mountains across a desolation of tree stumps, charred from frequent burning, with new bright green bushes and saplings springing up between, because it had not yet been cleared this year.

The Northerners stopped at the edge of the trees. Moril did not at first know why.

"The Lord of Mark, I think," Keril said to his captain. "Tholian must have set him to watch for the cart."

Moril leant round Egil, and his stomach fluttered at the number of the horsemen drawn up across the pass in the distance. They were clearly Southerners, and in war gear, and there were at least twice as many of them as there were Northerners in Keril's band.

"He can't be expecting us," said the captain. "I'll take an oath no one saw us come through. It'll give him a fair old shock when we ride out at him."

"I know," said Keril, "but I'd be more comfortable if we were twice the number."

"Oh come!" said someone else, laughing. "One Northerner's worth ten Southerners. Any day."

Moril thought for a moment. Yes. Everyone believed that. None of the band was particularly worried, and even Brid was looking confidently at Keril, sure they would get past the Lord of Mark without trouble. Northerners were famous fighters. But Keril was evidently thinking it was more important to get through to the North than to get courageously killed on the way.

"Would you like there to seem more of us?" Moril called over to him. "I think I can do it."

Keril made a bit of a face. "I only wish you could."

"I bet he can," said Kialan.

Moril slung the cwidder round his neck and began to

play the *Eighth March*. It was never played in the South, for obvious reasons. But, as Clennen often said, it went to such a brisk time that only the North thought of it as a march.

"We are the men of the North, the North,
And I'll tell you how much we're worth, we're
worth –
One man is as good as ten Southern men
And each of us marches as ten."

For a moment, until the cwidder began to hum, Moril was afraid he had got it wrong after all. But the hum increased and became almost like a light-hearted whistling, and the wood was suddenly full of men, horses and wagons. Some of the Northerners cried out in alarm.

Kialan burst out laughing. "Oh, well done, Moril! Only nine more pink carts are a bit much!"

Moril glanced from side to side and could not help laughing. There were indeed nine more pink carts. One of them had a tree apparently growing through it. And a false Moril sat in each playing an illusory cwidder. What he had done was to reflect their own band nine times over, just as the song said. After all, it was an illusion that one Northman was worth ten Southerners. And the riders and wagons were exactly that, like reflections in a mirror. The Northmen realised. People began to laugh and wave at their own reflections. Consequently, the false nine-tenths waved and laughed also.

Keril laughed with the rest. "Keep playing, Moril. Off we go."

Moril played on gaily, and they moved out from among the trees, the real and the false men together. They rode among the bushes and stumps under a stormy sky, towards the road, and the real men had to go round saplings and the larger stumps, but Moril's illusions went straight through everything in their path. When they reached the road, there was a good deal of confusion and much laughter. The Northmen tried to get out of the way of their own shadows, until they grasped that there were four reflections on the left and five to the right, and that the fifth band from the left was the real one, entitled to use the road. Once they had sorted that out, they trotted on in fine style, many of them singing the *Eighth March* as Moril played. And on either side the nine repetitions went straight through the landscape, pink carts through bushes and horses through saplings.

Moril sat in the midmost pink cart beaming with

elation. It was the most splendid proof that he had done his thinking right. The whistling hum of the cwidder in his hands, calling the strange army into being, took on an extra note, like a sort of purring, as it reflected Moril's pleasure and amusement. Behind him, Brid and Kialan thought it one of the funniest things they had seen. They thought it even funnier when Olob sensed enemies near and began prancing about, setting the nine other Olobs prancing too, and the nine other Kialans grabbing at his bridle to help Brid control him.

By the pass the Lord of Mark's force drew uneasily together, seeing five hundred apparent Northmen riding merrily towards them. As Keril's band drew nearer, they could see the enemies' uneasiness mounting. Ordinary Northerners maybe they could face. But what was to be done with enemies who went straight through small trees and seemed none the worse for it? When they were near enough to distinguish faces, and only a hundred yards from the camp the Lord of Mark had set up to the right of the road, a group of the Southerners panicked and had to be brought back by some others. Moril could see a man who must be the Lord of Mark riding up and down imploring his men to keep calm. He laughed. Then two shadow wagons and a pink cart went right through the camp without disturbing so much as a guy rope. A number of the Southerners wailed with terror. Moril thought, *Why not?* and threw in the lowest string. *Run!* it boomed beneath the gay tune.

The Lord of Mark broke and ran, and his men with him. They galloped frantically away to right and left along the mountains and vanished in the bushes, leaving Flennpass open. A roar of laughter went up from Keril's band.

Brid's voice cut through it. "Moril! *Look!*"

Moril glanced back. Huge numbers of horsemen were on the dark edge of Mark Wood, and more were among the trees. The horses' legs were all moving steadily, but they were too far away for sound to carry, and the riders seemed to glimmer along as if they were an illusion too. Only they were no such thing. They were the forefront of Tholian's army.

CHAPTER THIRTEEN

MORIL GAVE THE alarm with a sweep of his hand on the cwidder. Though Keril also looked over his shoulder, it was only to confirm what the cwidder said. In that same moment they were all going hell for leather for Flennpass and Fort Flenn at the other end of it. The ghostly nine-tenths had gone as if they had never been. Moril knew there was no time for illusions. As the cart bucked and wove along, he hung on to the side and looked back.

Tholian's army was coming at a steady speed across the cleared stretch. If anyone saw the cart, or the sudden decrease in the size of their band, there was no sign of it.

The host of horsemen simply came onwards. It might be pursuing Keril, but it looked more as if their band would be merely the first incident in the invasion. Tholian had no need to hurry, since the North was unprepared. Olob knew the army was behind and Brid could not control him. Kialan had taken the reins and was dragging him along with Egil's horse. Moril thought this might well make Olob worse. Olob had never really accepted Kialan. But there was nothing Moril could do.

They swept into the pass with a gathering thunder of hooves. It held a good road between cliff-like walls, which narrowed at the Northern end. They had to string out as they went, with the cart and the wagons bouncing in the rear. Egil and the other drivers were using their whips. Brid was smacking Olob. Moril thought they would just make it to the fort, though it would be a close thing – and it seemed closer every second. The army behind had no wagons with the vanguard to slow them down. They were catching up steadily. As Keril's troop came to the narrowest part of the pass, where the fort stood chunkily above on the skyline, Moril looked round to see the first line of Tholian's cavalry coming into the wide end of the pass, and multitudes of others milling behind.

Keril had reached the fort, when Moril looked back,

and was shouting to the people inside. There was a moment's delay. But the defenders must have seen all that happened. A sudden black space appeared where the great gate had been, and some of the Northmen rode into it. The space between the cliffs was filled with noise, the huge drumming of a mass of hooves, and some sharper sounds. Moril thought the fort was firing on the enemy.

Things began to fall around the cart and bounce off the wagons. They were not from the fort, but from the advancing army. Moril could do nothing but hope. It was long-range, and he thought it must be difficult to fire from a cantering horse. But to Olob, struggling against Kialan's impatient hand on his bridle, it was the last straw. In his terror, he turned clean round, dragging Kialan and Egil's horse with him. Brid lurched and hung on to his mane. A number of the Northmen saw what was happening and turned back to help. And the narrow end of the pass at once became a dangerous bottleneck, full of riders trying to go two ways at once. Egil roared out a curse and pulled the cart up. Moril jumped down, with the cwidder slung across his shoulders, and ran towards Olob.

"Let him go!" he shouted to Kialan. "Olob, stop it!"

Luckily, Kialan had the sense to let go. For, as Moril ran up, Olob reared, frightened out of his wits. There were just too many enemies for him. Moril had to dodge his lashing front hooves, and Brid slid helplessly down his back, over his tail and on to the ground. And as Olob stood high above them, screaming and slashing, an unlucky bullet took him clean through the head. His great brown body came down between Moril and Brid with the force of a falling oak. He was dead before he hit the ground.

They stared at one another over the huge corpse.

"Olob now," said Brid.

"Right!" said Moril. "That does it!"

Keril's captain had been sorting out the bottleneck. Now he galloped up and held down his hand to Brid. "Catch hold, lass! Up you come!" Brid caught hold and scrambled up behind him.

Kialan shouted to Moril and held down a hand to him, but Moril did not attend. He raced to the cliff at the side of the pass and climbed it like a maniac with the cwidder bumping and booming on his back. He was at the top in seconds – how, he never knew. Heaving deep breaths, he went scrambling along the cliff edge until he had a view down into the pass. He saw Kialan, not very far below him, at the gate of the fort, waving and shouting something. He seemed to mean there was a door in the fort at the top of the cliff. Then he went into the fort, and the gate shut.

But Moril, now he knew the Northmen were in the fort, was not interested in the door. He looked Southward along the pass. It was packed with Tholian's horsemen more than halfway along. They were going more slowly now, because of the narrower space, and beyond the wide end of the pass, as far as he could see, there were more riders coming. It was truly an invasion.

Moril stood up and slung the cwidder in front of him. He felt a spatter of rain. There looked to be a storm coming, which was all to the good. For a second he gazed up at the heavy bruise-like clouds, feeling a little awed. He thought anyone would who was about to use the cwidder as Osfameron had used it.

Then he looked down into the pass where Olob's body lay in the middle of the road. The nearest riders were not so far from it now. He struck one sharp, rolling chord, and the power in the cwidder swelled with it. There was no humming, but he could feel the power. "You're not coming North," he said to the jostling riders. "And this is why." He struck two more chords. The power almost choked him. The answer was a great dagger of lightning, green and perilous, lancing down over the cliffs. A peal of thunder followed, and Moril led it on, pealing the lowest note of the cwidder, so that the power in it could grow.

When it stopped, he spoke, in the way the singers spoke an incantation. He said:

> "*Kialan and Konian were caught in a storm.*
> *The one you hanged in Holand had not harmed*
> *anyone,*
> *Nor had Kialan when you caught him.*
> *This is for Konian first.*"

He struck another chord, followed by a swinging, hanging, frantic phrase, and felt the power in the cwidder grow again. Then he said:

> "*Unlucky Clennen lies by a lake in Markind,*
> *The singer you stabbed on suspicion only*
> *And prevented him performing.*
> *This is for the Porter Clennen.*"

He struck a sharp chord and a rolling one. The first horsemen were now right beneath him. They did not pause when they came to Olob but trampled over him and on. Moril saw, but he looked beyond them, to the centre of the pass. Tholian was there, jostled on either side by his favourite friends. Moril waited, quite confident and implacable, and let them come on while the power in the cwidder grew yet again. Then he spoke his last stave:

> "There was no mercy shown
> by the magistrate in Neathdale
> To Dastgandlen Handagner. There was death in the South
> And weeping in the Uplands. Now war comes North,
> And all through Tholian. This is for Tholian."

He struck the cwidder again, and again, and yet a third time, vengefully. The power grew enormous, until it possessed Moril, the sky, the clouds and the entire pass. Then, as Moril had known they would, the hills began to walk.

They started mildly and slowly, as if the mountains on either side of the pass were shrugging their shoulders. But in a second or so, the shrugging was a deep rhythmic jigging. The tops of the cliffs bent and marched, regularly inwards and downwards, walking, piling, inescapably trudging together to fill the pass. The thunder pealed and was drowned in the grinding of ton after ton of rock, moving and jogging inwards. Almost lost in the greater din was the lesser screaming of men and horses. At the far end of the pass Moril could see riders swirling and struggling to get back or get out. But leisurely, sleepily, rhythmically, the mountains were filling the centre. The cliff Moril was on marched with the rest, downwards and forwards. Moril leant backwards to keep his balance and let it take him, until he was standing at the head of a heap of jumbled rocks, almost over the place where Olob had been shot. The rocks were piled into the rift, choking it so that it was no longer a pass.

Moril did not spend long looking, because the rain came down, and the torn surfaces of the rocks were black with it. But he knew, as he turned round to keep the cwidder from the worst of the wet and stripped off his coat to cover it, that Tholian was underneath somewhere and Barangarolob had plenty of company. He looked across to see that the fort was safe, as he had intended. It was there, standing on a steep-sided block of steady rock, and Keril was picking his way over the ruin of the cliff towards him.

"I've just done something really horrible," Moril said to him. "Haven't I?"

Keril jumped from one rock to another and then on to the one where Moril stood. "I don't think we had much chance of holding the pass otherwise," he said.

"You don't understand," said Moril. "I did it because of Olob." He leant against Keril and burst into tears. Keril took off his own coat, wrapped it round Moril, and led him quietly back over the rocks to the fort.

They left the fort the following day, after a big force of men from the North Dales arrived there to make sure the Southerners did not attempt to attack over the fallen rocks. Moril did not see as much of the journey to Hannart as he would have liked. He was exhausted and spent most of the time asleep in one of the wagons. Every so often he woke to find they were on a green road, or in a wood where the trees were still only budding in the later spring of the North, and went to sleep happy. He was awake to see the Falls at Dropwater, which he would not have missed for worlds. And by the time they reached Hannart he had come to himself again.

He was disappointed, but not really surprised, to find Hannart a city far larger than Neathdale, in the centre of a big valley. Flags were flying in honour of their arrival. There were crowds of people carrying flags or flowers. Hannart was full of flowers in fields, in gardens, on trees and growing wild, thick as the grass on the steep sides of the mountains. Moril could smell them as soon as they entered the valley. At the end of the valley was a great tall thing, like a castle four times life-size, picked out in gold and blue and green.

Moril stared at it. "Whatever is that?"

"That's the steam organ," said Kialan. "Haven't you heard about it? They'll probably play it tonight. It makes the most splendid noise."

"I wish someone had told me," said Moril.

There was a feast that night, in their honour, and as Kialan had thought, the steam organ played. In a strong steamy smell of coal and oil, it thundered out well-known tunes, like a mountain singing, or the grandfather of all music, and made Brid and Moril laugh. It seemed most fitting that Hannart should own such a thing, because the place was full of music, not only then, but at all times. Cowbells clinked in the steep meadows. Women called the cows home in a kind of song, not unlike Brid's *Cow-Calling* song. In the city there were tunes for crying everything that was on sale and for telling the hours of the watch. There was singing and dancing somewhere almost every night. The saying was that you could tell someone came from Hannart because whatever they did, they sang, and if they did not sing, they whistled.

Keril lived right in the centre of the city, in a house

twice the size of Ganner's. Unlike Ganner's house, it was always open. The cheerful people of Hannart seemed to use its front courtyard as another part of the main square. There was always someone there, gossiping or selling something, and, if anything unusual happened, they came on into the rest of the house to tell Keril about it. Since there were also large numbers of people who actually lived in the house, Moril found it almost impossible to sort out who came from where.

Brid loved it. She had never been happier in her life. "I often remembered it, but I didn't think it was real!" she was fond of saying.

Moril enjoyed it too. He liked the liveliness, the carelessness and the way people rushed up to Keril and said what they pleased. He could not imagine anyone doing that in the South. Moril liked Keril. He liked Halida, Kialan's mother. He enjoyed being with Kialan, and he loved the perpetual music. But he was too hot in the city and far too hot in the house. He kept having to go out on the hillsides. At night it was worse, and he slept in one of the gardens when he could. When Halida realised this, she gave him a room on the ground floor, opening on one of the gardens. Moril was grateful, but he hardly went into the room, and he only slept there if it was raining.

Brid and Kialan consulted about it and went to see what Keril thought.

"Yes," said Keril. "I'm afraid he'll be off again, one of these days. I hope not yet, though. I owe it to Clennen to see he has an education."

After that Brid watched Moril like a hawk. Moril showed no sign of wanting to leave. He seemed perfectly happy getting the education Keril thought he should have. He spent long hours playing his cwidder with Kialan, arranging songs and trying to make new ones. He rode with Kialan and Brid and walked on the hills with them. It was just that he was too hot indoors, and there was something at the back of his mind he did not want to think about yet.

Now Flennpass was blocked, there was very little news from the South. It was nearly a month before some fishermen brought news that Tholian had indeed been killed by the fall of rocks, and his army, most of it having been unwilling, anyway, had packed up and gone home. Some time after that, a trader arrived to say that things had gone very quiet in the South. Yes, he said, when Keril questioned him, the lords and earls were very shaken. But the cause of the quiet was the ordinary people. They did nothing, but they seemed powerful. The earls were afraid of them. They dared not even try for peace with the North, in case that stirred up a revolution.

A month later still a cart drove into Hannart. By the black mud on its axles, it had clearly come north through the Marshes. Apart from the mud, it was gaily painted in green and gold, and trim enough. It was driven by a very pretty girl. Beside her on the driving seat sat a dreamy-looking man with a thin face and a thin, greying beard, who smiled round at the gaiety of Hannart with a look of mild pleasure. The small gold lettering on the side of the cart said he was HESTEFAN THE SINGER.

The people of Hannart realised that here would be both music and more news of the South. Numbers followed the cart as it jogged through the streets and drove into the front court of the Earl's house.

"Oh look! A singer!" Brid said to Kialan.

"Do you know him?" Kialan asked Moril.

"I've heard of him," said Moril. He looked at Hestefan's mild face and dreamy eyes, and it came to him that he would probably look like that when he was older.

The cart stopped. The mottled grey horse blew, as much as to say, "Good – that's enough for today, thank you." The canvas cover came back a little, and a third traveller rather hesitantly stood up in the cart.

"*Dagner!*" shrieked Brid, Moril and Kialan.

They rushed up and hurled themselves on him. Dagner, grinning and blushing mauve with pleasure, climbed out of the cart and was thrown against it by their onrush.

"What happened?" said Brid.

"How did you get out of prison?" said Moril.

"Ganner got me out," Dagner said when he had got his breath back. "Ganner's a good fellow. I got to like him a lot. He did follow us, you know, but he went back to Markind when he didn't find us. Then – I don't know what you said to that old snob of a Justice, Moril, but when they had me up in front of them again, they didn't seem at all sure I was guilty and kept asking me about Ganner. So I told them he was marrying Mother, and they sent all the way to Markind to ask if it was true. It was marvellous. As soon as Ganner heard I was in prison, he came to Neathdale and raised a real stink. And while he was doing it, news came that Tholian was dead. Ganner upped and sacked the Justice, and said he was in charge now. It was marvellous! He let half the other prisoners go too. But seeing that I really had been passing information, Mother thought I'd better go North for a while and got Hestefan to take me."

"How is Mother?" asked Moril.

"Terribly happy," said Dagner. "Runs about all the time laughing. I don't know why – she laughed when she heard Flennpass was blocked and said you and Brid must have made it to the North. She sent me with a letter for you both."

Brid and Moril snatched the letter and bent over it eagerly. It was a good long letter, all about Lenina's doings in Markind. Lenina wrote of everything from the speckled cows to the roof where Moril had walked, and reminded Brid of this and Moril of that, and sent Ganner's love – and to Moril, it was like a letter from a distant acquaintance. He felt it might just as well have been written to the baker's boy round the corner. He was sad that he should feel like that, but he could not help it.

"What a lovely letter!" said Brid. "I shall keep it."

While they were reading it, Hestefan's pretty daughter had driven the cart away to the stables. Moril was annoyed, because he had wanted to talk to Hestefan. He dashed away to the stables, but the green cart was already standing empty in the coach house beside their battered and faded pink one. Moril went back to the courtyard, where Dagner, delighted to see them all again, was being uncharacteristically chatty.

"Shall I tell you something really silly?" he said to

Kialan as Moril came up. "You won't believe this!"

"Try me," said Kialan.

"Well," said Dagner, "I'm the Earl of the South Dales. They won't have me," he said hastily, as Kialan burst out laughing. "Nothing will possess them to invest me. But it's true. Tholian wasn't married, and all his cousins were killed too, when Flennpass collapsed – you *must* tell me about that, by the way – and the only living heir left was me. And Moril after that. Honestly."

Moril stood silent in the crowded courtyard and left Brid and Kialan to do the exclaiming. Now he knew what it was that he had not wanted to think about. He had done that. He had worked a huge destruction and killed so many people that Dagner was now an earl. Everyone no doubt thought he had done right. He had saved the North, prevented a war, and avenged Clennen and Konian. But Moril knew he had not done right. He had done it all because Olob was killed. With the cwidder in his hands, he had behaved as if it was for Konian, for Clennen, for Dagner and for the North, but it had all been for Olob, really. He was ashamed. What he had done was to cheat the cwidder. That was the worst thing. If you stood up and told the truth in the wrong way, it was not true any longer, though it might be as powerful as ever. Moril saw that he was neither old enough nor wise enough to have charge of such a potent thing as that cwidder.

That night, there was a feast in honour of Dagner, Hestefan, and Fenna, Hestefan's daughter. Keril asked Hestefan to sing. Hestefan sang, old songs, new songs and many that Moril had never heard. When he sang, you forgot it was Hestefan singing and thought only of the song. Moril was impressed. Then Hestefan told a story. It was one Moril did not know. And while Hestefan was telling it, he found he forgot who was telling it and simply lived in the story. Moril realised he still had a lot to learn.

After that they wanted Dagner to sing. Dagner was nervous, but surprisingly ready to perform.

"Huh!" said Brid. "He just wants to impress Fenna, that's what."

Whatever the reason, Dagner took his own cwidder, fetched for him by Kialan, tuned it, and sang the song Moril had tried to finish for him. He did it nothing like the way Moril had made it go. The new parts of the tune were quite different from Moril's, and he had changed the beginning. It now went:

"*Follow me, follow me.*
The blackbird sings to follow me.

No one will know where we go –
All that matters is we go."

Kialan looked at Moril and made a face to show that he liked Moril's version better. Moril smiled. Everyone had to do things their own way. While Dagner went on to sing his *Colour* song, Moril slipped quietly away, fetched the old cwidder, slung it on his shoulders, and went to where Hestefan was refreshing himself with beer beside an open window. Hestefan looked as if he was too hot, just like Moril.

"Please," Moril said to him, "will you take me with you when you go?"

"Well," Hestefan said dubiously, "I was thinking of slipping off now, while nobody's noticing."

"I know you were," said Moril. "Take me too. Please."

Hestefan looked at him, a vague, dreamy look, which Moril was positive saw twice as much as most people's. "You're Clennen's other son, aren't you?" he said. "What's your name?"

"Tanamoril," said Moril. "I'm called Osfameron too," he added, as an inducement.

Hestefan smiled. "Very well then," he said. "Come along."

A Guide to Dalemark

Aberath, the northernmost earldom of North Dalemark; also the town on the north coast, situated on the Rath estuary at the mouth of the river Ath.

Aden, the small river running north to the sea at Adenmouth, thought by some to be all that remains of the great River of the spellcoats.

Adenmouth, a small town and lordship in the extreme northwest of North Dalemark, and part of the earldom of Aberath.

Adon, a name that seems to mean "High Lord" and has several applications:

1. One of the secret names of the One.

2. The name or title of the heroic King of Dalemark about whom there are many songs and legends. The Adon was an Earl of Hannart who married Manaliabrid of the Undying as his second wife and went into exile with her and the Singer Osfameron, during which time he was murdered by his jealous half-brother Lagan and brought back to life by Osfameron. He then became King, but on his death his two children disappeared, leaving Dalemark without a King and riven by civil war.

3. The title of the eldest son and heir of the Earl of Hannart.

The Adon's gifts, the legendary gifts Manaliabrid brought to the Adon as her dowry. These are:

1. A ring said only to fit the finger of one with royal blood.

2. A cup which was believed to acknowledge the true King and also to shine in the hands of anyone telling the truth.

3. A sword which, it was said, only the true King could draw from its scabbard.

The Adon's Hall, one of the old-style songs composed by the singer-mage Osfameron, in which Osfameron seems to be thinking not only of the Adon in exile in a ruinous hall but of his own cwidder and of the Sayings of King Hern.

Al, the most common short form of Alhammitt, the commonest name in South Dalemark. The name of a castaway picked up by the yacht *Wind's Road.*

Alda, the wife of Siriol; a confirmed alcoholic.

Alhammitt

1. The true name of the Earth Shaker.

2. The most common man's name in South Dalemark.

3. Mitt's actual name.

Alk, a lawman from the North Dales who took office under the Countess of Aberath and shortly married her.

His status then became that of Consort of Aberath, with the courtesy title (which was seldom used) of Lord. Alk devoted his time to inventing steam engines and eventually, almost single-handedly, brought about the industrial revolution of Dalemark.

Alksen, Major, the head of security at the Tannoreth Palace.

Alk's Irons, the name given by the people of Aberath to the steam machines invented by Alk. The most notable of these were a plough, a hoist, a press, a pump and a locomotive.

Alla, the elder daughter of Alk and the Countess of Aberath.

Allegiances, the personal ties of primitive Haligland. A man or woman would be born into one clan, sent as foster child to a second, swear friendship to a third and marry into a fourth. This formed a network of friendship and obligation which you were bound to tell to a stranger when you told your name. Allegiances defined you as a person. If you did not tell, or had no allegiances, you were either a criminal or a social outcast.

Almet, the son of the Adon and Manaliabrid, who declined to be King after his father.

Amil, one of the secret names of the One, which

appears to mean either "Brother" or "River". It later became the name of the line of kings that began with Amil the Great.

Ammet, a straw image thrown into the sea every year at the Sea Festival in Holand in South Dalemark, which was said to bring luck to the city. Small images were also made and sold for luck. Even greater luck was supposed to come to any boat that found Ammet floating beyond the harbour and brought him aboard. The name is a corruption of Alhammitt, one of the names of the Earth Shaker. See also **Poor Old Ammet.**

Andmark, the earldom in the centre of South Dalemark which was probably the wealthiest in Dalemark. Henda was Earl of Andmark until he was killed in the Great Uprising.

Anoreth of the Undying became the wife of Closti the Clam. The name means "unbound".

Ansdale, a remote valley east of Gardale. The birthplace of Biffa, whose family kept the mill there.

Arin, a senior lord of the (Heathen) invaders from Haligland and chief warrior-minister of Kars Adon.

Armour was markedly different in the two halves of Dalemark.

Southern soldiers wore helmets and breastplates with

exaggerated curves designed to deflect bullets, over tough leather, with knee-length boots and big gauntlets. Many carried guns as well as swords, and foot soldiers carried pikes.

Northern soldiers still used chain mail under sleeved jerkins of leather or tough cloth. The mail was long enough to protect the wearer to the wrists and knees, and the helmets were round, coming low enough in the back to protect the neck. Gloves were leather with mail or studs on the backs. Weapons were usually crossbows, swords and daggers. Guns were few and could only be spared for picked hearthmen.

Arms inspectors were employed by all the earls of South Dalemark to keep strict watch on gunsmiths, armourers and weapons makers, who were not allowed to work without the inspectors' seal on all their equipment. The earls rightly feared that the craftsmen might otherwise sell weapons to the common people or make weapons for the earls that were deliberately flawed. Despite the inspectors, many armourers seem to have done both these things.

Arris, a rough spirituous liquor brewed throughout South Dalemark from discarded grapes and sprouting corn. All that can be said in its favour is that it was much cheaper than wine.

Ath, the river that runs north into the sea at Aberath. It is thought to be one of the remnants of the great River of prehistory.

Autumn Festival, the usual name in the South of Dalemark for Harvest, the feast that celebrated the gathering of crops.

Autumn floods in the prehistoric Riverlands were as regular as spring floods but never so large. They were due to the rains that fell in the autumn storms.

Autumn storms were a regular feature in Dalemark. In historic times they reached as far north as Gardale and could be very severe. The worst lasted for days, with the gale swinging from northwest to southwest. With a shorter storm the winds tended to gust even stronger but not veer so much. If the gale was southerly, the storms came repeatedly for several days.

Bad luck gave rise to many superstitions all over Dalemark. Those which require explanation are:

1. Giving. It was considered disastrously unlucky to give, or promise to give something and then not give it. This is why Ganner was forced to give Lenina to Clennen and also why he seems to have been certain she would one day come back; he had not incurred bad luck

by refusing to give her away.

2. Festivals, feasts and ceremonies. Enormous bad luck was incurred if anything happened to interrupt these. Note that the Heathens interrupted the One's fire ceremony; that both Mitt and Al interrupted the Sea Festival; and that Fenna interrupted the Midsummer Feast by fainting.

3. A death brought great bad luck and could only be countered by a marriage on the same day. Lenina and Ganner take advantage of this belief.

4. Speaking a falsehood to the Undying brings more bad luck than any of the foregoing.

5. An unlucky person can bring bad luck to others. Gull was considered to be doing this, and Kialan believed he was such a person.

6. A person or group can carry their own cloud of bad luck around with them and nothing will go right for them until the cloud passes away.

Barangarolob, the full name of the horse that pulled Clennen the Singer's cart. Clennen, who loved long names, named him after the Adon's horse Barangalob, with the inserted superlative particle *ro* meaning "youngest" or "much younger".

Barlay, Lawschool slang. "No barlay" means

"no quarter given".

Beat the water, as part of the Holand Sea Festival in South Dalemark. People pretended to beat the sea with garlands of fruit and flowers. The ancient aim seems to have been to subdue the sea for the following year.

Beer was drunk throughout the North of Dalemark instead of water, wine, or coffee until near the end of Amil the Great's reign. One of Navis Haddsson's many profitable enterprises was to set up a large brewery in the Shield of Oreth, but the best beer came from Hannart and still does. The lager brewed in Kinghaven is to be avoided at all costs.

Bence, captain in chief of the fleet of the Holy Islands and commander of the *Wheatsheaf.* Bence was not a Holy Islander. He was born in Wayness in the earldom of Waywold.

Besting, Lawschool slang for best friend.

Biffa, pupil at the Gardale Lawschool, a native of Ansdale and best friend of Hildrida Navissdaughter. The name is a shortened pet-name form of Enblith.

Big Shool, one of the larger of the Holy Islands.

Black Mountains, the highest range of mountains in prehistoric Dalemark. It is possible, though not certain, that they were thrown higher in the mountain-folding at the start of the reign of King Hern, to become the Black Mountains of historic Dalemark, in which case the name may refer to the large deposits of coal to be found there.

"Both hands cut off..." refers to the law of primitive Haligland, whereby any member of the High Lord's (King's) family who was suspected of treason could be legally deprived of both hands, not as a punishment but as a precaution against a threat to the throne.

Bradbrook, a lordship on the coast of Waywold in South Dalemark.

Brid, daughter of Clennen the Singer and sister of Moril and Dagner, who fled North with Moril. Soon after her arrival Brid went to Gardale and trained as a law-woman, and thence to a professional appointment in Loviath. After the Great Uprising she became Countess of Hannart and eventually the first head of the Royal Dalemark Academy of Music, which she helped her brother Moril to found.

Bull, the most usual form in which the Earth Shaker appears. For this reason bulls' heads are carried in the Holand Sea Festival. It is said that the Bull is most frequently seen in the Holy Islands.

Canden, the younger of two brothers from Waywold in South Dalemark, devoted to freedom fighting. He moved from Waywold to Holand, where conditions were much worse, deliberately to foment rebellion. In Holand he joined the secret society of the Free Holanders and shortly proposed the firing of one of the Earl's warehouses. The older Free Holanders refused and stayed at home, while Canden led the younger ones to the warehouse. There he found that they had been betrayed and that soldiers were waiting for them.

Canderack, the earldom on the west coast of South Dalemark, where the best wine was grown. Until the reign of Amil the Great, Canderack owned a fleet that rivalled Holand's.

Canderack Head, south of Canderack Bay, an important landmark for shipping on the South Dalemark coast.

Carne Bank, a mudbank at the far east of the prehistoric Rivermouth, notorious for quicksands and shallows.

Cenblith, a queen of prehistoric Dalemark who first took the One for her lover and then bound him to the will of mortals, apparently either by forcing him to make the great River or by carving an image of him.

Cennoreth, one of the Undying, known in legends as a witch and often called the Weaver. It was said that whatever she wove became truth. She was sister to the legendary King Hern and mother of Manaliabrid, wife of the Adon.

Chindersay, one of the outer ring of the Holy Islands, notable for the dark colour of its rocks.

Cindow, a village northeast of Markind in South Dalemark.

City of Gold, King Hern's lost city of Kernsburgh, which gave rise to the saying "The City of Gold is always on the most distant hill", meaning that your ideal is never *here*, under your hands, but always out over *there*.

Clans, the tribe families of the Heathens of Haligland. The clans are very large and contain all classes, from aristocrat to lowborn. For instance, Kars Adon and Ked both belonged to Clan Rath, but Kars Adon was King while Ked was lowborn and had no real relation to the royal family.

Clennen Mendakersson, one of the most famous and characterful of the old-style Singers; a musician, composer, and teller of tales. He married Lenina, niece of the Earl of the South Dales, and was the father of Dagner, Brid and Moril. He was murdered near Markind in South Dalemark on suspicion of being a spy, and bequeathed to Moril a cwidder with strange powers, which he claimed had been handed down to him from their ancestor Osfameron.

Climbers, Lawschool slang name for the cloistered court with steps.

Closti the Clam, father of Tanaqui the weaver and a native of Shelling in the prehistoric Riverlands kingdom of Dalemark. He was called the Clam for his extreme uncommunicativeness, which may have been caused by the early death of his wife, Anoreth, or perhaps by the command of the One. He was killed in the invasion of the Heathen Haliglanders before he could tell his children many very important facts.

Collen, one of the two Southern forms of the name Kialan; a name fairly common in Markind.

Collet, the steward of the King of the Riverlands, whose duty was to memorise the King's debts for lodging and provision.

The Colour Song, composed and sung by Dagner Clennensson.

Come Up the Dale with Me, an apparently innocent love song from South Dalemark which was actually urging rebellion. It was banned.

Come with Me, a song being composed by Dagner Clennensson, which Clennen objected to on the grounds that it could be seen by spies as urging rebellion.

Coran, a townsman of Derent in Waywold in South Dalemark, later well known as a freedom fighter.

Countess

1. A female who is earl in her own right, like the Countess of Aberath.

2. The wife of an earl.

3. Mitt's name for his bad-tempered horse, which was not even female.

Cow-calling, a traditional patter song to a lively tune. Each verse is two lines longer than the last, until the singer is addressing the whole herd of cows.

Crady, a large town in the south of Andmark in South Dalemark.

Credin, the tidal wave which, at certain seasons, runs up the river Aden from the sea. A lesser wave usually runs up the river Ath at the same time. It is thought the name derives from memories of the mage Kankredin.

Cressing Harbour, a small fishing port to the northeast of the Point of Hark. It was the nearest landing for ships from South Dalemark and much involved in smuggling goods and people from both sides.

Cruddle, one of the traditional instruments played at the Holand Sea Festival, a sort of triangular fiddle with three gut strings. The player held the cruddle under his chin and scraped the strings with a loose horsehair bow. Cruddlers were seldom musicians. Their sole aim was to make as much noise as possible.

Cuckoo Song, a comic song with rather indecent words composed by Clennen the Singer.

Cwidder, a musical instrument rather like a lute but with some of the properties of an acoustic guitar. Cwidders are found in all sizes, from small trebles to medium-sized altos and tenors to large bass and deep bass. Moril's cwidder was a large bass, but it could be used as a tenor. Cwidders were much used by Singers because they were both versatile and easy to carry.

Dagner, the elder son of Clennen the Singer and a noted composer. Dagner became Earl of the South Dales very early in his life but was so reluctant to leave his life as a travelling Singer that he only took up his earldom after fifteen years, at the urgent request of Amil the Great.

Dalemark, the fifteen earldoms of Aberath, Loviath, Hannart, Gardale, Dropwater, Kannarth, the North Dales, the South Dales, Fenmark, Carrowmark, Andmark, Canderack, Waywold, Holand and Dermath, with the so-called King's Lands (the Holy Islands, the

Marshes and the Shield of Oreth), that, together with their peoples and history, make up historic Dalemark. For prehistoric Dalemark, see **Riverlands.**

Dapple, the mottled grey horse belonging to Hestefan the Singer. It was blind in one eye. There was usually something amiss with Singers' horses because they could only afford to buy them cheap.

Dark Land, the place where the souls of the newly dead gather before they make their way to the constellation of the River and on to oblivion.

Dastgandlen Handagner, the full name of Dagner Clennensson, who was named for the twin brothers of the Undying encountered by the witch Cennoreth. It was said that Clennen could not resist long names.

Derent, a prosperous town in the northeast of the earldom of Waywold in South Dalemark.

Dermath, the earldom in the extreme southeast of South Dalemark.

Diddersay, one of the Holy Islands.

Dideo, a fisherman of Holand in South Dalemark, one of the older members of the Free Holanders, who knew how to make bombs. Dideo put this knowledge to use for Mitt, and again in the Great Uprising, when he had a hand blown off by one of his own bombs, but he survived this and ended his days on the City Council of Holand.

Dike End, the birthplace of Mitt, farmed by his parents for the first six years of Mitt's life. The name comes from the situation of the farm and the nearby village at the end of the great Flate Dike, quite near where it runs into the sea about ten miles west of the port of Holand.

Doen, one of the Holy Islands.

Doggers, Lawschool slang for top of the game league.

Doreth, second daughter of Alk and the Countess of Aberath.

Dropthwaite, a secluded valley at the source of the river Dropwater where the Adon is said to have hidden as an outlaw. A centre of tourism in modern Dalemark.

Dropwater, after Hannart, the richest and most influential earldom of North Dalemark, situated facing southwest astride a wide fjord that is ideal for shipping, and sheltered by the mountains from the normal harsh weather of the North. The chief riches of Dropwater come from wool and leather goods, but it was mostly famous for its strong plum brandy and, above all, for the spectacular giant waterfall at the head of its dale.

Duck, the pet name of the youngest son of Closti the Clam, who later became famous as Mage Mallard.

Duke of Kernsburgh, a new title created by Amil the Great and bestowed upon Navis Haddsson. It was designed to ensure that Navis outranked all the earls.

Earl

1. The aristocratic ruler of one large segment of Dalemark. In the old days, prior to the reign of the Adon, earls held their places as officers of the King but, when Dalemark ceased to have kings, each earl became a small king in his own right, with absolute authority over everything in his earldom. Many misused this power, some brutally, and all went to great lengths to keep it.

2. The title of a clan chief among the Heathens of Haligland. This later became the modern title.

Earldom, a division of Dalemark ruled by an earl. It was said that earldoms came into being when King Hern divided his kingdom into nine and set nine men in charge, whom he called earls after the name of the clan chiefs, to govern under him. These divisions he called marks. Later six more marks were added in the South when Hern's conquests had reached that far. The system worked well, provided the King was strong. The common people traditionally regarded the earls as only the officers of the King and continued to think this way even after there were no kings.

Earth Shaker, the title of Alhammitt, one of the elder Undying, who had become the god of corn and of the sea. The title might describe the sea, but it possibly also refers to what happens if any of the Earth Shaker's secret names are spoken.

Edril, the younger grandson of Amil the Great and one of Maewen's ancestors.

Egil, a hearthman in the service of Earl Keril of Hannart.

The Eighth March, the last of a set of marching songs usually called "The Seven Marches," and only sung or played in North Dalemark because the words were offensive to the South.

Eleth of Kredindale, the mother of Noreth, who died soon after Noreth was born, declaring to the end that her daughter was the child of the One.

Elthorar Ansdaughter, keeper of antiquities at Hannart in North Dalemark in the time of Earl Keril, a law-woman of great learning who gave up the law in order to study the history and prehistory of Dalemark. She was present at the discovery of the spellcoats and translated them, sometimes rather inaccurately.

Eltruda, the Lady of Adenmouth, wife of Lord Stair, and younger sister of Eleth of Kredindale. Being childless herself, Eltruda brought Noreth up when Eleth died. On the death of Lord Stair, Eltruda married Navis Haddsson and became a considerable force in Dalemark politics and almost legendary for her quarrels with her stepdaughter, Hildrida.

Enblith the Fair, Queen of Dalemark some hundreds of years after the reign of King Hern, daughter of the Undying and said to be the most beautiful woman who ever lived. The musician-mage Tanamoril found Enblith living as a pauper in the woods and tricked the King into marrying her.

Falls

1. In prehistoric Dalemark the great River rose as a waterfall said to be half the height of a mountain. This was the site of Hern's battle with the mage Kankredin.

2. In historic times the falls at the head of the dale of Dropwater, where the river Dropwater fell nearly three hundred feet to the floor of the valley, were among the most admired sights of North Dalemark.

Fander, a revolutionary in Neathdale in South Dalemark, a grocer by trade, who provided the family of Clennen the Singer with bacon, lentils and, for some reason, a large bunch of rhubarb.

Farn, the southernmost of the Holy Islands.

Fayside, one of the dormitory houses in the Lawschool at Gardale.

Fenna, the daughter and apprentice of Hestefan the Singer.

Fenner, Ganner Sagersson.

Fervold, captain of Earl Henda of Andmark's private army.

Fire, a ritual bonfire which had to be lit for the One every spring as soon as the River ceased to flood. The fuel had to be specially arranged with the image of the One at its centre and kindled with coals from the hearth of the officiators. The lighting of the fire was celebrated with a feast. When the fire died down and the One was revealed in the ashes, only the eldest male of the family was allowed to remove the image.

Firepot, a clay pot with a lid and cunningly placed vents in which a fire could be kept alight and carried until needed. Until the invention of the wheel-and-flint tinderbox, firepots were in use all over Dalemark and continued in use by Singers and travelling traders until some time after the reign of the Adon.

Fishmarket, a broad thoroughfare in Holand in South Dalemark where fish was sold until the days of Amil IV.

Flags were considered potent symbols in Dalemark

from prehistoric times onwards:

1. In the old Kingdom of Riverlands flags were religious symbols and only carried in the holiest ceremonies to honour the Undying.

2. To the Heathen invaders from Haligland flags were equally holy as expressing the honour and status of a clan. They were carried at all times and defended to the death in battle.

3. In historic Dalemark flags were nearly taboo. They were only flown at Midsummer Fairs and by ships at sea. No earls and few kings dared fly flags until Amil the Great designed the royal standard of the crowned wheatsheaf. To this day only the monarch flies a flag.

"Flaming Ammet!", an oath peculiar to Holanders and a favourite of Mitt's. Since Ammet was an image of the Earth Shaker made of wheat straw, the notion of it on fire amounted to blasphemy.

Flapper, Ganner Sagersson.

Flate, the general name for the flatlands surrounding Holand in South Dalemark, most of which were at, or below, sea level.

Flate Dike, the main drainage ditch for the lowlands around Holand. It was wider than most roads and ran dead straight for nearly fifteen miles, the water in it flowing like a river to an outlet ten miles west of the port of Holand.

Flate Street, a street in a poor but respectable district to the west of the city of Holand in South Dalemark, where Earl Hadd provided Hobin the gunsmith with a house and workshop.

Fledden, a small town to the north of Andmark in South Dalemark, the birthplace of Earl Henda and one of the few places where Henda could rely on absolute loyalty. The inhabitants held the curious belief that the colour yellow was unlucky.

Flennpass, the last of the passes open in the mountains between North and South Dalemark. It was said that the musician-mage Osfameron had closed the other three passes at the time of the Adon.

Flind, a common name in South Dalemark.

1. A vintner outside Derent in Waywold, who brought Kialan and a supply of wine to Clennen the Singer.

2. A non-existent person mentioned in a password as part of Siriol's plans for Mitt's escape.

Flower of Holand, the boat belonging to Siriol on which Mitt served as apprentice, part of the fishing fleet that sailed regularly from the port of Holand in South Dalemark.

Follow the Lark, a song about bird catching whose secret meaning was "overthrow the earls," composed during the last rebellion before the Great Uprising.

Fort Flenn, the fort at the northern end of Flennpass, in the hands of the North and designed to hold the pass against incursion from the South.

Fredlan, one of the Singers, who travelled in a cart with his family, giving performances all over Dalemark.

Free as Air and Secret, a song pretending to be about the delights of the countryside which secretly urged rebellion, composed during an early uprising in South Dalemark.

Free Holanders, one of many secret societies of freedom fighters in the city of Holand in South Dalemark, the one to which Mitt belonged from the age of eight. Its members were mostly fishermen who believed ardently that they should free South Dalemark from the tyranny of the earls but who could seldom agree how this should be done. However, when the Great Uprising finally came about, all the Free Holanders were active in it, both in the fighting and in the reshaping of the government afterwards.

Gander, Ganner Sagersson.

Gann, a great hero in the legends from South

Dalemark who performed many great feats with his sword, Soulmaker, which was forged for him in secret by the Undying smith Agner while both were captives of the mage-king Heriol. Some stories give Gann as the brother of the witch Cennoreth. See also **Gull.**

Ganner Sagersson, Lord of Markind in the earldom of the South Dales, who had been betrothed to Lenina Thornsdaughter as a young man. When she left him for Clennen the Singer, Ganner did not, despite pressure from his household, marry anyone else. He seems to have expected Lenina would eventually come back to him (see **Bad Luck**). Ganner was a just and efficient administrator and one of few Southern lords to survive the Great Uprising untouched. He became regent for the South Dales on the death of Tholian.

Ganter Islands, a cluster of three islands in the Holy Islands.

Gardale, a prosperous valley, town and earldom in the southeast of North Dalemark, site of the famous Lawschool.

Garlands of apples, corn and grapes were worn by all those taking part in the Holand Sea Festival and afterwards thrown into the sea.

Golden Gentleman, the name given by the King of

the Riverlands to the image of the One when he finally found it in the keeping of Robin Clostisdaughter.

Gosler, Ganner Sagersson.

Gown, the distinguishing garment of the mage among the Heathens of Haligland. The gown had spells woven in it which appeared as words and, once put on by a mage, was never taken off, even for washing.

Grand Father, the most respectful of the titles of the One, possibly derived from the fact that most kings and many earls claimed to be descended from the One.

Great Girl (or boy), Lawschool slang for the pupil who comes top in the oral examinations held just before Midsummer.

Great Ones, the term for the Undying in the Holy Islands.

Great Uprising, the name for the countrywide revolution in Dalemark which brought Amil the Great to the throne. The Uprising began in the North around Kernsburgh and, almost simultaneously, in the South in the city of Holand, where a mob stormed the palace of the Earl and then had to fight a bloody battle with soldiers hastily sent by Dermath and Waywold. In the North a number of lords and earls who did not at once side with the rebels were killed or forced to go overseas.

Green roads, the system of highways said to have been made by King Hern. They remained for many centuries, being remarkably well engineered, never steep, despite running through the peaks of North Dalemark, and deliberately grassed for ease of travel by horseback. Many people believed that the Undying made and maintained the green roads, particularly as they continued to exist long after the main centres of civilisation had moved down to the valleys. The roads were used as drove roads and by those who wished to travel quickly from dale to dale, until Alk took them over as railways in the reign of Amil the Great.

Gregin, Alk's valet in Aberath in North Dalemark.

Grittling, the traditional ball game of the Lawschool at Gardale.

Guilds, organised companies of craftsmen and merchants in South Dalemark. Most guilds were formed at the time of the Adon, when the men of many trades realised that the South was becoming increasingly estranged from the North, while the Southern earls grew ever more powerful. Almost every trade, including the Singers, took hasty steps to obtain the protection of the law, usually by petitioning the Adon for a Royal Charter, so that in after years the earls could not easily disband them. The guilds generally kept a low profile, looking after their own members and the widows and orphans of members, training apprentices, educating children, saving money and paying taxes promptly. They had considerable power and were suspected by the Southern earls to be quietly financing the various uprisings, though nothing was ever proved.

In the North guilds were almost unknown.

Gull, eldest son of Closti the Clam and Anoreth of the Undying, the only one of Closti's sons to go to the wars. Gull was captured early in the fighting by the Heathen invaders and interrogated by the mage Kankredin, who returned him to his own side little better than an idiot. Gull is thought to be the same person as the Southern hero Gann, and if this is the case, it seems that Gull did eventually recover from Kankredin's treatment of him.

Guns were invented at the time of the Adon but never much used in North Dalemark. The South used guns extensively, although they were forbidden to all but earls, lords and their hearthmen. The early guns were clumsy and inaccurate and used mostly for sport until Hobin invented the rifled barrel, which had a spiral groove down the inside that caused the gun to shoot far more accurately. There was then a rush to buy guns. Waywold and Canderack drove a thriving trade smuggling guns to the North.

Gunsmiths' Guild, to which Hobin belonged, together with all other gunsmiths, was a very sober and respectable body of men who, in fact, spent the majority of their meetings laying careful plans for the Great Uprising.

Hadd, the angry and tyrannical Earl of Holand in South Dalemark who, after a lifetime of injustice, quarrelling with Earl Henda, terrorising his family, and overtaxing and suppressing his subjects, was murdered at the Sea Festival by an unknown marksman.

Halain, a spy for the Earl of the South Dales who had infiltrated the freedom fighters in Neathdale in South Dalemark.

Halian Tan Haleth, Lord of Mountain Rivers, is an old name for Tanamil. A legend about him was woven into the rugcoat given by Anoreth to Closti on their marriage but is otherwise unknown.

Halida, the wife of Keril, Earl of Hannart, who was born a poor relation of a lord in Canderack in South Dalemark. When Keril was taking part in an uprising in South Dalemark as a young man, Halida helped him escape capture and fled North with him.

Haligland, a country on the other continent, peopled by emigrants from prehistoric Dalemark several centuries before the reign of King Hern. Once in Haligland, they developed a clan system, a science of magery and a religion of the One. Modern Haligland is an oil-rich republic, still with a clan system and a fanatical religion, but one which denies vehemently any connection with the uncanny.

Ham, the partner and mate of Siriol aboard the *Flower of Holand.* Ham's full name, like so many in Holand, was Alhammitt. He was a large, good-natured, unintelligent man who was killed in the violence following the storming of the palace in Holand during the Great Uprising.

Hammit, a South Dalemark name, one of the many abbreviations of Alhammitt.

Hand organ, a musical instrument with pipes, bellows and keyboard, like a very small church organ. It had a sweet, piping tone, strong enough to be heard above the noise of a crowd. The player carried the organ on his or her right arm and pumped it with the left hand while playing the keyboard with the right.

Hands to the North, an unknown group of secret freedom fighters in Holand in South Dalemark. They were quite possibly invented either by Harl Haddsson as cover for his attempt to assassinate Earl Hadd or by

Harchad Haddsson as an excuse to pull down buildings to give *his* assassin a clear shot at Earl Hadd.

The Hanging of Filli Ray, a popular ballad about a young outlaw who was hanged for having the temerity to court a lord's daughter. The version sung in the South concluded with the arrival of the Earl, who reveals, too late, that Filli Ray is his son. In the North it is the King who arrives too late.

Hannart, the leading earldom of North Dalemark, famous for its music, its flowers, its buildings and the frank, outspoken nature of its people, and reputed to be the first civilised area of Dalemark. Certainly some of the buildings in the town of Hannart itself are thought to date back to the days of King Hern. Throughout much of history Hannart stood for freedom, justice and opposition to the South and its ways. Its heyday was from the reign of the Adon to that of Amil the Great, when it was also a centre of learning, but it became steadily less important from the time of the Great Uprising until it passed by marriage into the royal family and was adopted by the Crown Prince as his country retreat. Nowadays Hannart is mostly famous as a beauty spot and for the remains of the giant steam organ at the north end of its dale.

Harchad, second son of Earl Hadd of Holand in South

Dalemark, head of Hadd's secret police and master of his spies, said to be the cruellest man in Dalemark.

Hardimers, the name given to disciplinary officers at the Gardale Lawschool.

Harilla Harlsdaughter, eldest girl cousin of Hildrida and Ynen and betrothed at an early age to the Lord of Mark by her grandfather, Earl Hadd.

Harl Haddsson, the eldest of the Earl of Holand's three sons, a fat and seemingly indolent man, who became Earl of Holand for a year following the death of Hadd, during which time Holanders took to saying that Earl Hadd was preferable. He was killed when the mob stormed the palace in Holand during the Great Uprising.

Harvest, the Northern term for the Autumn Festival.

Headman, the leader or chieftain of a village in prehistoric Dalemark. The office combined the functions of major, priest and judge and was usually handed down from father to son.

Hearthmen, a privileged band of soldier companions sworn to a lord or earl and personally responsible to him only, who lived in their hearthlord's mansion with him and formed a private army when need arose. A lord was also said to be the hearthman of the earl who was his overlord if he had sworn to follow the earl to war. In the

South of Dalemark hearthpeople were always men, but many lords and earls of the North swore in women too. The maintaining of hearthpeople was forbidden by royal decree in the reign of Amil II.

Heathens, emigrants from Haligland who invaded the prehistoric kingdom of Dalemark and eventually intermarried with the natives. They brought with them their women and children and the mage Kankredin and his college of lesser mages, intending to settle, and introduced to the country both the worship of the One and many magical practices that were previously unknown. Their main, disastrous invasion is described in the spellcoats, but it seems certain that small boatloads of Heathens had been arriving for decades previously, compelled by the harsh conditions in Haligland to find better living and possibly inspired by legends of their former home in the Riverlands.

Henda, Earl of Andmark in central South Dalemark, a violent and paranoid man who spent much of his time quarrelling with the Earl of Holand and lived in constant dread of plots from the North. He was beheaded by his own hearthmen during the Great Uprising.

Herison, Lawschool slang meaning "the right to start grittling until the next full moon".

Hern, the second son of Closti the Clam and Anoreth of the Undying, who became the first known King of Dalemark. Most of what is known of him is legend, like the story of his defeat of the mage Kankredin, but numerous laws, customs and sayings are said to be his, and it is fairly certain that he founded the city of Kernsburgh, moving the seat of the throne there from his early base in Hannart and constructing the system of roads now known as the green roads or the paths of the Undying.

The name Hern means "heron".

Hestefan, one of the travelling Singers, of whom little is known beyond the facts that he befriended both Dagner and Moril Clennensson and became a follower of Noreth of Kredindale during her bid for the crown of Dalemark.

High Mill, a village twenty miles northeast of the port of Holand, on the rising ground towards Dermath, well known as a beauty spot.

Highside, the dormitory house at the Gardale Lawschool to which Hildrida Navissdaughter belonged.

High Tross, one of the islands of the Holy Islands, so called from its high and rocky outline.

Hildrida Navissdaughter, one of the company who

sailed North to Aberath in the yacht *Wind's Road*, granddaughter of Hadd, Earl of Holand, betrothed to Lithar, Lord of the Holy Islands, at the age of nine. After spending several years at the Lawschool in Gardale, Hildrida was able to annul this betrothal, and practised as a law-woman in the North Dales until Amil the Great appointed her Warden of the Holy Islands upon her marriage. Hildrida seems to have preferred living in Kernsburgh, however, where she became a leader of fashion and notorious for her quarrels with her stepmother, Eltruda.

Hildy, the pet name of Hildrida Navissdaughter.

Hobin, known as Bloody Hobin, the elder of two brothers devoted in different ways to freedom fighting. He was born in Waywold in South Dalemark of a family which seems to have been secret hereditary guardians of the kingstone, and he became a brilliant and innovative gunsmith, highly respected by his guild and much in favour with the earls of Holand, Waywold and Dermath. He then moved to Holand, where he married Milda, Mitt's mother, and bided his time, building up a hidden stock of weapons and an organisation of sober revolutionaries like himself, until word came from the North that Amil the Great had seized the crown. Hobin sensed the time was ripe and at once led a massive revolt in Holand, which spread to Dermath and Waywold and rapidly became a bloodbath. Hobin killed so many people, many of them innocent, that Amil himself was forced to intervene. It was said that Hobin shot himself rather than submit to a King. This may be true, but the story that he shot his wife and daughters at the same time is probably a fabrication.

Hoe, a village on the rising ground west of Holand in South Dalemark.

Hoe Point, the second major landmark for ships sailing northwest out of Holand. Sailors took care to know it well because a strong current flowed northwards from there.

Holand, the leading earldom of South Dalemark, a sizable city, a flourishing seaport, and the seat of Earl Hadd, situated in the extreme south of Dalemark.

Hollisay, one of the Holy Islands, named from the number of holly bushes that grow there.

Holy Islands, a scatter of islands in the bay between the Point of Hark and Carrow Head, famous as a haven for shipping. The islands are home to a strange, fey people and full of legends of the Undying. They are part of the King's Lands and owe no allegiance to any earl, but in the long interregnum between the Adon and Amil the Great they were regarded as part of South Dalemark and claimed by whoever was the strongest earl. Amil the Great rectified this by appointing a Warden of the Islands and spent much time there himself helping Ynen Navisson build his new fleet and experiment with steamships.

Holy Isle, the centremost island of the Holy Islands and rightly named. Only those who are meant to go to it can find it.

Honker, Ganner Sagersson.

Horsehair drums, traditional crude drums made of horsehide with the hair still on it, beaten loudly at the Holand Sea Festival, probably because Old Ammet was thought to govern the wild horses of the sea.

Horses of the sea were said to belong to Old Ammet and to appear galloping round a ship that was doomed.

Hurrel, Lawschool slang for a big push at grittling, a real scrimmage.

Incantation, a measured alliterative way of speaking, passed down from Singer to Singer and only used on the most solemn occasions.

Irana Harchadsdaughter, one of Earl Hadd's many grandchildren, cousin of Hildrida and Ynen, betrothed at an early age to Agnet, third son of the Earl of Waywold in South Dalemark.

"I sent the hidden death…", one of Kankredin's two chief mages, who seems to have had no name apart from the boastful spell woven into his gown.

"I sing for Osfameron, I move in more than one world" are the words inlaid in Moril Clennensson's cwidder in the old writing, by which the cwidder describes itself. Compare Tanaqui's weaving. It is possible these words cause the cwidder to behave as it does.

Island people, the inhabitants of the Holy Islands who are something of a race unto themselves, being small and brown, with dark eyes and pale hair. Their singsong accent is unlike any other in Dalemark. They are said to be remnants of the first people ever to settle the country.

Isle of Gard, the ruling island of the Holy Islands where the Lord's mansion and the main fleet are.

"I tortured the beast…", one of Kankredin's two chief mages, known only by the words woven in his gown.

Jay, herald and captain to the King of the Riverlands. Jay seems to have started as a minor, though trusted, herald, but he distinguished himself in the wars with the Heathens, when he lost an arm and endeared himself to the King by his cheerfulness, and became the favourite of the King in exile.

Jenro, a Holy Islander, coxswain aboard the flagship *Wheatsheaf.*

Jolly Holanders, a sea shanty that was known and loved all over South Dalemark.

Justice, an essential part of the corrupt legal system of South Dalemark before the reforms of Amil the Great. A justice was appointed and paid by an earl and did the earl's bidding, sitting as a magistrate and hearing only such cases as interested his employer or could bring the justice himself a bribe. The South had no access to the Lawschool of the North, and justices seldom had any legal training. They had to rely on their clerks, who were equally corrupt, to tell them what the law was.

K at the beginning of a personal name was only used in North Dalemark. In the slurred and softer dialect of the South a *K* becomes either *C* (pronounced *KH*) or *H*. For instance, the Southern form of the name Keril is Harl; or there are sometimes two forms of a Northern name, as in the name Kialan, which appears in the South both as Collen and as Halain.

Kanart, an Earl of Dropwater killed in battle during the Adon's wars.

Kanarthi, the conjectured Northern form of the name Cennoreth.

Kankredin, an evil magician, sometimes called the mage of mages, who accompanied the Heathen invaders from Haligland, intending to use them to help him usurp the power and position of the One. Kankredin was himself of the Undying and had increased his powers by magically passing through death, which made him virtually impossible to kill. Though legend claims that King Hern overthrew him, Kankredin appears again in stories long before the time of the Adon and was later said by the North to be the cause of all the evils in the South. It is claimed that Amil the Great frustrated an attempt by Kankredin to take over the North too.

Kappin, Lawschool slang for fighting to hold the team's position.

Karet, a hearthman of Aberath.

Kars Adon, son of Kiniron, who became clan head and High Lord after his father died in the invasion of prehistoric Dalemark. Though Kars Adon was barely fifteen and crippled from birth, he was held in great honour by all his subjects. This was partly due to the custom of the clans, but mostly to the character of Kars Adon himself.

Kastri, the Adon's son by his first wife and ancestor of Earl Keril of Hannart, who accompanied his father and Manaliabrid into exile.

Ked, a lowborn member of Clan Rath, aged about eight, who had a bad reputation as a liar.

Keril, Earl of Hannart, descended from the Adon and generally considered the most influential man in North Dalemark. As a young man he had high ideals and set out to free the South by helping in an uprising. The rebellion failed, and Keril had to be rescued and smuggled North by Halida, whom he married. He arrived back in Hannart to find his father dying and himself with a price on his head in the South. This seems to have given Keril a strong distaste for revolution of the violent kind. As an earl he supported the Southern freedom fighters surreptitiously, with money and advice, apparently hoping for a peaceful political solution, no doubt with himself as chief negotiator, for he possessed a lively and devious political mind. Unfortunately this same deviousness caused him to miscalculate gravely in the case of Navis Haddsson, and he had, as a result, to watch the gradual fading of Hannart as a power in the land.

Kern, the Northern form of the name Hern.

Kernsburgh, the capital city of Dalemark, situated nearly at the centre of the country. Kernsburgh was founded by King Hern and flourished for many centuries until the kingship shifted to Hannart, Canderack and elsewhere, after which it fell into ruins. At the time of the Great Uprising it was little more than grassy humps in the ground. Amil the Great's first act as King was to rebuild Kernsburgh, and from then on the city grew continually, to become the seat of government, centre of commerce and international metropolis it is two hundred years later.

Kestrel, the husband of Closti the Clam's elder sister, Zara, an old man who married late in life when Zwitt refused to marry Zara after Closti had jilted Zwitt's sister. Kestrel, it seems, did not wish to see Zara suffer through no fault of her own.

Kialan, younger son of Keril, Earl of Hannart, and later his heir.

King of the Riverlands of prehistoric Dalemark. Tanaqui never gives his name, perhaps out of respect, or perhaps because she never knew it. She clearly shows that he was not the correct man for dealing with the Heathen invasion, although he seems to have done his best at first, until his family was killed and his spirit broken.

Kinghaven, in the earldom of Loviath, the main port city of North Dalemark and otherwise notorious for brewing bad lager.

King's Sayings, a collection of proverbs and wise thoughts memorised by all Singers and supposed to be the words of King Hern himself.

King Street, the main thoroughfare in Kernsburgh.

The King's Way, a traditional song with a rousing tune which celebrates the customary journey of the new King down the green roads of North Dalemark to Kernsburgh to claim his crown. This song was banned in the South, where the earls did not wish to remind people there had once been Kings.

Kiniron, the younger brother of the King of Haligland who led the main invasion of the clans to prehistoric Dalemark, where he died of wounds from the fighting.

Kintor, Lord of Kredindale and cousin of Noreth Onesdaughter.

Knots and crosses, one of the oldest and most potent charms of binding and, of course, the basic pattern of a net. See also **Nets**.

Konian, the elder son of Keril, Earl of Hannart, executed in Holand in South Dalemark after a travesty of a trial.

Korib, son of the miller in Shelling and an excellent shot with the longbow.

Kredindale, a valley, town and lordship in the extreme northwest of North Dalemark where deposits of coal were found very early in history. From the reign of the Adon, mining became the main occupation of the valley until the mines were closed in the reign of Amil III. Kredindale was the birthplace of Noreth Onesdaughter. Its name is thought to be derived from Kankredin.

Labbard, King of Dalemark prior to the Adon, an indolent and incompetent man who openly declared that he would rather sit and drink cider than rule the country.

Ladri, one of Kankredin's mages, whose task was to collect the souls caught in the soulnet.

Lady, the wooden image of a woman which the family of Closti the Clam kept, according to the customs of prehistoric Dalemark, in one of the niches reserved for the Undying.

Lagan, the villainous half-brother of the Adon, a student of sorcery and, some legends say, a pupil of Kankredin. Lagan seems to have been consumed with jealousy both of the Adon's status and of the Adon's love for Manaliabrid. Having conspired to have the Adon sent into exile, Lagan then followed him, disguised himself by sorcery, and stabbed him to death. The Adon was recalled from death and later killed Lagan.

Lake, a large body of water in the centre of prehistoric North Dalemark, which must have been extensive even when the River was not flooding, to judge from the petrified remains of freshwater life to be found all over the central peaks. By historic times this lake had shrunk to a row of small tarns, the largest of which is Long Tarn.

Lalla, housekeeper at Lithar's mansion in the Holy Islands and an aspect of Libby Beer.

Lament for the Earl of Dropwater, an old ballad song composed during the Adon's wars, mourning the death of Kanart, who was one of many earls who opposed the Adon.

Lathsay, one of the Holy Islands.

Lavreth, a coastal town northwest of Hannart in North Dalemark.

Lawman, a position of great power and prestige in North Dalemark. Lawmen served earls, lords and town governors as advisers, justices, or planners for the future and in many other ways, often for very large fees. Quite a few lawmen married into the families of lords or earls. Since the law was open to everyone, however lowborn, training as a lawman was a favourite way to rise in the world.

Law of the sea was very largely unwritten but was held throughout Dalemark waters to be much more binding than the law of the land. It stated, among other things, that all ships must go to the assistance of any boat in trouble.

Lawschool at Gardale in North Dalemark, the only such school in the country until the reign of Amil the Great, very famous and much sought after. It took only those pupils who could reach a very high standard in its oral entrance exams, but a pupil could join the school at any age from nine to fifteen and then be assured of the very best education, both in law and other studies, and nobody ever failed to get a job after graduating. The Lawschool was well endowed with funds and gave quite a number of scholarships to poor students every year. Students entering the school found it a world in itself, with many strange customs and words that were not found anywhere else.

When Amil the Great founded lawschools all over the country, the status of the Gardale school diminished. In the reign of Amil III it became simply a part of Gardale University.

Law-woman, a female lawyer, had even more prestige in North Dalemark than a lawman and could command an even higher fee.

Lengday, Lawschool slang for Midsummer Day.

Lenina Thornsdaughter, niece of Earl Tholian of the South Dales, wife of Clennen the Singer, and mother of Dagner, Brid and Moril. Lenina was brought up as an aristocrat in the Earl's household in Neathdale in South Dalemark and left there when she became betrothed to Ganner Sagersson. Clennen saw Lenina at the betrothal feast and persuaded her to marry him instead.

Libby Beer, the name of the image made of fruit that was yearly thrown into the harbour in Holand in South Dalemark at the Sea Festival. The name is certainly a corruption of one of the little-known names of She Who Raised the Islands, the Undying mother of fruitfulness and wife of the Earth Shaker.

Licence, a legal document with the seal of an earl attached, showing that the holder was allowed to exercise his or her trade anywhere in South Dalemark. Licences were expensive. Their main value was the unspoken assumption that the holder was allowed to travel between the South and the North. Without a licence, a traveller would be arrested at the border.

Liss, Maewen's aunt, who ran a livery stable near Adenmouth in the north of Dalemark.

Litha, a woman of the prehistoric Riverlands who was killed by the Heathen invaders from Haligland.

Lithar, Lord of the Holy Islands, who was of special value to the earls of South Dalemark, both because of his fleet and because, as lord of the onetime King's Lands, he was not the subject of any earl. He was betrothed to Hildrida Navissdaughter when he was twenty and she was nine years old.

Little Flate, a village on the slightly rising ground southwest of Holand in South Dalemark, which was the first landmark for ships sailing out of Holand. Sailors gave it a wide berth because of the shallows just offshore.

Little ones, the name Holy Islanders give those mortals under the special protection of the Undying.

Little Shool, one of the Holy Islands, barely yards from its neighbour, Big Shool.

Lord, a lesser ruler under the earls, who owed allegiance to the earl in whose earldom his lordship was, paying taxes and providing fighting men when his earl required him to. A lord was also supposed to obey every other command from his earl, but not all lords did so. Otherwise a lord lived in his mansion, kept hearthmen, and ruled his subjects just as an earl did, but on a smaller scale.

Lord of Mark, lord of the northernmost lordship in South Dalemark, a plump and middle-aged widower, betrothed to Harilla Harlsdaughter when he was thirty-eight and she was ten years old.

Lovely Libby, one of the big merchant ships sailing out of Holand in South Dalemark. Like most of the tall ships of Holand, she was named from the Sea Festival for luck.

Loviath

1. The earldom on the northwest coast of North Dalemark.

2. The name of Maewen Singer's physics teacher.

Luck ship and shore, the ritual reply to the traditional greeting "The year's luck to you" at the Sea Festival in Holand in South Dalemark.

Lucky ship, any ship sailing out of Holand that could retrieve the image of Poor Old Ammet from the sea. The yacht *Wind's Road* was doubly lucky from having accidentally brought the image of Libby Beer as well. Anyone noticing this fact had to be a Holander.

Luthan, Earl of Dropwater and cousin of Noreth of Kredindale. Because of his almost accidental support of the King's side in the Great Uprising, Luthan – and

Dropwater with him – became extremely important in the reign of Amil the Great. Luthan was made chancellor and was twice elected prime minister.

Lydda, Siriol's daughter, a plump, good-natured girl who married a sailor from the merchant fleet of Holand. Her husband later took over Siriol's boat and business.

Maewen Singer, a teenage girl hijacked from modern Dalemark to take the place of Noreth of Kredindale. See also **Mayelbridwen.**

Mage Mallard, the Undying musician-mage, youngest son of Closti the Clam and brother to the Weaver and King Hern. See also **Duck.**

Mages were fairly common in primitive Haligland and much respected because much feared. No one dared insult a mage of any kind, but the greatest fear and respect were reserved for the so-called college of mages, which was always made up of fifty of the strongest and most experienced enchanters in the land. When Kankredin came to head this college, he seems to have made it a condition that every mage should have passed ritually through death before he joined, which was not the case before his time. College mages were always male, but female mages also existed, with a coven of fifty of their own.

A man came over the hill..., a rhyme woven into the skirt of Robin Clostisdaughter by her sister Tanaqui, but hopelessly garbled. As far as can be understood, the rhyme seems to be about the meeting of Closti with Anoreth, or else it refers to a much older but very similar story.

Manaliabrid

1. The Undying wife of the Adon, daughter of Cennoreth the Weaver.

2. The full second name of Brid Clennensdaughter (her first name was Cennoreth).

Manaliabrid's Lament, a song in the old style, said to have been composed by Osfameron after Lagan killed the Adon. It has a tune of strange broken phrasings, so unlike the usual style of Osfameron that many consider that Manaliabrid may have composed the *Lament* herself.

Mansion, the large semi-fortified house of an earl or lord, always the most prominent in the area. Besides housing the lord's family and many servants, the mansion had to be big enough for a band of hearthmen, advisers, lawyers, clerks and numerous other assistants.

Markind, an area in the very south of the South Dales, the lordship of Ganner Sagersson, and notable for its many little hills and valleys, which are, in fact, the worn-down remnants of volcanoes.

Marks, an old name for the fifteen divisions of Dalemark that later became the earldoms.

Mark Wood, a large forest at the northern edge of the third and highest Upland in the earldom of the South Dales, part of the lordship of Mark. It was full of clearings stockaded against possible invasion by the North, where wood was cut and charcoal was made. The inhabitants hated the North heartily and put up the stoutest resistance met by the army of Amil the Great at the start of the Great Uprising.

Marriage by proxy, a custom among earls of holding a wedding without the bride's being present. Her place would be taken by a woman who was married already. The practice probably originated to save the nobly born bride the trouble and expense of a journey, but it was widely used if the bride was unwilling, or a child, or both.

Marshes, a huge area of volcanic swamp to the east of Dalemark. Throughout historical times the Marshes were considered worthless, remarkable only for curious plants and birds, and they became King's Lands because nobody else wanted them. When, in recent times, oil was discovered there, they remained the property of the crown but added considerably to the wealth of the country.

Mattrick, chief among the freedom fighters in Neathdale in South Dalemark.

Mayelbridwen, a form of the name Manaliabrid from Fenmark; Maewen Singer's full name.

May the clay purge from you..., the start of the ritual spoken when the image of the One was put into its yearly fire. The speakers of this invocation had, for generations, no idea that what they were uttering was a spell for the unbinding of the One.

Medmere, the valley where Clennen the Singer was murdered. The round lake in the middle is the centre of an old volcano.

Middle vokes, Lawschool slang for the second stage of the training course.

Midsummer flags, traditional bright banners flown at Midsummer Fairs all over Dalemark. The devices on them – the Eye, the Sheaf, the River, et cetera – are versions of the Old Writing. The flags are thought to be the debased remnants of flags once carried in religious ceremonies.

Milda, the mother of Mitt and afterwards the wife of Hobin the gunsmith, who was the father of her two daughters. Sadly, neither Milda nor her daughters survived the Great Uprising. Though there are several highly coloured stories about their deaths, the most likely theory is that they perished in the terrible violence and confusion after the mob stormed the Earl's palace in Holand, when the earls of Dermath and Waywold sacked the city in reprisal.

Mitt, short for Alhammitt. Mitt was born at Dike End in the earldom of Holand in South Dalemark, on the day of the Sea Festival. He moved to the city of Holand as a child, where he became a freedom fighter and was forced to escape to the North to avoid arrest. After just under a year in Aberath, in training as a hearthman, he left to follow Noreth of Kredindale in her bid for the crown.

Modes, Lawschool slang for a progress report on the term's work.

Moril, younger son of Clennen the Singer. Clennen bequeathed to Moril a cwidder said to have belonged to the minstrel Osfameron. After the death of his father, Moril went to Hannart in North Dalemark, where he briefly joined Hestefan the Singer before leaving to take part in the Great Uprising. He played a considerable part in the Uprising and afterwards became court musician and chief architect of the Royal Dalemark Academy of Music, collecting travelling Singers from all over Dalemark and gathering them together in Kernsburgh. This caused such changes and improvements in the making of music that by the end of Amil the Great's reign the old travelling Singers had ceased to exist.

Mount Tanil, a very tall volcano on the edge of the Marshes southeast of Gardale, thought by unlearned people to be the home of the One.

Mucks, Lawschool slang for gloved hands, the gloves often weighted by being stuffed with metal or stones.

Natives, the term given by the Heathen invaders to the prehistoric inhabitants of Dalemark, who were mostly dark and squarely built. After the invasion many of these people went South, where they intermarried with the settlers there to give rise to the average Southerner, pale-skinned and brown-haired. Those who stayed in the North interbred with the invaders to produce the brown-skinned, light-haired Northerner.

Navis Haddsson, third son of the Earl of Holand, a brilliant and efficient soldier and a ruthless politician, who was forced to escape North from the palace plots in Holand (he was disliked by both the old Earl and the new for having shown too much sympathy for the plight of the common people of Holand). He spent nearly a year as a hearthman in Adenmouth before leaving to follow Noreth of Kredindale and to take part in the Great Uprising. It was probably thanks to Navis that the bloodshed was not greater. Early in the reign of Amil the Great, Navis was made Duke of Kernsburgh, partly in reward for his services and partly because he then outranked the earls it was now his job to control. A year later he married Eltruda, widow of Lord Stair of Adenmouth.

Neathdale, a large market town in the South Dales, the seat of Earl Tholian. Because it was the last major town before the North, Neathdale flourished both on legal trade and by smuggling goods and people in and out of North Dalemark. The earls' spies and security forces were particularly active there, which led to the Siege of Neathdale during the Great Uprising.

Nepstan, a country in the far South.

Nets, a potent item of magecraft, akin to weaving. The netmaker, working with power, could design his net to perform various tasks. Kandredin's soulnet, besides trapping departing souls, was intended to draw Gull's soul to him *and* to bind the One. Tanamil's nets likewise had several purposes: concealing the army, blocking the mages and forcing them to assume their true shapes.

New Flate, the drained flatlands some miles west of Holand in South Dalemark, where Halain, grandfather of Earl Hadd, was supposed to have had dikes dug and drained the sea marsh. In fact, the New Flate was probably older than that. It was very fertile farmland but was denied prosperity until the reign of Amil the Great by the ridiculously high taxes imposed by the earls of Holand.

Noreth, known as Onesdaughter, of whom it was said that the One spoke to her all her life, telling her she was to take the crown when she reached the age of eighteen. She was born in Kredindale to the Lord's unmarried daughter, Eleth, who died soon after Noreth's birth, declaring that the child's father was the One himself. If this was true, it gave Noreth the strongest possible claim to be Queen. She was educated first in Adenmouth, where she was left in the care of her aunt Eltruda, and then at the Gardale Lawschool, from which she graduated early, then spent the next two years at Dropwater as junior law-woman to her cousin Luthan. The Midsummer after her eighteenth birthday Noreth returned to Adenmouth, where she formally declared her intention of riding the royal road to claim the crown.

North, the seven earldoms of Hannart, Gardale,

Aberath, Loviath, Dropwater, Kannarth and the North Dales, all these being north of a line drawn east and west from the Point of Hark. This was the earliest part of the kingdom of Dalemark and also the most mountainous, where the people, though generally poor, had a long tradition of independence and freethinking. The earls of the North quickly learnt that injustice was not to be tolerated (quite a few earls lost either their lives or most of their subjects to the mountains while this lesson was being learnt), and the laws of the North were therefore fair and lenient, applying to earl and commoner alike. From well before the reign of the Adon, the North was known as the place of freedom. It was also, perhaps because it was the oldest-settled part of Dalemark, renowned for strange old beliefs and even stranger happenings.

North Dales, the earldom immediately to the north of South Dalemark. Though it was cut off from the South by a range of high mountains, the people there were used to dealing with the South (often as smugglers) and were in some ways more akin to the South than to the North.

Northern Cross, the most noticeable constellation in the night sky at all seasons, invaluable to sailors because it revolved round the true north. Other well-known constellations are Enblith's Hair, the Flatiron, the Big Cat, the Kitten, Hern's Crown and the River. Astronomy was not much studied in Dalemark until the reign of Amil the Great, so that although it was known that the world was round and circled the sun, little account was taken of the planets. Sailors called them the Unreliable Stars, for always moving about, or the Unchancy Ones.

Old Flate, the flatlands towards Waywold in South Dalemark, part of the earldom of Holand which had once been drained and farmed but allowed to return to marsh in the course of the two centuries before the Great Uprising because of the ruinous taxes imposed by the earls of Holand. The Old Flate became the haunt of snakes, criminals and disease.

Old Man, the highest mountain in Hannart, at the south end of the dale, thought to be named for the One.

Old Man of the Sea, a seeming priest who appeared to certain people in the Holy Islands, an aspect of the One.

Old Mill, across the River from Shelling in prehistoric Dalemark, where the first spellcoat was completed and the second begun. It had become a forbidden place for the villagers after the marriage of Closti and Anoreth. Some said it was haunted by the ghost of a woman, others that it was the abode of bad spirits, and still others that the River had cursed the place. As the King's men found mussels being cultivated on a system of ropes in the millpond, it appears that not everyone in Shelling believed these tales.

Old Smiler, Mage Mallard's derisive name for the King of the Riverlands.

Old Writing, a system of syllabic signs in use before letters were developed, which came to be thought of as magical. It was often used in spells or for inscriptions intended to be potent.

Olob, the shortened name of Barangarolob, Clennen the Singer's horse, which Clennen often said he would not part with for an earldom.

Ommern, one of the Holy Islands, the greenest.

Ommersay, one of the larger of the Holy Islands.

One, the greatest of all the Undying, whose face could not be looked upon and whose names could not be spoken. The One was said to have fathered the human race by his union with the witch-queen Cenblith, at which time he made the great River of prehistory and was for centuries bound by magic at its source. He was at length unbound by the Weaver and shook the country into its present mountainous state when he defeated the mage Kankredin.

The One was worshipped as a god by the invaders from Haligland and for a long time remained a god in the North of Dalemark, where many beliefs and customs about him still remain, but he was almost unknown in the South. Nowadays he is regarded simply as an old superstition.

Or, er, ro, a particle inserted into a name to give the meaning "younger" or most often "youngest". Compare Barangalob and Barangarolob, Tanamil and Tanamoril, Osfamon and Osfameron, et cetera.

Oreth, one of the secret names of the One, the least known, meaning "he who is bound".

Orethan the Unbound, the name by which the One was known after the Weaver released him from the spells of Cenblith and Kankredin. This name is almost never spoken.

Oril, one of several names taken by Mage Mallard to disguise the fact that he was of the Undying.

Orilsway, a town which grew up at the junction of the green roads in the far north of Dalemark, possibly taking its name from Mage Mallard in his guise as the Wanderer. When the green roads were abandoned as highways, Orilsway fell into ruin and was only rebuilt and resettled after the coming of the railways.

Osfameron, one of the two names taken by Mage Mallard in his guise as a minstrel and meaning "Osfamon the younger". It is not known who Osfamon was. Under this name Mallard became the friend of the Adon, whom he raised from the dead, and also created the cwidder with which he is said to have made mountains walk, later bequeathed to Moril Clennensson.

Palace of Earl Hadd in Holand in South Dalemark. Most earls, even in the South, lived in much humbler mansions, but Earl Hadd, perhaps because he insisted on his entire family's living with him, enlarged and renamed his dwelling. The palace was largely destroyed in the Great Uprising.

Pali, a prison guard in Neathdale in South Dalemark who was a secret freedom fighter.

Panhorn, an intricately curled horn with four mouthpieces and eight valves, very difficult to play.

Paths of the Undying, a name for the green roads of North Dalemark used by those who believed that the Undying created and maintained them.

Peace-piping, a very difficult form of musical magecraft in which the mage must first use his pipes to echo the anger of combatants and then reduce their feelings to calm and shame. Moril Clennensson unwittingly used a form of peace-piping on Tholian, Earl of the South Dales.

Peelers, Lawschool slang for willow wands with the bark peeled off.

Penner, Ganner Sagersson.

Pennet, a village between Waywold and Holand in South Dalemark.

Piper, the name most often used, from the time of the Adon onwards, for Tanamil of the Undying, onetime lord of the Red River. It was said that being released from bondage at the same time as the One, Tanamil went to the Holy Islands, where his piping may still sometimes be heard on calm evenings.

Point of Hark, the high rocky peninsula that divides North from South Dalemark waters.

Poor Old Ammet, the full name of the image made of plaited wheat decorated with fruit and flowers and ribbons which was thrown into the harbour in Holand in South Dalemark each year at the Sea Festival. Opinions vary as to whether this ritual echoes some personal sacrifice by one of the Undying or is simply a charm for improving the harvest, but what is certain is that any boat which picks up Poor Old Ammet beyond the harbour has good luck ever after. This is rare; the tides and currents have to be exactly right. Usually the image sinks in the harbour.

Portable organ. See **Hand organ.**

Porter, the main spy for North Dalemark, operating under the noses of all the earls of the South, and the most wanted man in the South. He reported to Hannart almost everything the Southern earls wished to keep secret, organised freedom fighters, and ran a rescue service for wanted men and women. The Porter was operating for most of the eleven years prior to the Great Uprising.

Prest, one of the Holy Islands, large, with high crags.

Prestsay, a small rocky island in the Holy Islands.

Proud Ammet, a big merchant ship based in Holand in South Dalemark, where Earl Hadd's assassin seems to have been when he fired. Like all the big merchant ships, this one was named from the Sea Festival.

Ratchet, a cat found by the children of Closti the Clam on their journey up the great River, named from the sound of her purring.

Rath Clan, sometimes called the Sons of Rath, the royal clan of primitive Haligland into which Kars Adon and Ked were born. The clan colours, which appeared on banners and in clothing, were red and blue.

Rattles, rotating wooden rattles, where the noise is produced by a wooden flange meeting a ratchet, which are traditional at the drowning of Old Ammet in the

Holand Sea Festival. The rattle users are always small boys dressed half in red and half in yellow.

A Reader for the Poor, a book designed to teach working people to read. It was written by a clerk in Carrowmark who had little imagination. A typical page begins, "Ham beats the cask. He knocks in five nails. Will that make it hold water?"

Red One, one of the names for Tanamil the Piper.

Riss, a seaman aboard the flagship *Wheatsheaf* in the Holy Islands.

Rith, a boy's name, fairly common in North Dalemark.

River, the mighty prehistoric watercourse which flowed north through Dalemark from a source somewhere near Hannart. It was said that the One made the River, and that the River was both the One and the soul of the land, and that it was the path of souls on their way to the sea. The River was destroyed by the One when he shook the land to rid it of the evil mage Kankredin. It only remains nowadays as two small rivers, the Ath and the Aden, and in the belief that the souls of the dead travel down the constellation of the River to oblivion in the sea of the universe.

Riverbed, the spirit land behind the great River, otherwise called the River of Souls.

Riverlands, the correct name for the prehistoric kingdom of Dalemark.

Rivermouth, the place where the great prehistoric River of Dalemark ran out into the sea in the north, through a delta of marsh, quicksand, and changing tides and currents. Its remains can be seen today in the bay between Aberath and Adenmouth, where there are still treacherous currents and constantly changing shoals.

Robin, the eldest child of Closti the Clam and Anoreth of the Undying, whose birthright was knowledge. Unlike her brothers and sisters, Robin passes clean out of all history and legend after the narrative of the spellcoats. It is possible that stories about her have been lost or attributed to her more spirited sister, Tanaqui.

Royal road, the green roads of North Dalemark between Adenmouth and Kernsburgh. Tradition said that each new monarch should make this journey on the old roads before claiming crown and kingstone at Kernsburgh.

Rugcoats, the poncho-like garments of woven wool worn by men and women over their other clothing in prehistoric Dalemark.

Rugcoats for weddings were presented by a girl's family in prehistoric Dalemark to a husband-to-be as a sign that the two were officially betrothed; the groom then wore the rugcoat at the wedding. These rugcoats were always of specially fine weaving, usually with words all over. It was believed that the coat brought luck to the wedding, and possibly children too. If the bridegroom did not wear the coat at the wedding, it was a sign that the bride would soon be either deceived or a widow. If the groom gave the coat back before the wedding, the betrothal was broken off.

Rushing people, the souls of the dead that hurry along the Riverbed towards the sea.

Rush mat, woven by Mage Mallard to deceive the King of the Riverlands. Weaving in any form is a potent spell.

Rusty, a ginger tomcat found by the children of Closti the Clam on the journey up the great River.

Sailing in grybo, Lawschool slang for being in the clear, without black marks.

Sard, a trusted soldier of the King of the Riverlands – trusted because he enjoyed killing.

Scap, Lawschool slang for the spring solstice.

Scarnel, a pipe made of pea or bean stalks, hollowed and varnished, traditionally played at the Sea Festival in Holand in South Dalemark by any number of amateur players. The sound is indescribably horrible.

Sea Festival, celebrated in autumn and called the Autumn Festival or Harvest elsewhere in Dalemark and peculiar to Holand in the South. Two images, one of straw and one of fruit, are carried down to the harbour in a procession of men clothed in red and yellow, draped with garlands and wearing traditional hats, accompanied by music from traditional instruments and by other lesser images; at the harbour with solemn words the two greater images are thrown into the sea. This is followed by feasting.

The Second March, one of seven tunes used by soldiers to march to all over Dalemark. *The Second March* has a jaunty tune and is generally more in favour in the North.

Sein right, Lawschool slang for the right to start grittling. The team with sein right could choose weapons and set up the first move.

Sending Day, at the Lawschool, the day on which pupils returned home for the summer. Pupils' families were asked to attend the closing ceremony before they removed the pupils.

Sessioning, the Lawschool word for school term.

Sevenfold, a merchant ship based in Holand in South Dalemark which had the good luck to pull Poor Old

Ammet out of the sea. Every man aboard was said to have made his fortune subsequently. *Sevenfold* herself was sold when she became old to a merchant in Waywold who renamed her *Fair Enblith* and was not particularly lucky with her.

Sevenfold II, a merchant ship sailing out of Holand in South Dalemark, so called when the first ship of that name was sold. Her cockboat was found by the yacht *Wind's Road*. Like most Holand shipping, both *Sevenfolds* were named from the Sea Festival.

The Seven Marches, the set of lively tunes to which soldiers marched in both North and South Dalemark. Each march had well-known words.

Shelling, a village much like other villages on the west bank of the great River of prehistoric Dalemark, the birthplace of Closti the Clam and his children.

Shelling River Procession, held once a year at Midsummer to honour the River as a god. This was one of four yearly ceremonies in which flags were carried, and probably gave rise to the custom of flying flags over the stalls at Midsummer Fairs all over historic Dalemark.

She Who Raised the Islands, the most common term for the lady of the Undying who, as wife of the Earth Shaker, has power nearly equal to his but is, on the whole, more benign. As Libby Beer she provides fruit and nourishment, but in her stronger aspects she is the earth itself and the only one of the Undying able to control the Earth Shaker. She is adored particularly in the Holy Islands, where she takes the shape of a beautiful red-haired woman dressed in green.

Shield of Oreth, a mountain plateau in the southwest of North Dalemark that faces the milder weather of the sea. The name is from the least known of the secret names of the One, and it should perhaps be noted that at least three of the Undying and the Adon's sword were to be found there. In early historic times the Shield was well farmed and populous, but it fell into wasteland during the Adon's wars. Navis Haddsson was given ducal lands here and was fond of saying that of all his achievements, the one which gave him most pleasure was the restoration of the Shield to farmland and prosperity.

Singers, a race of men and women, most of whom claimed descent from Tanamoril or Osfameron, who travelled the country of Dalemark singing, playing music and telling stories. Because singers were among the few people able to move freely between North and South, they also carried news, letters and often fugitives. Some even acted as spies, but this was rare: singers had their own rigid customs and standards, chief among which was always to tell the truth and never to perform a vile or a violent act. They also passed down by word of mouth innumerable old customs, sayings, beliefs and incantations, many of which were lost when Moril Clennensson disbanded the Singers in the reign of Amil the Great.

Siriol, the owner of the *Flower of Holand,* a fisherman and a prominent member of the Free Holanders, the society of secret freedom fighters to which Mitt also belonged. Mitt was apprenticed to Siriol for a while until his indentures were bought out by Hobin the gunsmith. Siriol greatly distinguished himself during the Great Uprising and afterwards became first a councillor and then semipermanent Mayor of Holand.

Six steps up to a front door were standard in Holand in South Dalemark, where the land is only inches above sea level and there is constant danger of flooding, particularly during the autumn storms.

Skreths, Lawschool slang word for the cloister to the east of the school.

Small Western clan, any of several minor clans that sailed from Haligland to prehistoric Dalemark during the years before the main invasion.

Soulboat, a small skiff specially enchanted to hold the souls of the dead once they had been retrieved from Kankredin's net.

Soulnet. See **Nets.**

Souls of mortals were believed until quite recently to be the prey of witches and sorcerers, whether joined to a body or not. The mages of primitive Haligland claimed to be able to steal a man's soul while he slept, and Kankredin is said to have been able to take someone's soul at any time he wished. Souls of the Undying and those descended from them were a different matter because they were believed to be combined not only with a body but with the entire country too.

South, the eight earldoms of Dermath, Holand, Waywold, Canderack, Andmark, Carrowmark, Fenmark and the South Dales. This part of Dalemark has a warm climate, a rich soil and few high mountains. In early historic times it was very wealthy, but it became steadily poorer under the oppressive rule of the Southern earls, until, shortly before the reign of Amil the Great, the South was actually often poorer than the North and only ruled by fear. The North regarded this regime with disgust; the South was deeply suspicious of the North; and each considered itself superior to the other. The

South, in fact, was noted for a number of virtues not seen in the North: efficiency, cool-headedness, perseverance and clear-sightedness, combined with a strong sense of humour.

South Dales, the earldom closest to North Dalemark and in many ways not unlike the North in climate and geography. But being this close to the freethinking North had a bad effect on the earls of the South Dales: They were the most tyrannical, warlike and unjust of all the Southern earls.

Spannet, a stablehand in Adenmouth in North Dalemark.

Specials, guns made secretly by Hobin of Holand in South Dalemark which he sold only to a chosen few. Each gun had some unusual feature, and all were better than any of the weapons he sold in public.

Spellcoat, a poncholike garment woven with word pictures that either told a story or stated facts. The garment, in the weaving, became the spell that made the story or fact come true. See also **Weaving; Words.**

Spirits were thought to be everywhere and to govern everything in prehistoric Dalemark, and it was necessary to please or soothe them every day. Some of the more powerful spirits almost had the status of gods and were confused by many with the Undying. The unusual thing about Closti's family is that they did not share this belief. Hern, in fact, rejected spirits out of hand as "unreasonable".

Spring floods, as a result of the snow melting in central Dalemark, are extensive even in modern times. In the uncontrolled River of prehistoric times there was always much flooding, which not only devastated homes but also brought fertile silt, driftwood and fish. This violent mixture of destruction and benevolence caused many people to regard the River as a god.

Square rigging, the old type of sail which is simply a sheet of canvas hung between two yards across the mast and swivelled at both ends to catch the wind. South Dalemark very early gave this up in favour of the far more efficient fore-and-aft-rigged triangular sail, but the North still clung to the old rig right up to the reign of Amil the Great, when Ynen Navisson reorganised all shipping to form his fleet.

Square-topped pillar, a waist-high primitive altar only found in the Holy Islands.

Squarks, Lawschool slang meaning "being too bumptious".

Stair, Lord of Adenmouth in North Dalemark, a confirmed alcoholic.

Stapled, Lawschool slang meaning "to be posted on a notice board as a wrongdoer". Any pupil who was stapled lost certain privileges for a month.

Steam organ, at Hannart in North Dalemark, a huge music-making machine built into the side of the mountain, operating like a church organ but powered by steam. It was said to have been the brainchild of the Adon and brought sightseers to Hannart from the moment it was built. It is clear that the people of the Adon's time knew all about steam power two centuries before the industrial revolution but considered it only worthwhile for providing entertainment.

Stirring, Holy Islands dialect for rowing a boat.

Stork, the totem standard of the King of prehistoric Dalemark, where birds had a significance and potency which it is now hard to define. No one but the King or his accredited agents dared carry the Stork. Thus the people of Shelling knew at once that the messengers were there by royal decree.

Surnam, Lawschool slang for the one who spearheads an attack at grittling.

Sweetheart, a black cat rescued from an island by the children of Closti the Clam on their journey up the great River.

Sweetrush, a pet name for Tanaqui the weaver.

Talismans, charms for keeping the soul in the body made for King Hern's army by Tanamil the Piper. Many centuries later Dalemark people still call pebbles found with a chance pattern of cross-hatching piper's pieces.

Tally, the Lawschool term for its list of prizes.

Tan, a particle added to the front of a personal name to mean "the younger", as in Tanabrid, Tankol, Tanamil, et cetera.

Tanabrid, the daughter of the Adon by his second wife, Manaliabrid of the Undying, who married the Lord of Kredindale after the death of the Adon.

Tan Adon, Young Lord, one of the names for Tanamil the Piper.

Tanamil, one of the elder Undying, whose name means "younger brother" or "younger river". It is said that Tanamil was enslaved by Cenblith at the same time as the One and forced to create the Red River. There are many legends about him, some of which confuse him with Tanamoril, the mage-musician. Tanamil, however, is earlier than Tanamoril, for he is said to have played a major part in King Hern's defeat of Kankredin, after which he is said to have gone to the Holy Islands, where he can sometimes be heard playing his pipes at sunset.

Tanamoril

1. Moril's full second name. He was called after his famous ancestor.

2. The name taken by Mage Mallard in his earliest disguise as a minstrel. Under this name he assisted Enblith the Fair to become Queen because, according to some stories, she was his daughter.

3. The name means "youngest brother" and also refers to both Mallard's and Moril's position in their families.

Tanaqui

1. The second daughter of Closti the Clam and Anoreth of the Undying. She was a skilled weaver who made the two spellcoats which were dug up from the hillside above Hannart in North Dalemark. Her name is a punning one, meaning both "scented rushes" and "younger sister". There has been speculation as to whether Tanaqui is herself of the Undying and, if so, is to be identified with Cennoreth the Weaver, but this is probably without foundation: Tanaqui was plainly a real person. See also **Weaving**.

2. The scented rushes that are nowadays rare, growing only in certain habitats in North Dalemark.

Tankol, otherwise known as Young Kol, head foreman of the mineworkers at Kredindale in North Dalemark.

Tannoreth Palace, built by Amil the Great in Kernsburgh at the start of his reign, to Amil's own design, and still the royal palace although the present monarch seldom lives there. Amil appears to have invented the name Tannoreth himself (as he invented so many other things in the course of his long reign). It means, if anything, "the younger Noreth".

Tanoreth, the "young bound One", a name for Tanamil the Piper.

Tears, a potent magic. When Mitt weeps on an image of Libby Beer, he unknowingly invokes her protection.

Termath, the southernmost port in South Dalemark, the seat of the Earl of Dermath.

"The year's luck to you", the ritual greeting between Holanders on the day of the Sea Festival.

"This is my will", a form of words used by a dying King to name the next King. These words had the force of law. King Hern, having named his son Closti as King, is said to have continued, "and it is my will that I name all Kings after you".

Tholian, the name of several earls of the South Dales. After the last Tholian perished in an abortive invasion of the North a year or so before the Great Uprising, the name was discarded as unlucky.

"To tide swimming…", the ancient charm of invocation to the Earth Shaker and She Who Raised the Islands, spoken as part of the Holand Sea Festival. Any who doubt that this is indeed a charm should note that the words *Go now and return sevenfold* are thrice repeated in it.

Trase, Lawschool slang for a team attack at grittling.

Trethers, Lawschool slang for roll call, for which all pupils had to be present to answer their names.

Tross, one of the largest of the Holy Islands.

Trossaver, one of the Holy Islands, held to be the most beautiful.

Tulfa, the Southern spelling of Tulfer Island.

Tulfer Island, a large island some eight leagues off the coast of Dropwater in North Dalemark, closely allied to Hannart by marriage.

Undying, immortals. There are three kinds:

1. The gods and closely related spirits of prehistoric Dalemark, whose images were kept in niches by the hearth and worshipped and placated daily.

2. The Elder Undying, who had the status of gods and whose souls were supposed to be enmeshed in the land. They were worshipped in numerous rituals throughout Dalemark which still remain as fragmentary customs

and superstitions, particularly in the North. Though there never was any organised religion and only a few buildings were dedicated to the Undying, it is clear that everyone in early historic times, from the King downwards, joined in rituals of worship or invocation to the Undying at certain times of the year. The Elder Undying can be distinguished by their ritualised names e.g. the One, whose names are not to be spoken; the Weaver of Fates et cetera.

3. People who live for ever. There seems to be a gene of true immortality in the blood of Dalemark. Such people – for instance, Tanamoril or Manaliabrid – are born rarely, possibly one every three or four centuries, but do seem to exist. They nearly always possess unusual powers or abilities and often claim descent from the Elder Undying. It has been said that these immortals are the same as the Elder Undying, except that the Elder Undying unwisely allowed themselves to be bound into godhead by mortals wishing to worship them, but there is no proof of this theory.

Undying at Midsummer, a very ancient tune of invocation to the One at the time of his greatest power.

Updale, a small village in the centre of the second Upland, north of Neathdale in South Dalemark.

Uplands, the most northerly section of South Dalemark. The land here rises in three steep escarpments to meet the mountains of the North.

Virtue, power, life force, or magic.

Wailers, mourners, women who traditionally sit over a dead person making sounds of grief. The sounds have strict rules, which have to be learnt. Wailers are usually elderly women or those without children who have had time to learn the rules.

Wanderer, the one of the Undying who walks the green roads of North Dalemark, keeping them in good repair. He is the patron of all travellers and invoked even in the South at the start of a journey.

Warden of the Holy Islands, the title bestowed on Hildrida Navissdaughter by Amil the Great.

Warm Springs, mentioned in the spellcoats, halfway along the southern stretch of the great River and certainly of volcanic origin. Dalemark lies across two tectonic plates, and the land has always been prone to earthquakes and volcanic upheavals. Most historians believe that the shaking of the land by the One was in fact caused by the colliding of the two continental plates. There is evidence in Markind of a much earlier upheaval accompanied by massive volcanic activity.

Wars in Dalemark were frequent, but three only need concern us:

1. The prehistoric invasion by Heathens from Haligland.

2. The Adon's wars when the Adon claimed the crown, one of the few civil conflicts in which earls from both North and South appeared on either side.

3. The Great Uprising, when Amil the Great took the crown, which ended in the establishment of modern Dalemark as one kingdom.

Watersmeet, in the prehistoric Riverlands, the junction where the Red River flowed into the great River.

Waystone, a flat, round stone with a hole in the middle, set up on its narrow edge to mark the start of a green road in North Dalemark. It was the custom to touch the waystone for luck at the start of a journey.

Waywold, the earldom next door to Holand on the south coast of South Dalemark.

Weaver, the lady of the Undying who weaves the fates and fortunes of mortals. She is said by some to be the same as the witch Cennoreth.

The Weaver's Song, a well-known nursery song that may originally have been an invocation to the Weaver.

Weaving was always to some extent a magical skill and not simply to do with making cloth. In early historical times each pattern woven was held to have significance. Note that Tanaqui takes it for granted that whatever she weaves will contain at least some words, usually at the hem or wrists of the garment, but quite often in bands throughout. See also **Words**.

"Welcome aboard, Old Ammet, sir!", the traditional greeting from the crew that found Old Ammet floating in the sea, showing respect proper to one of the Undying.

Wend Orilson, assistant curator at the Tannoreth Palace in Kernsburgh, who claims to be one of the Undying.

West Pool, the second harbour of Holand in South Dalemark, shallower than the main harbour and protected by walls and gates, where the rich have always kept their pleasure boats. Harbour dues here are very high.

Wheatsheaf, the flagship of the Holy Islands fleet.

Wheatsheaf crest, the badge of Holand in South Dalemark, much feared in the time of Earl Hadd, when Harchad Haddsson gave each of his paid spies a small gold button stamped with this crest.

"Wider than the world, or small as in a nut", a quotation from a song by the Adon, sung by Kialan on the road north. The song is called *Truth* and, at one level, describes the working of the cwidder bequeathed to

Moril Clennensson.

Wind's Road

1. An archaic term for the sea, used in spells and invocations.

2. The name of the yacht in which Mitt and his friends escaped north.

Wine, made all over South Dalemark. The best vintages, red and white, are from Canderack, and the worst from Holand, and there are one or two superb reds from Andmark. The Holy Islands make a strange sparkling white and a brandy so good only earls can afford it. Apart from this, everywhere north of Markind tends to make cider instead and distill from it the spirits called gley. The main drink of the North is beer, except in Dropwater, where they make a sort of plum brandy.

Winthrough, Lawschool slang for a scholarship student.

Wittess, one of the Holy Islands, low and green.

Words, a term used by Tanaqui and Kankredin for the clusters of woven signs in the spellcoats which only the learnt or the initiated could read in the cloth. These signs not only formed words in the normal sense but were also potent ingredients of a mage-weaver's spell.

Wren, the headman of an unknown village in

prehistoric Dalemark who led his people northwards, fleeing from Kankredin. He was the first man to swear allegiance to King Hern.

Yeddersay, one of the outer ring of the Holy Islands.

Ynen, son of Navis Haddsson, who became Amil the Great's admiral in chief. Ynen not only experimented with steamships but built the conventional navy up to the extent that Dalemark quickly became an important sea power.

Ynynen, the lesser of the Earth Shaker's two Great Names. Readers are strongly advised not to say this name beside the sea or in a boat.

Young One, the red clay image of a smiling young man which the family of Closti the Clam kept in one of their fireside niches reserved for the Undying.

Zara, the sister of Closti the Clam, who was to have married Zwitt, the headman of Shelling, if Closti had not jilted Zwitt's sister. Zara was then forced to marry Kestrel or remain a spinster. Zara never forgave Closti or his family for this, though she seems to have retained a strong fondness for Zwitt.

Zwitt, the headman of Shelling beside the great River of prehistoric Dalemark. When Zwitt was young, he was betrothed to Closti the Clam's sister Zara, while Closti was betrothed to Zwitt's sister. Closti, however, fell in love with Anoreth and married her instead. Zwitt, in revenge, refused to marry Zara. This caused continuing bad blood between Zwitt and Closti's family.